BOUND BY HER PASSION

BOUND BY HER BLOOD BOOK 2

MARA LEIGH

Half Dome Press

This is a work of fiction. Names, characters, places, and incidents are the product of the author's imagination or are used fictitiously. Any resemblance to actual events, locales, or persons, living or dead, is purely coincidental.

Cover design: Covers by Juan
ISBN: 978-1-989318-07-2 Print Edition

CHAPTER 1

Selina

I wake in the dark, head thick, mouth dry, and my entire body craving blood.

My night vision reveals concrete walls that seem to go up forever, like I'm at the bottom of a deep shaft. No windows are visible, but the air is fresh and I sense the faint sound and vibrations of the city, high in the distance.

I'm trapped. Underground. Again.

Kidnapped by Pike, the monster that tortured me for over a year when I was King Xavier's captive fiancée.

Xavier's not even a king, not a real one, I know that now, but it doesn't change the fact that I've been captured by the most vicious member of his Guard.

Pike's not here now, at least I can't see him, but the entire space is thick with his presence as if the walls are painted in his blood.

I sit and my hip sinks into an unexpectedly soft and clean mattress, and chains rattle as I brush back hairs from my face. Shit. My wrists are shackled, so are my ankles.

This part's more expected than the soft mattress. More like Pike.

Gathering my diminished strength, I tug against my constraints, but the chains are securely bolted to the concrete floor.

I'm bound, captive, trapped. But I am a vampire—and more powerful than the one Pike remembers, strengthened after feeding from my lover, the elegant Gray.

Even hungry as I am now, needing to feed after being unconscious, I'm no longer the weak, baby vampire that Xavier and Pike held captive.

Standing, I tug on all four restraints at once, but they're spread out, and I can't get enough force on any single bolt. Concentrating on my right arm, I punch forward with the force of my entire body—over and over. The chains clank as I thrust back and forth, but my only accomplishments are making my wrist ache and further exhausting myself.

I kick with my left leg, working on that bolt for a while, then try my last two limbs, but make no headway.

All the bolts are well secured, but I will not give up.

Deciding to focus on one bolt, I choose the right arm, then fight and fight. I move close to the wall, surprised that the ceramic tiles next to the bed are covered in soft padding, and then I charge forward, combining my strength and speed with a sudden burst of power.

My wrist snaps.

My right hand hangs limp and useless, so I shift to the left arm. But on my eighteenth punch with the left, that wrist breaks too.

I gingerly cushion my hands as my bones knit back together, but even the first one's not healed. There are too many little bones in a wrist and hand for it to recover very quickly.

Resting my arms, I kick forward, but I don't have as much slack with my legs and it feels fruitless.

Not fruitless. I will not give up. I can't. I won't sit here like prey, a passive victim hoping compliance might make my punishments less brutal. Never again.

With every ounce of energy inside me, I kick and kick with my left leg. A splintering crack and searing pain joins the sound of the chain as I break my shinbone, possibly my femur, too.

I can fight through the pain while I heal, but can't kick without a strong base.

Trying the right arm again, I wince as sharp pain shoots through me, and I collapse to the mattress.

"Enough!" A loud male voice echoes through the cavernous space.

My body freezes. My heart gallops. Pike is here.

"Let me go!" I shout.

He steps from behind a tiled pillar. Above his massive and powerful frame, his amber eyes glare from his scarred face and I choke back a gasp, not wanting to reveal my fear. His worn leather pants, the uniform of Xavier's King's Guard, cling to his hips and the mounds of his thighs like the garment grew there, like the leather's his skin. A simple black T-shirt hides the scars I know slash across his chest to terminate at some mysterious place beneath his leather waistband.

"I will *never* marry him," I shout as strongly as I can through my weakened condition. "Not *ever*. There is no use in holding me. I'll die first."

"That's not why you're here." His deep voice crosses the twenty feet that separate us.

Goosebumps rise on my arms like I was bathed in the sound. "You're a monster."

He grunts. If I didn't know better, I'd think my words had hurt him, but if Pike ever had human feelings, he lost them long ago. If he had emotions, a hint of morality, he could never have served an evil sadist like Xavier, or tortured and violated me in that dungeon.

"No matter what you do to me," I shout, "you won't break me. I'll fight you. I'll escape. And my friends will come for me. They will find me and push a stake through your heart. Assuming you have one."

He leans back against the pillar, casually crossing one leg over the other. "You need blood?"

"Not *yours*!" My blood lust rises, pulsing with need. "Never."

He shakes his head slowly. "I meant from a human."

"I won't let you kill an innocent person."

"Who said anything about killing?" His chest rises and falls, and I'm mesmerized by the movement, knowing too well the power in his body, fearing what he no doubt plans to do to mine.

My fear, this anticipation, might be as bad as the actual torture, but I shiver imagining being raped by this vampire monster. Now that I've experienced the pleasures of consensual sex, rape will be so much worse.

"What are you waiting for?" I tug on the chains.

"You *are* hungry," he says softly. "You can barely move those chains."

"No I'm not! Well, yes." There's no point denying the obvious. "But stop toying with me. If you're going to kill me, get on with it." If he comes close enough, maybe I can use the chains to my advantage, get one around his neck and cut off his air supply. I'd still need to find a stake to finish the job, and a way to break free from the chains, but at least it would be progress, at least it would be something.

"I'm not going to hurt you," Pike says, his voice deep but gentle.

"Liar."

He shrugs. "I would *never* hurt you."

"Never hurt me?" A burst of laughter erupts from inside me. "Are you kidding me? What kind of sadistic game are you playing? Do you think that if you feign kindness, I'll let you use me for your sick pleasure?"

I shake my chains. "That will never happen. *Never.* I hate you. I will always hate you."

He sucks in a sharp breath, and I'm momentarily confused. Is it possible he *did* capture me for himself, rather than his so-called king?

The words he said to me the day I escaped Xavier's dungeon flash through my mind. They ripple through my body with fear and revulsion. He said that one day he'd fuck me. That I'd want it. That I'd ask for it.

Was this his plan all along? To capture me and hold me until I gave in like a victim of Stockholm Syndrome?

I sneer. "You're a disgusting animal. A monster. More repugnant than even the worst myths humans have imagined about vampires."

Eyes narrowing, he strides toward me. "You have no idea how right you are."

I leap to my feet, but my leg bones aren't yet fully healed and the pain is blinding. I fall back to the mattress and he's instantly at my side, catching me before I hit and crouching beside me.

His hand softly strokes my shoulder.

I shrug it off. "Don't touch me."

He places his wrist near my face. "Drink."

Holding my lips tight, I shake my head. But like it did the first time he offered his vein, my powerful blood lust invades. A lust so consuming I don't dare part my lips. My mouth and cheeks, my entire body starts to shake from the effort of keeping my fangs contained.

Coursing through Pike's veins, his blood calls to me with a song so alluring I can barely think of anything else. The force is like the rush of Niagara Falls pounding down, but instead of sounding like water, his blood is a chorus of voices, singing the most beautiful music in existence, so beautiful it could never actually exist except in the best of dreams.

My hunger is too strong. I can't fight my need for long. Suddenly I don't only need blood, I need *his* blood —*Pike's* blood. And so much worse than that, I'm wet. Desire pools between my legs.

He can probably sense it, and anger and humiliation rise inside my chest.

I suck short breaths through my nose, my jaw aching with the effort of keeping my fangs out of his vein.

This feeling—this deep, primal need—is even more powerful than what I felt that night in the club when I took Grayson's vein. The night I had my first taste of Gray's blood, I understood, for the first time, the power I could gain from feeding from another vampire. I understood, too, how my twin hungers for blood and sex are so tightly bound.

But it made slightly more sense that I wanted Gray. My body needed his blood, and even though I'd just met him, I had no reason to hate him. In fact, I liked Gray right from the start.

On the other hand, Pike is repulsive. He must be

using some kind of evil trick to make me feel this way, some vampire power no one has told me about yet.

His hand cups the back of my head, gently holding my lips against his other wrist. "Feed, Selina. Please."

As I shake my head, my lips brush over his skin, amplifying my desire to do as he asks.

I force my mind to concentrate on Rock, my giant, my love, my protector. And on Grayson, my passionate lover.

Some day I might love Gray too, if he ever shows me a glimpse of who he is deep inside. Beyond handsome, Gray's look is elegant and refined, even given his slightly long hair and sideburns, out of another time. And Gray's deep blue eyes dance with humor and wit, never able to disguise the mischievous, fun-loving young man he was before his transition, no matter how many years he may have walked the Earth since then.

But his appearance is nothing compared to the way Gray makes me feel when he's inside me… Or the experience of feeding from his vein.

Desire pulses through me, and my tongue pushes between my lips, its tip grazing Pike's rough skin.

"Yes." The word escapes from his lips in a long hiss. "Feed. Take my blood."

My mind snaps back to the present and I struggle against Pike's hold, pushing on the hand behind my head.

He lets me go and I fall to the mattress as he backs away.

Finally able to safely open my mouth, I gulp in air like I've been underwater for hours. My entire body's involved in each breath as I lie on my side, watching as Pike turns away from me, his expression seeming more sad than angry. What is he up to?

"Why?" I ask on a hard exhale.

"Why what?" he asks, his massive back to me.

"Why kidnap me? If you didn't take me for Xavier, why are you holding me here?"

He shakes his head slowly.

I push up to sit, glad to find my wrists are once again ready to support me without pain. "Even if you kill me, you'll be hunted, you know. Others will avenge my death. I'm no longer the lone baby vamp who got lured into Xavier's court. I have friends now. Lovers. People who care about me."

"Good."

The word comes softly but nearly knocks me back down. "Good?" Wincing against the pain of my nearly healed leg, I stand, putting my hands on my hips. "Why did you kidnap me? Tell me."

"I didn't kidnap you."

I shake the chains. "What the fuck do you call these, then?"

"I rescued you."

"Rescued me?" I tug on the chains, letting them clang. "Rescued me from my friends? From the men that I love?"

"I'll go get you some food." He strides into the darkness, turns a corner and disappears.

CHAPTER 2

Gray

Astrid—my friend and head of security for FJS, the centuries old vampire-run corporation we both work for—walks the prisoner into the interrogation room as I watch from the other side of a one-way mirror. My body's shaking inside, both from the adrenaline of the battle and the shock of Selina's kidnapping.

I raise my hand to confirm that I'm keeping the trembling inside. Keep calm and carry on.

After Selina was taken, Rock and I pursued, leaving Astrid and Malcolm to deal with the remaining vampires and dispose of the corpses of those we killed in self-defense.

But neither Rock nor I found any trace of Selina or the vampire who took her. They evaporated into the city.

Behind me in the viewing area, Rock clomps, pacing across the room for what must be the hundredth time in the less than five minutes we've been here, and each of the giant's steps vibrates through my body, exacerbating my tension.

I grab his arm as he passes, and his momentum pulls me along for a few fumbling steps before he stops.

"Take some deep breaths, mate," I say. "Your pacing is making the building shake."

Rock draws a long breath, and I can sense both of his hearts beating at a ferocious rate, like we're still in battle.

"You're acting like a caged animal." I state the obvious.

He grunts, and pain and anger flash in his eyes.

"How can you be so calm?" he asks. "Selina was *taken*, kidnapped by that monster who tortured and *raped* her, that means to *kill* her." His voice breaks.

"Hey." I clap his upper arm. "I am *not* calm. This is not what calm looks like. But your pacing won't help find her." I nod toward the one-way mirror. "Right now, Astrid and her team are our best bet."

I close my eyes for a moment, thinking of the lovely, lavender-haired Selina, and try to focus on her face, her smell, her taste, rather than thoughts of what that monster could be doing to her.

Selina is strong but she's already been through so much, and under enough pressure, even the strongest branch snaps.

Rock turns his massive body toward the one-way mirror and leans against it, arms overhead. His fingers rest at the intersection of the wall and the ceiling. Bloke's got to be over seven feet tall.

He presses his forehead against the glass. "Can you turn up the sound?"

"Sure, mate." I adjust a knob, low on the wall. "I forgot you have a hearing deficiency."

"Deficiency?" Turning toward me, he frowns.

I lightly punch his arm. "Compared to a vampire you're practically deaf."

He grunts. "In that case, *you* have a height deficiency."

"Not to mention a weight one." I wink.

His eyes narrow. "Did you just call me fat?"

"Walks like a duck…" I can't tell if he's amused or angry, but I'm betting on amused, so I grin. "Or should I say—walks like a mountain."

He chuckles as he turns back to the glass.

The woman I love loves this giant, but instead of harboring resentment or jealousy, I'm growing to like him more and more every day. It's not hard to understand what Selina sees in Rock, and although he can't provide everything a vampire needs in a mate, I understand why Rock makes her feel safe.

I pull over a chair, sit and lean back, trying to keep calm so I can concentrate as Astrid and her team work. They're skilled at interrogations, but Selina told me some of what went on while she was held in Xavier's dungeon, and I suspect she's told Rock even more. The two of us need to listen for clues—catch things Astrid and her team might miss.

Moments after Pike kidnapped Selina, Astrid's team from FJS arrived and arrested the two vampires who were still alive on charges of attempted murder and kidnapping.

The one who was badly burned by the silver net is healing, and the second is on the other side of the glass. One of Astrid's staff directs her into a cast-iron chair that's bolted to the floor—bolted into the skyscraper's foundation, if I had to guess.

Two of the security team members fasten clamps around the captured vampire's wrists, ankles and waist, and curved bars descend to rest over her shoulders, like she's strapped into a roller coaster chair.

"Will that hold her?" Rock asks.

I nod. "The clamps are made from a titanium alloy that even the strongest vampire can't break. And look. They're so tight she can't move."

"Comfortable?" Astrid asks the vampire.

The captive narrows her eyes and squares her jaw, like she's trying to look fierce, but I can sense the fear in her eyes. The vampire is dark-haired and -skinned, with dark red lips and warm brown eyes. Tall and athletic, she's the type of bird I might go for in the club, hoping for a quick shag.

Might have *gone* for, that is. Since finding Selina, I have zero interest in the casual fucks that used to fill my nights.

Astrid stands in front of the prisoner. "My name is Astrid. I'm head of security for FJS—Fides, Juris, Sanctorum. What's your name?"

The captive continues her fear-tinged scowl, but her fingers tremble and her lips look dry and tight. Astrid must see this too. How could she not?

"When did you last feed?" Astrid asks her.

The captive looks away.

Astrid presses a button near the door. "Our guest needs a meal."

She approaches the prisoner and touches her upper arm. "Let's get you fed before we talk. Is this too tight?" She adjusts the holster holding down the vampire's shoulders, and the prisoner's expression shows a brief moment of relief.

The door opens and a human male enters. The human's attractive, tanned, with well-coifed brown hair and clothed in what looks like a bespoke business suit worthy of Savile Row.

Astrid beckons him over. "Jason, can you feed our guest, please?"

The man nods, then quickly removes his suit jacket, tie and dress shirt, placing them carefully on the back of a chair.

"What the fuck?" Rock turns toward me.

"Astrid's going to give her some blood," I explain. "Probably to soften her up. Hoping to get her to cooperate. She's terrified. Don't you see how she's trembling?"

"Selina's missing! Why waste time?"

"Astrid knows what she's doing. Plus there are rules. Ethics."

Rock shakes his head. "Ethics? Give me a break. Who is this man? A blood slave?"

"That's an offensive term."

Rock rolls his eyes.

"Listen, mate. You shouldn't even be in here. Astrid made an exception, so don't go casting judgment."

"Then tell me what I'm looking at." Rock's voice booms, but there's no reaction from inside the interrogation room. The glass must be treated so that even vampires can't hear through it.

"What do you want to know?" I ask Rock.

He shakes his head. "What I see is an unsuspecting human about to have his neck pierced by vampire fangs, and then his memory of the trauma stolen. How is that ethical? Or do your rules only apply to those of your kind?"

"This man knows what he's doing," I assure Rock. "Blood donations at FJS are fully consensual, and the donors well compensated for their services."

Rock's eyes narrow. "Malcolm and Astrid have never mentioned anything about blood slaves. Not once." He looks down. "I mean, I know they need human blood..."

"Blood donor positions aren't something FJS typically advertises." I turn away from the one-way mirror as the human positions himself, exposes his neck and the prisoner starts to feed.

Rock stares through the glass. "Are they trapped inside the building?"

"The prisoners?"

"No, the man she's feeding from."

"Of course not."

"But then... They don't report you to the police?" Rock shakes his head. "Of course they don't. They forget they were bitten."

I lean against the glass beside the giant. "Even if this guy forgets parts of the feeding, he came into the room willingly. You saw that. You saw him prepare, right?"

Rock nods.

"The blood donors are carefully vetted, all long-time FJS employees, well trusted. Their positions are highly sought after within the corporation."

"Must be coercion or abuse of power."

"Trust me. The donors are good with it. Not in the five hundred year history of the corporation has a blood donor gone to the human authorities."

Rock shakes his head, his expression revealing conflict, as he looks back through the window. "Does everyone at FJS feed from these—donors?"

"Most do. It's safer. Easier."

"Easier for whom?" Rock narrows his eyes.

"Look." I shake my head. "Can we talk about the

ethics of blood donors later? It's more complicated than you think, and right now—"

Rock nods. "Selina is all that matters."

"You said it, mate."

"Feeling better?" Astrid asks the vampire in the interrogation room, as the human, clearly dazed, is guided into a wheelchair of sorts. An attendant collects his clothes, and he's taken from the room.

Astrid pulls over a chair and sits opposite the trapped vampire. "You're under arrest for attempted murder, kidnapping and a variety of other charges. It's an ironclad case. You're looking at a minimum sentence of a century behind bars."

The vampire blinks, clearly shocked at this news. "A century?"

"You must know vampire law."

The vampire shakes her head.

"When were you turned?" Astrid asks. "Didn't your Maker teach you?"

"I became a vampire six years ago." The vampire's voice trembles. "I've been in King Xavier's court the whole time."

"He's not a king, you know."

"He's not?"

Astrid shakes her head. "I'll make sure you get some basic lessons while you're serving your sentence."

"I didn't know," the vampire says, her voice cracking. "I was under orders. I didn't have a choice. That vampire we were sent to capture is King Xavier's mate."

"Again." Astrid holds up her hand. "Not a king. Not his mate."

"He sure *seems* like a king." The vampire shakes her

head, her expression changing as if her entire world has been upended.

"What's your name?" Astrid asks softly.

"Kwana."

"Kwana, you've got a lot to learn about vampire history and culture, but right now I need to find the vampire your buddies took. If you help, we can discuss a reduced sentence, rehabilitation."

"I'll tell you whatever you want to know." Her face twists like she's in pain. "I had no idea there were vampires like you. Places like this." She shakes her head. "This is a syndicate, right?"

"Not exactly," Astrid tells her. "But if all you've seen is Xavier's so-called court, then you have a very warped idea of vampire culture." She leans forward. "Where are they holding her?"

Kwana shakes her head.

"So you *want* to spend the next hundred years in prison?"

"No!" Kwana blurts. "I don't know where she is. Pike took her. He wasn't with us."

Astrid folds her arms over her chest. "I know for a fact Pike is one of Xavier's Guard."

"He is. He *was*. I guess he still is?" Kwana shakes her head. "But he wasn't with us tonight. He must have followed us." Her eyes close for a moment. "Maybe he was backup in case our team failed?"

"You're asking me?" Astrid tucks a stray lock of red hair behind her ear.

"I don't know why Pike was there tonight. Honest." She shivers. "Pike doesn't talk much. Everyone's afraid of him. Maybe even King Xavier. Pike's always been a loner, but none of us have even seen him since Xavier found out Selina was alive."

"How did Xavier find out? And how did your team find her tonight?"

"An informant," Kwana says. "A syndicate boss named Louis."

Astrid nods.

"Do you know who they're talking about?" Rock asks me.

"Yeah, I do. A real weasel." When we first arrived in the city, my old partner Andreas and I questioned Louis several times. He likes to act like he knows everything that's going on in the vampire world. "This Louis twat dresses like the Sun King."

"Louis the fourteenth?" Rock rubs his head. "Was the King of France a vampire?"

I laugh sharply, keeping one eye on the interrogation. "Not a chance. And this guy who calls himself Louis is a poser. Goes around decked out in velvet and lace, carries a walking stick that converts to a stake."

Rock's eyes open wider. "I *saw* him. He confronted Selina the same night I met her… I was following her to make sure she found a safe place to spend the day." Rock looks up. "Do you think it's been him, not Pike, who's been following her since?"

I shrug. "Could be. If it was Pike, I don't get why he didn't make a move before tonight."

I turn my attention back to the interrogation on the other side of the glass.

"If you were in Xavier's Guard," Astrid says to Kwana. "How could you know so little about getting in and out of his lair?"

"Tonight is the first time I've been out of the palace since I was taken down there as a human."

Astrid turns toward us, and I see skepticism on her face, but it disappears when she turns back to the vampire she's questioning.

"How did you become part of his Guard?"

"I was an athlete when I was human," Kwana answers. "Strong. My Maker was in his Guard, and he recommended me to Xavier."

"And once you were in the Guard, you got free run of the palace? Access in and out?"

She shakes her head. "No. Neither. Only the commanders know the way out."

"But you know now," Astrid says softly. "You got out tonight. Kwana, will you help us get into Xavier's compound?"

She looks down.

"Help us," Astrid says, "and we'll be able to lighten your sentence."

Kwana's eyes rise and they're filled with fear. "I can show you how to get in, but I don't think you'll find Selina down there."

"And why is that?" Astrid leans onto the table.

"Pike told Xavier he'd killed Selina. If Pike let her live…I doubt he took her for Xavier."

Listening to Kwana speak, I stagger back and drop down into a chair. She's right. Pike showed up after the others. He took her—but he took her for himself.

Rock pounds the glass, and the vampires inside the room turn toward us.

"Careful, mate," I tell the giant. "You're going to break that glass."

He turns toward me. "What the feck do we do now? She could be anywhere!"

Drawing a deep breath, I rise to my feet. "What we do is find her. That's what the fuck we do. We find her and we save her from that monster."

CHAPTER 3

Selina

I slump against the padded wall, waiting for my wrists and ankle to heal for the third time. The bolts haven't loosened a bit.

In addition to the padding at my back, other things about my cell are surprising. The mattress is comfortable and has clean sheets and even a soft pillow, and now that I've been able to study the space more closely I can tell that it's clean—without the rats or bugs I'd expect underground. The tiles on the walls and floor were recently scrubbed, and someone draped fabric between a few of the pillars to make the space seem more like a room than a dungeon.

Was this Pike's doing? I try to imagine him cleaning or hanging makeshift curtains, but can't. Does he *live* down here?

I shake my head. Pike lives in Xavier's compound with the rest of the Guard, and even if he comes here when he's outside the court, he didn't decorate it like this for his own tastes. Nothing about it seems like Pike.

My stomach roils with revulsion. If anything, this is a place he uses to trap females for his sadistic pleasure.

I sense Pike before I see him.

The thick velvet curtains part, and Pike strides toward me, a human man slumped over his shoulder.

"You're awake," he says. "Good."

I press my back against the wall, wishing I could push myself into the padding, disappear into the wall—anything to keep out of Pike's reach.

"I brought you food."

He strides toward me, carrying the man, then gently lays his body down on the mattress beside me.

I swing my arm, hoping to punch Pike in the temple with an iron shackle, but my still-broken wrist betrays me. I cry out.

Pike's eyes fill with what looks like pain. "Stop hurting yourself."

"Hurting *myself*? That's rich."

He steps back, leaving the human beside me. "I hate to see you in pain."

"Pain you haven't inflicted yourself, you mean?"

He stares at the floor. "I will never, ever hurt you."

"But you *have* hurt me! Many times, you monster."

He steps back, still not raising his gaze from the tiled floor. "I can't change the past. I can't change who I am. But I will never hurt you, and I would die before I let *anyone* hurt you. Ever again."

Something in the tone of his voice is convincing, but I refuse to believe it. "So, what's your plan here?"

"To keep you safe."

"Safe? How is this safe?"

"Xavier can't find you down here."

I tremble, realizing his twisted logic. "So you expect me to live out my life in this dungeon? Is that it? Locked away and alone so that he can't hurt me? That's twisted. You're even more of a monster than I thought."

He turns away.

"I can't live in this dungeon. I won't." I shake the chains. "I'll keep breaking my bones until I can make the pieces small enough to slide through these shackles. And if that doesn't work, then I won't feed. You say you'd die to protect me? Well *I'll* die before I let you hold me captive."

"You need to feed." He backs away and disappears behind a curtain.

I stare down at the man. He's young. Probably in his early twenties and around the same age I was before I transitioned, the physical age I will remain forever. Dressed in scruffy jeans and a torn T-shirt, at first glance the man looks like a homeless person, but I soon realize his clothes are expensive; his skin and hair are clean.

And his blood is calling me to feed.

Accepting this "gift" from Pike feels like giving in on some level, but on the other hand, maybe if I feed it will remove the risk that I'll give in to something much worse —feeding from Pike's vein.

Plus, I need to stay strong. I need to do everything I can to escape, to get back to Rock and Gray, who must be frantic with worry.

Yielding, I adjust my position on the mattress, tip the man's head to the side and dig my fangs into his neck. He reacts in his slumber, tensing, then relaxing with a deep moan as my venom floods his body with the chemical that calms humans and makes the feeding pleasurable.

His blood cascades into my system, nourishing me,

healing me, making me feel whole and alive. I wasn't rationalizing when I chose to feed. I need this. I love this. I can barely remember a time before I needed human blood to survive, before I longed for it.

Sensing I'm on the verge of taking too much, I pull back and lick his wounds closed. The man sighs in his sleep, and I wonder how Pike made him unconscious. Probably the same way he rendered me unconscious last night.

I touch the man's face. His skin is slightly warmer than a vampire's, his chin scratchy with razor stubble, and I sense each tiny whisker on my palm. I run my finger over his slightly chapped lips.

Aroused by my feeding, I can't help but recognize that this human is attractive, his shoulders and chest well muscled beneath his baggy T-shirt.

"Wait until he's awake to fuck him."

I jump at the sound of Pike's voice, my back striking the padded wall. "Fuck you."

"If you wish." His hand rests on his thigh, close to the obvious bulge at his crotch, and I'm not sure whether the bulge just appeared, or whether it was there all along and I've just become aware. Very aware.

Heat shooting through me, I turn my gaze from Pike, disgusted with myself. Why would my mind go anywhere near there? It's the aftereffects of my feeding.

"You done?" he asks.

"Yes."

"Okay if I get him?"

I nod.

He lifts the man over his shoulder like he weighs nothing and then turns to go.

"Don't kill him!"

He turns toward me. "I would never."

"Why was he unconscious when you brought him down?" I ask. "What did you do to him?"

"No more than you did," Pike replies. "I had a quick feed so he'd forget all of this."

"Oh." Something inside me stirs, realizing that both Pike and I have fed from this man. There's something intimate about that idea, and it makes me squirm.

"You okay?" he asks.

I glare at him, embarrassed that my emotions might have shown on my face. "I'm fantastic, thanks. What girl wouldn't *love* being chained up in a dungeon?"

CHAPTER 4

Rock

Gray and Malcolm are chatting, sitting on Eames chairs in the corner of the small room off the FJS lobby, and I approach Astrid as we wait for the security staff to bring the vampire prisoner.

"Do you really trust her?" I ask Astrid.

"I never trust anyone," Astrid replies after a pause. "Not fully." Her long red hair is tied back from her face, and she reaches behind to twist it into a bun that she secures with a long pin as she talks. "But my instincts say that Kwana's telling the truth. She was terrified during the interrogation."

"Terrified of you, or of Xavier?"

Astrid shrugs slightly. "Probably both. But even if she's lying, she's the best lead we've got."

"This is bonkers!" Gray shoots to his feet. He crosses the room toward me and Astrid. "Malcolm just told me that you're letting the prisoner go free."

Astrid crosses her arms over her ample chest as she

turns to face Grayson. "We're not *letting her go*. She's going to show us the entrance to Xavier's compound."

"What if it's a trick?" Gray yells. "What if we're ambushed?"

Standing, I clap Gray on the back. "Don't you think it's worth a shot? We need to try everything we can to find her."

"It's a fool's errand." Gray narrows his eyes and shakes his head. "I'm shocked you could be so stupid, Astrid. You're supposed to be a professional."

Red spots rise on Astrid's pale cheeks, but that's the only clue that the head of security is angry. "Do you have a better suggestion, Grayson?"

"Look for her!" he shouts. "Search the fucking city! That vamp already told us that Pike *didn't* take her to Xavier's. So which is it, Astrid? Do you trust her word or not? Because if Kwana's telling us the truth, Selina's not there!"

I nod in support. "Gray's got a point." My mind bounces like a ping-pong ball, bashed back and forth by fear and anger. Nothing feels right to me tonight. The entire world tipped on its edge when my love was taken, and it's taking every ounce of my willpower not to smash down the walls, to take this building, the entire city, apart brick by brick until I find her.

"Showing us the way into Xavier's compound is part of the deal we made with the prisoner," Astrid says calmly.

"So capturing Xavier's your priority?" Gray asks. "Not finding Selina?"

"Xavier held Selina captive for over a year," Astrid replies. "He *tortured* her. He's done it to others. He needs to face justice."

"But Selina's not fucking there!" Gray yells.

His anger transfers to me. Turning, I punch the wall and my fist goes straight through and into the lobby. "Fuck. Sorry."

"It's just a couple of layers of drywall," Astrid says. "It can be fixed."

Through the hole my fist made, I see two of Astrid's security team members in the lobby, flanking Kwana. Another dozen security officers follow them. I turn toward the others. "She's coming."

"This is a wild goose chase." Gray shakes his head. "Selina's in danger, and we're wasting time."

I've never seen Gray lose his temper, never seen him in anything less than total control over his emotions, and the display further unnerves me.

The door opens and Astrid shakes Kwana's hand. "Ready?"

She nods, but her lips tremble. "If Xavier finds out I showed you—"

"We've got your back." Astrid adjusts the holster she's wearing over her leather blazer. Her holster is loaded with at least a dozen wooden stakes. With a vampire serial killer on the loose, no one will look sideways at a woman openly armed with stakes.

"Everyone ready?" Astrid asks, and Malcolm strides over to join the group.

"Fuck this!" Gray says. "Fuck you all. I'm going to look for Selina." He turns to me. "You coming?"

"I…" I look toward Astrid, then Kwana, then back to Gray. "We don't know where to look for her."

"Fine!" Gray glares at me. "I'll find her myself."

He pushes past the security team and into the lobby alone.

"Let's head out," Astrid says, like she's unaffected by Gray's outburst or quick departure.

The moment we're outside the FJS building the team spreads out, spacing themselves in small groups along both sides of the street, some of them disappearing from my view entirely. But if I know anything about vampires I know that just because I can't see them, it doesn't mean they're not there.

As we walk through the nearly abandoned downtown streets, Kwana changes her route and doubles back a few times.

"I… It's been a long time since I've been in the city," she says, her voice shaky. "I was down there for six years. And when we came out last night I was part of a group. I was following, not leading."

"Just concentrate," Astrid says firmly, but not harshly. "Trust your instincts. You know the way."

After leading us around the city for nearly two hours, Kwana stops short.

"What is it?" Astrid asks.

"This is it." Kwana points a trembling hand toward a construction site. "The entrance is down there. In the subbasement."

I lean close to Astrid. "Selina told me she came out in an alley, somewhere downtown."

"Kwana says there's more than one way in and out," Astrid answers. "But she only knows the way she came." She turns to her team. "Check for cameras and guards."

I pace along the construction fencing, trying to release my pent-up energy. Should I have gone with Gray? What if he's already found her? What if he's in trouble?

I stare through a gap in the fencing but it's hard to see much. Based on the crane overhead, it looks like they're ready to start the above-ground stories of this future condo building.

Light rain starts to fall, and I tip up my face, letting the cold dampness soak my skin. The sky erupts in light, followed by thunder, and the clouds burst with a heavy downfall.

Astrid's team members return, and I dash back to find out what they're saying to her.

"Cameras are disabled," a short, stocky vampire reports. "There's no security team on site. I'd say we've got at least fifteen minutes before someone comes to check why the camera's failed."

"Let's go, then." Astrid gestures for Kwana to show us the way.

Kwana leads us to the back of the site and then jumps over the twenty-foot fencing.

"What?" I turn toward Astrid, but she's already jumped, too. Her team follows.

Shaking my head, I punch a hole in the plywood, break it apart, then pry open a space in the metal fencing behind it. I can jump twenty feet, but not without a run to build power and who's got time for that? When the space is wide enough, I step through, but a wire tears the back of my shirt, scratching my skin.

The last of Astrid's team disappears from view and I head to where they last were. Damned vampires. They move too fast and jump too high. At least I can match them in strength.

I glance down. They all jumped down a future elevator shaft at least four floors deep. If I jump, my ankles will shatter.

Finding iron scaffolding rungs along one side, I use them like a ladder and quickly descend a floor at a time.

The team is at the far corner of what will be a parking garage once the building's constructed, and as I approach, Kwana turns her head toward me in alarm.

I realize my heavy footsteps are shaking concrete loose from the ceiling, leaving a small trail of pebbles behind me.

"It's through there." Kwana points to a steel door.

Astrid tugs on the handle, but it's locked.

"Let me." I tear the door off its hinges and toss it onto the floor, and the sound echoes through the cavernous space.

The shallow room contains a series of drainage pipes that disappear under the concrete, likely leading to the sewer system.

"It's back there." Kwana points to wall on the right.

The FJS security team takes out wooden stakes and, wearing thick leather gloves, they adjust the silver handcuffs that hang off their belts.

Astrid leads Kwana toward the spot. "Where's the door?"

"It was right here." Kwana shakes her head as she runs her hands over the wall. "I swear it was here."

"The wall here is new," Astrid says. "Look. The cement is darker in this section, and the blocks don't line up."

"Let's take it apart," one of the vampires says.

"We don't have time," Astrid replies. "Someone will investigate the downed security cameras soon. We'll come back tomorrow night."

My uncertainty about whether or not I should have gone with Gray disappears. I am meant to be here. "Get out of the way."

Astrid and Kwana step back. I take off my jacket, wrap it around my fist, and then slam the concrete. The concrete brick I strike crumbles, and I take out more bricks the same way. Once enough are gone, I start pulling them out, and they reveal a steel door.

I clear more of the wall and then tear the steel door from its hinges. Behind it is a huge pile of rocks and rubble. My entire body strains with the effort of pulling out a monstrous boulder, but then more rocks fall to fill the space I created.

"They've collapsed the tunnel," Astrid says. "It's no use."

I pull out another rock, then another, but they're quickly replaced by other ones falling. I pause, shaking my head. Astrid is right. I pound against the rocks.

The pain in my fists is excruciating. I don't care.

"Rock! Stop it!" The sound of Astrid's voice barely penetrates my anger and the sound of rocks crushing under my fists.

"The building is shaking!" she yells. "If it collapses, we'll all get buried down here."

I thrust both fists against the rocks one final time, then rest my forehead against a stone stained with my blood.

Willing my hearts' rates to slow, I struggle to catch my breath and calm down. The only lead we had to find Selina is a literal dead end.

CHAPTER 5

Selina

I wake in darkness, my heart rate high, my body hot and humming, and wetness pooling between my legs.

Holy shit!

I scan the room to make sure Pike's not here, then close my eyes, not sure whether I want to forget or relive the dream I just woke from. The *very erotic* dream I just woke from. I don't think I could forget it if I tried.

The dream is still so vivid in my mind, it's like the events are happening now. I can almost feel the padding on the wall against my cheek as Pike, in the dream, positioned me spread-eagled, facing the wall of the cell, my chains taut, my back arched with my ass pushed back.

In the dream, Pike's hard body bent over mine, his mouth on my throat as he fed, and his hardness pressed against my ass and my sex. I didn't fight him in the dream. Instead, I yielded, let him feed from me willingly, and the act brought me to a state of rapture, as every ounce of blood he hadn't yet consumed rushed down to my slick sex.

Pike offered me his wrist, and I bit down, gulping the most glorious elixir, building both my strength and sexual desire. And while I was still feeding and the wound was open, he pulled his wrist away and bathed my body in his blood.

His blood on my skin was like a hot massage oil, simultaneously soothing and exciting every inch of my body, and I writhed in pleasure and anticipation, rubbing back against his hardness, wanting him more than I knew I could want anything.

In the dream, Pike's huge, rough-skinned hands cupped my breasts. They squeezed and kneaded and teased my nipples, and somehow he had more than two hands, because while the first two remained on my breasts, another one cupped my sex, and long thick fingers stroked through my folds. And the heel of his yet another hand pressed hard against my mound, nearly lifting me off the ground, his fingers circled my entrance and flicked over my clit as his hands, everywhere at once, pinched my nipples.

"Fuck me," I yelled in the dream. "Fuck me hard. Take me like an animal."

And he did. Somehow his hands stayed on my breasts and my clit while another clamped over my mouth. The hand on my mouth pushed a thick finger between my lips at the same moment that an impossibly huge cock drove into my pussy from behind.

I sucked hard on the finger as the cock relentlessly pounded inside me, as fingers continued to pinch and tease my nipples and fondle my clit, and another set of hands gripped my hips, tugging me back to meet each thrust. Pike consumed my body, used me for his pleasure, but it was my pleasure too. Pleasure like I've never known, never thought attainable.

As the cock continued to drive inside me, so hard, so fast, so deep, I came, over and over and over, as if orgasms were my new state of being, as if my climaxes would never stop. I could barely see, barely breathe, there was nothing but his thick cock filling me as my pussy contracted around it, hundreds—millions—of explosions going off in my body and mind as I lost control of my limbs, as my torso convulsed and bucked within the constraints of the chains, his hands all over me and his huge body pressed against my back as he rammed hard inside of me.

Panting, I come back to the present and realize my mental reenactment of the dream brought me to another orgasm. I squeeze my legs together to draw out the contractions.

What is wrong with me?

Shame overtakes my pleasure as the climax ends and my breathing rate slows. Is this Stockholm Syndrome? Is it working? Is Pike's strategy of feigned kindness, of making me as comfortable as possible, actually working?

Is that why I'm sexually attracted to a monster?

Sitting, I lean back against the padded wall, and the chains clank as I settle. There's no chance these will ever break. There's no chance I'll get out of this bondage without his help.

Just like the restraints in Xavier's dungeon, there is no escape.

I only got out of there because my restraints were left open. Left open by Pike. On purpose?

Again, I consider his motives. At the time, the only logical explanation was that he wanted a hunt—that he wanted to chase me—because there was no way he'd have been so careless as to leave them open by accident.

Are we still playing that game? Did he give me a few weeks of freedom intending to capture me again?

Back in Xavier's dungeon he said that if he ever fucked me I'd want it. That I'd beg him for it. Is that his goal? Holding me captive, treating me with kindness until I cave?

In that scenario, meeting Rock and Gray, my sexual experiences with them—feeling true sexual pleasure for the first time—could that have been part of Pike's plan?

Now that I've experienced that kind of pleasure, I *crave* it. I need it like I need blood, and Pike's put himself in a position to be the only one who can provide either.

My insides squeeze, thinking back to the dream.

But that theory's crazy. All of it. There's no way Pike could have planned everything that's happened to me since I escaped. And if he wanted me for a fuck toy, he could have just taken me out of Xavier's dungeon and brought me here right from the start.

When it comes to Pike, the only thing I'm sure of is that I'm not sure of anything.

His appearance and demeanor are terrifying, ferocious. I know he's capable of brutality and yet…he's been so gentle and kind, bringing me a vein to feed from, giving me my space down here.

And he did help me escape from Xavier's dungeon, there is no questioning that at this point, and when he took me from the warehouse—took me from my friends and the men I love—he also took me away from vampires who had wooden stakes aimed at my heart.

The curtain parts and Pike steps through the opening.

My heart gallops, and it's not just fear.

Terror, anger and lust mix inside me in a potent combination that leaves me confused and breathless. My hatred for Pike and my utter fear are now mixed with highly erotic feelings, plus grateful ones. Pike did save my life. Possibly twice.

As he steps further into the space, I'm overwhelmed by the sound and scent of his blood, and the power of the thick hot fluid coursing through his body overtakes my mind. I can't hear anything else, smell anything else, taste anything else.

Pike takes a step toward me, and I lick my fangs and squeeze my legs together to relieve the tension. Or perhaps to increase it.

Please. I try to regain my sanity. *This vampire is a monster. He's hurt you. He's holding you captive. Get a grip on your libido and smarten the fuck up.*

CHAPTER 6

Pike

My cock is like a steel rod. The sight of her, the sound of her heartbeat and the scent of her blood—combined with her unmistakable arousal—are too much to bear. If she were any other woman I'd take her right now. I'd relieve this need hammering inside me, relieve her obvious need, too.

But I won't touch Selina. Not without her invitation. And that invitation's not likely to come.

I watched her, so turned on in her sleep and her daydreams after. But those dreams weren't about me. She dreamed about the large human, or that fancy vampire who's so hot for her. Her desire was not, is not, will never be for me.

"Why?" she asks, her voice raspy, like she's just woken.

"Why what?"

"Why did you bring me here?"

"I told you. To keep you safe."

Her eyes narrow and her expression hardens. "It

doesn't make sense. You let me escape from the dungeon. If your plan was to trap me down here, then why let me go in the first place?"

"The situation has changed. You're in grave danger."

"No shit! From you!"

I step back, blinking against the pain of her words. She's not entirely wrong. The attack at the warehouse was my fault, and she was almost captured. Xavier's Guard must have followed me there another night and discovered her. I got careless.

"Xavier is the danger," I say softly.

"And you're one of his Guard!"

"Not anymore." And now they want me dead, too. "I told Xavier you were dead once. He won't believe me again."

"Liar." Her expression shows that she's thinking. "You were with the others when they attacked."

I shake my head. "I saved you from them."

She blinks a few times. "If Xavier wants me dead, why am I still alive? I had stakes at my heart."

When I crashed into that warehouse, I wondered the same thing. And my only conclusion chills my bones. "Xavier doesn't trust anyone else to kill you," I tell her. "Or he wants to watch it happen. He wants to see you suffer."

I shudder at the memory of what I've seen Xavier do to others. Even if I didn't commit any of those murders, I was complicit. Selina called me a monster, and it's true. I was a monster, even as a human, and now I've literally become one.

She tips her head to the side as if considering my words, then stands and leaps forward. Her chains clank as she hits the edge of her range. "You can't hold me here. My friends will come for me. They will kill you."

"If I let you go, *Xavier* will kill you."

"My friends can keep me safe."

"If that's true," I ask her, "then why are you here?"

She frowns. "So you're going to keep me trapped down here forever? Torturing and raping me like you did in the dungeon?" The hate in her eyes is a million stakes to my heart.

Things much worse than murder happened in Xavier's dungeons.

I lift my gaze from the tiled floor. "I will never hurt you."

"Bullshit." Her chains clank. "You've hurt me before, you'll do it again. You're a monster. I hate you. I will always hate you."

"I only want to keep you safe."

"Safe? At what cost?"

Unable to bear the hate in her eyes, I look down. She'll never love me like I love her. She'll never forgive me, and as much as that hurts, I understand. I don't deserve her. I don't deserve forgiveness. And I certainly don't deserve love.

I've done terrible things. Unforgivable things. And she's right. I can't keep her here forever. It's wrong to keep her apart from the men she loves. I've caused her enough pain.

But if I let her go she'll be killed, and that would kill me, too.

So we're stuck here, and I need to bear the pain of her anger, of her unhappiness. Her hatred.

I long to tell her the truth, that I *never* hurt her and kept others from hurting her on many occasions, but sharing that truth wouldn't ease her trauma; the truth would only unburden me.

And besides, my attempts to protect her, to lessen her pain, weren't enough—not nearly enough. I don't deserve to explain.

"You don't trust me," I say as calmly as I can. "I understand that. But know this." I force myself to look straight into her accusing eyes. "I will never, ever hurt you. And I will never let anyone else hurt you again."

CHAPTER 7

Grayson

I slump against the wall inside the warehouse, letting the cold from the bricks penetrate my back. I have no idea why I came here, to the last place I saw her. If she escapes, she's more likely to go to Rock's bar. At least there I know she'll be safe, able to hide in his subbasement.

But nothing in this world seems safe anymore.

The windows, high in this warehouse and smashed when Xavier's team broke in, have already been repaired, no doubt arranged by Astrid or Malcolm. I've been part of FJS for close to twenty years, but at times I'm still taken aback by their efficiency.

If only I'd asked Astrid to assign a security team to guard this warehouse every time we trained. But we were trying to keep Selina on the down low. Or I certainly was. I did not and do not want anyone else to suspect who she really is. I still can't believe it myself.

If I'd done my sworn duty, she'd be captive somewhere else.

I slam the back of my head against the brick wall a few times, hoping the pain will snap me out of my terror- and grief-induced fog. I was foolish to leave the others and head out on my own. Did I think I'd just find her by randomly searching?

The city is huge, millions of people, and by now Pike could have taken her out of Toronto, he could have taken her anywhere.

Seeing stars from banging my head, I turn and punish my fists against the wall instead of my skull.

I am an idiot, a failure. I'm so weak. I know better. I should have taken Selina away the first night we met. I should have turned her over to the Order. I swore an oath, but then let lust overrule my sacred duty.

I squeeze my eyes shut to mirror the tightening in my chest. I'm kidding myself to claim it was just about lust. Even on that first night, there was more. And my intense initial reaction to Selina is quickly turning into love. Not that I'd ever tell her I love her. And not that she'd ever love me back.

Even if she didn't already love Rock—which she obviously does—as soon as I tell her who she is, who I am, and return her to her rightful place, Rock will lose her too. She'll hate me for it but neither Rock nor I are worthy of being her mate.

Sensing the air moving, I spin around.

"Who's there?" I call out.

Pike steps onto the warehouse floor.

I pull out a stake and leap forward to attack, but stop with my weapon an inch from his heart.

Pike stands, arms extended to the side, chest open,

head tipped back, throat exposed. It's the universal vampire posture for submission, surrender. And my training and instincts stopped me from killing him instantly.

"Where is she?" Hatred floods through me, my own heart pounding so hard I can barely hear my voice. "Why did you come back here? Did you already kill her?" I press the stake against his T-shirt, nestling it between two ribs, ready to drive forward at any moment.

"She's alive," he says. "Unharmed. Safe."

Relief dilutes the hatred in my heart. Even though I've been a vampire less than sixty years, as a Knight of the Order of Sanguis the rules of engagement are a part of me. Killing is against the law unless it's in self-defense, and to kill a vampire in this submissive pose is worse than illegal, it's immoral.

I knee him in the balls.

I may be schooled in the rules of gentlemanly combat, but I'm no angel.

His scarred face barely reacts to the pain, but anger burns in his eyes, his irises such a light brown they're almost yellow. In other circumstances the shade might look striking, but at the moment it evokes pure evil.

Grabbing him by the throat, I lift the fiend off his feet and smash his back into the pillar closest to the door. The fiery anger in his eyes threatens to erupt, but he keeps it contained.

I fight to hold back my stake, and my arm shakes from the effort.

My stake *wants* to be piercing his heart. I want it there, too. "Why did you come here?"

"To tell you she's safe."

"Safe? Like she was safe when you were raping her in that dungeon?"

He casts his gaze down. "I would never hurt her." His voice is strained against my hand that's constricting his airflow.

"But you *did* hurt her, you asshole! And for that you will die."

His body goes slack, held up to the wall only by my hand at his throat and the pressure of the stake jabbing at his chest. If I'm not careful, I'll choke him, or stake him, but why be careful?

Because murder is the highest crime in the vampire world. Even with the most lenient sentence, I'd spend the next two or three hundred years in prison. But no one is here to witness. If I told Astrid that Pike attacked first, Astrid might believe me.

My stake arm twitches. "Give me one reason I shouldn't drive this stake through your heart."

"If you kill me…" he can barely talk now "…you'll never find her."

I drop him and drive the stake against the wall. The splinters scatter onto the floor.

"What do you want?" I ask, knowing I'd give my life to find her.

"I want to protect her." He coughs and rubs his throat. "She's being hunted."

Yeah. By my Order. But I quickly realize that's not what he means. He means Xavier.

"Xavier won't rest until he finds her," Pike says. "He wants to see her suffer. He wants to see her dead."

This mirrors what Kwana said. She claimed Pike wasn't part of their team. I wonder if Pike will contradict that.

"How do I know you haven't already taken her to him?"

"I would never." He looks down.

"Liar."

"I will die before I let him touch her again." His gaze rises to meet mine.

Pain and shame are palpable in his eyes, in his entire expression and posture.

His emotions hit me straight in the gut and make me want to trust him, even though I know I shouldn't, even though I know I'm looking at the vampire who tortured the woman I love.

"Why should I believe you?"

"Why else would I be here?" He stretches out his arms again and exposes his chest, lifts his chin.

"I can't erase the past," he continues. "I tried to lessen her pain, but it wasn't enough. Not near enough." Dropping his arms, he punches his leather-clad thighs. "I won't make that mistake again. Xavier must die for what he has done to Selina."

"*You* should die for what you've done to Selina."

He nods an acknowledgement, and it almost knocks me off my feet.

"I do deserve to die," he says, "but first I've got to know that she's safe."

"Why take her if you meant to let her go?" My suspicion won't let me feel hope.

"I took her to keep her from Xavier," he growls. "Something *you* failed at." His eyes flash, revealing the warrior, the man capable of despicable things. It reminds me with whom I am dealing. I cannot trust Pike. Not this easily.

"If the Guard took her back to Xavier, you can't imagine…" His voice trails off.

"Why did you turn on your own team?" I ask.

"My team?"

"The group you attacked this place with."

He looks down, shaking his head. "It's my fault they found her. They followed me."

Interesting. That's the first thing he's said that contradicts Kwana's story. She said that creep Louis told them where we were. But Pike's guilt is obvious. He *thinks* he led Xavier's Guard to Selina.

I can use that guilt against him. "Take me to her."

He nods.

I blink. It can't be so easy. This must be a trap.

"I'll get the others," I say. But if they managed to get inside Xavier's compound they may still be down there—or dead.

Pike shakes his head. "Just you. Come. Right now."

"Why the sudden urgency?" Narrowing my eyes, I square my stance.

He drops his head. "She's hurting herself."

My heart rises to my throat. "You fiend!" I grab his throat again.

He shakes his head over my hand. "Please. There's no time for this. I'm afraid of what she might do."

He sounds desperate. Looks desperate.

I've replayed the events of last night over and over in my mind and I can't deny that his explanation fits with the facts.

I signaled Astrid the second the warehouse windows broke, and if her team had arrived moments earlier, Selina would have been safe—I have to believe that. But it's also true that when Pike swooped in and took her, she had a stake aimed straight at her heart. Rock and I were caught up in combat. I can see how Pike might believe that he saved her life.

Maybe he did.

And if he's willing to take me to her now, I can't let that opportunity pass, even if I walk into a trap.

CHAPTER 8

Selina

Pike has been gone for hours. I tried three more times to pull the bolts from the wall, but it's time to admit that the effort's futile. I need another plan, but what?

One of my wrists has just healed, the other is mending, but my ankle and shin are fully smashed and sending so much pain through me it's still hard to breathe.

I close my eyes against the pain, trying to go somewhere else in my mind while I heal, but it drifts to even worse places.

What if I never see Rock and Gray again? After just a few weeks, I can no longer imagine my life without both men.

Rock has my heart, fully, and while Gray remains a mystery—his emotions, his past fully guarded—he's so much a part of me already that I can almost sense him here with me now.

I draw a long breath, amazed at how vivid my memory of Gray can be. I can smell his scent like he's near.

"Selina!" His voice comes into my daydream.

My eyes snap open.

Within an instant, Gray's on the mattress beside me, holding me tight. But this is no dream.

"Are you hurt?" He looks down to my ankle. Shock fills his eyes and he springs up, grabs Pike—who I hadn't realized was with him—and throws the large vampire against the wall.

"You bastard!" Gray says to Pike. "You said you didn't hurt her."

"He didn't," I call out. "I broke my ankle and wrists while Pike was gone. I was trying to get free."

Gray drops Pike and pulls out a stake. "Release her. Now."

Pike crosses the room, slowly, hands out in a submissive gesture.

Looking up into his amber eyes, something inside me stirs. He is doing this for me, and it's causing him pain.

Good. He *should* feel pain. And once I'm released I'll kill him, if Gray doesn't do it first.

Pike pulls a key from the front pocket of his leather pants and unlocks the shackle around my broken ankle. I gingerly test the movement. It's starting to heal, but I don't think I can stand.

Gray puts his stake away and I give him a questioning look.

Pike moves to release my right wrist, and with his body so close, his scent is overwhelming. He's so close I could lick his skin, sink in my fangs to feed. I shake my head to force the thoughts from my mind.

My arm drops to the mattress.

In an instant, Gray pushes Pike out of the way and rubs my arm.

"Does it hurt? Look at the bruising." He glares at Pike.

I cup his face to turn it back to me. "The bruising will heal quickly."

Gray takes my lips softly, unlike the way he usually kisses me. He's so tender it's like he thinks my mouth is bruised too, and I moan, my tongue darting out to catch the edge of one of his soft nibbles.

My left arm drops from its shackle, and I wrap it around Gray's neck to deepen our kiss, needing the taste of him even more than I need blood.

Gray gathers me into his arms and my good leg wraps around his back as he kneels beside me. Freed from bondage, I want Gray. I want him right here, right now. I need to have him inside me. I reach between us to find his cock.

He moans, then I hear another groan.

My eyes snap open.

I forgot that we aren't alone. Pike is standing a few feet away, lust obvious on his face, but the moment our eyes meet, he drops his head.

That's right, I think. *You* should *feel shame, you perverted voyeur.*

I move my lips close to Gray's ear. "Kill him. Kill him now."

Gray pulls back to look into my eyes. He shakes his head.

"Then I'll kill him." I grab Gray's discarded stake and stand, ignoring the intense pain as I leap toward Pike.

Gray grabs me midflight.

I struggle against him. "He needs to die. He's been

holding me prisoner, and now he's got you trapped down here too."

Gray's hold on me tightens, his arms trapping mine at my sides. "Princess," he whispers in my ear. "Pike brought me here."

"It's a trap."

"Don't you think I thought of that?"

I struggle against Gray, unable to believe that Pike would just let me go, even though I realize he's done it before. There's no denying he's the one who let me escape from Xavier's dungeon.

"Princess, I know exactly where we are," Gray says. "Abandoned tunnels that two hundred years ago housed FJS offices. I've got my phone. Astrid could have a security team here in a flash."

I look up at Pike. He's standing in that submissive position again, except that his head is down, face toward the floor. He looks so sad, so defeated.

I relax in Gray's arms. "Why would he let me go?"

Pike raises his gaze to meet mine, and the look on his scarred face shows so much pain, so much conflict. My anger melts into compassion.

"Your vampire and that big man will keep you safe," Pike says. "You'd be safer here, but I can't bear to see you unhappy. Or hurting yourself."

I test my broken ankle. It's still stiff, but the bones are healed. I lean back into Gray and his tight hold on me loosens.

"Where are the others?" I ask him, over my shoulder.

"They're looking for Xavier's compound."

"No!" Pike shouts.

Gray grabs another stake from the holster on his back. "You *are* still loyal to him!"

Shaking his head, Pike assumes the passive position, ready to be killed by Gray. "I fear for your *friends'* lives, not his. Xavier must die for what he's done to Selina, but that won't be easy. He's well protected. Everyone in his court is brainwashed, most trapped there for decades, some centuries. Many don't know another life."

The way Pike says this, the anguish in his voice, makes me believe that he's telling the truth. I want to ask more. I want to know how he ended up in Xavier's court—and most of all, why he let me go.

But if my friends and my love are in danger, I must go to them.

"Take her somewhere safe," Pike says to Gray.

"Of course." Gray turns toward me. "Can you walk?"

I test my ankle again and then nod.

Gray takes my hand. "I have somewhere she can hide until Xavier's dead."

"Good." Pike nods. "Best if you don't tell me." He looks down. "If they follow me again…"

"How many are there?" Gray asks. "How soon will they come?"

Pike draws a long breath, as if thinking. "Xavier doesn't allow his subjects outside. Not even most of his Guard. The ones last night, most of them had never been outside court. You killed the only ones who had. It could be weeks or months before Xavier selects others he trusts enough to leave. But he will. He will come for her again."

"Thank you," Gray says. "You've done the right thing. Keeping her safe is my highest priority, my sworn duty, my life." Gray's words stir inside me. He cares for me more than he lets on.

Pike nods just perceptibly as he backs away from us, and still holding my hand, Gray leads me through the curtains toward the darkness. Before the velvet falls back down, I catch it and turn back. Pike is slumped, crouched against the wall with his head in his hands, and the sight is a stab to my heart.

If he's told the truth, Xavier's Guard is now after him too. "Will you be safe here?" I ask.

"Go," he says. "If they find me, I'll get what I deserve."

Selina

I JUMP INTO ROCK'S ARMS, THE INSTANT HE WALKS through the door into Gray's foyer. The big man's hearts beat hard against me, and surrounded by the warmth and strength of his huge body I'm safe, I'm home. Tonight is the first time I've seen the inside of Gray's house, but now that Rock's here it is home.

"Welcome." Gray claps Rock on the arm while the latter still holds me aloft.

"You live here all alone?" Rock asks scanning the huge foyer with its marble mosaic floor and the twin oak staircases that lead up to a balcony-style hallway on the second floor. Across from that, high above us, are a series of massive stained-glass windows.

As he looks around, Rock whistles through his teeth. "Guess you two will have to keep clear of this space once the sun comes up."

"Nope." Gray shakes his head. "Every window in the house is treated. Less UV light than what reflects from a full moon. Want the grand tour? Selina insisted we wait until you got here."

"You guys have been standing here in the entrance?" Rock looks at me with skepticism.

"We just got here." I press a quick kiss to Rock's cheek. A place I'd never be able to reach if he weren't still holding me in his arms. "I'm so glad you're safe," I say against Rock's neck. "When I heard you'd gone to find Xavier…"

"The entrance was sealed." He shakes his head. "The only one Astrid's informant claims she knows."

"You don't believe her?" Gray asks.

"To be honest, I don't know what to believe anymore."

The tall, elegant vampire leans against the round table at the center of the room, his fingers strong against the highly polished wood surface. "Shall we do the tour?" He gestures to his left. "I've got five guest bedrooms, each with an en suite, so you can each choose your favorite room, or… share if you prefer?"

Rock grunts and it vibrates through my whole body. "Haven't said I'd move in yet. Don't know that Selina has, either."

"Let's look around." I stroke the back of his neck.

I've already decided that I want to move in, and hope Rock will choose to live here too. Living above ground, with daylight—safely—is like a fantasy, but I can't bear the idea of no longer sleeping in Rock's arms. The last two nights were long enough. Never again.

"I don't use these principal rooms much." Gray flips on the lights in a large sitting room to one side of the foyer. "Guess this is the parlor?"

"Set me down?" I whisper in Rock's ear.

He lets me slide down the side of his hard body, and I brush my hand over his chest as I step away from him to explore the beautiful space. "Did you decorate this yourself?"

"No." Gray laughs. "The place came furnished. Why? Does it look like me?"

"It kind of does." I wink at him. "Victorian elegance."

"*That's* how you see me?" Gray plops down in a soft-looking sofa upholstered in red velvet. "How old do you think I am?"

Rock is at the edge of the room, checking out a beautiful piece of furniture, so I plop down next to Gray, and the sofa's so soft that I'm tossed against him.

"If you want to jump me, princess, all you have to do is ask." He kisses my forehead.

I place my hands on his chest for leverage to put some distance between us. "How old *are* you?" I ask.

"Which age to you mean?"

I shrug. "Both, I guess."

"I was twenty-four when I turned. And it was 1967."

I cock my head to the side, trying to decide if he's pulling my leg. "But you said your Maker was one of the Ancients."

"She was. Doesn't mean *I'm* one of the Ancients." He laughs. "Did you really think I was thousands of years old?"

I shrug. "How did it happen? When you turned?"

"I was traveling in Morocco, doing what young men and women did at the time—smoking hash, eating couscous and trying to figure out what I was going to do with my life."

I turn toward him on the sofa, bending up one leg. Rock sits down on a leather chair opposite the sofa.

"What was your family like?" I ask. "Did you have brothers and sisters?"

Gray shakes his head. "Only child. And I suppose that made it even harder."

"Made what harder?"

"Disappointing my father." Gray looks away from me.

I touch his shoulder. "How?"

He jumps off the sofa. "Enough about me. We've got a house to see." He points to the right and I spot a small door hidden in the paneling.

He opens it and steps through. "Servants' staircase." He points to the stairs, then starts down a hall leading right.

"You have servants?" I haven't seen anyone since we got here.

"Nah." Gray shakes his head as he leads us through the narrow corridor.

"Not even blood slaves?" Rock's voice booms in the small space that his shoulders nearly fill side to side.

"Rock." I nudge him, shocked at his rudeness.

"The servants' staircase leads up to the attic," Gray says. "The only part of the house that's not fully sun proofed. Don't go up there in daylight."

I nod, and he takes us about ten feet to the right, through a door that leads to a room lined with shelves and cupboards.

"Pantry." He strides through it. "I don't use this room. Actually haven't been in here for ages, but it's a shortcut to the kitchen."

We turn the corner into a large kitchen with two gas cooktops, three ovens and a modern fridge with glass doors revealing not much inside.

"Guess we'll need more food once the giant moves in." He grins back at Rock who just grunts, but I can tell he's impressed.

There are windows above huge ceramic sinks, and

moonlight peeks through the leaves of massive maple and oak trees in the yard.

"Those windows are treated for daylight too. In case you ever want to use the kitchen." He points toward a door. "Back garden is through there. And the stairs to the cellar."

"What's in the cellar?" Rock asks.

"Gym. Screening room. Boiler room. Laundry. I've been thinking of finishing more of it, maybe putting in a billiard table. Now I've got a housemate—" Gray smiles at me.

Rock grunts, and I stroke his arm to reassure him that even if I move in here with Gray, I'll still love him. Always.

Gray leads us through a narrow space housing more counters and cupboards filled with beautiful dishes and glasses.

"Butler's pantry," he says, and then we step into an incredibly beautiful dining room. Moonlight streams through an intricate stained glass window that fills most of the back wall and reaches up to the ceiling that must be at least twelve or more feet tall, given how high it rises above my giant's head. I could probably stand on Rock's shoulders without hitting the ceiling.

The table's long enough to seat at least twenty, and three crystal chandeliers hang above the table, the one in the center the largest of the three.

"Do those work?" I ask, and within seconds they're on. Light dances through the crystals to brighten the room, and it's marvelous. "They're amazing. How do you keep them clean?" I try to imagine Gray housecleaning, but can't.

"I've got a housekeeper. She comes in Tuesdays and Thursdays."

"Does she know?"

Gray shakes his head. "She came with the house. She gets a full-time salary, even though I've cut her hours to two days a week."

"She's not suspicious about that?" Rock folds his arms over his chest. "I thought you said Selina would be safe here. That no one would see her."

"Do you want to clean this place?" Gray asks. "Because you're welcome to do it."

"Where do you go when the housekeeper's here?" I ask.

"She thinks I work nights." He shrugs. "Which I suppose I do. If I'm here and sleeping, I leave her a note letting her know which room to skip that day. Besides, I don't need much sleep."

I nod. I've noticed that I can get by on fewer of hours of shuteye since I fed from Gray. I've felt so much stronger, more powerful since that night, and I wonder when he'll let me feed from him again.

The idea makes my fangs ache and wakes a stronger ache between my legs.

I take Rock's hand. I want him inside me in any way that we can. He claims we aren't compatible, that we can never have sex, but although the obvious size of his cock is intimidating, the mere idea of having him inside me makes me wet. So wet.

Squeezing my legs together, I know that my panties are soaked, and I resist the urge to pull Rock's hand and put it between my legs. Something I plan to do the moment we're alone.

The dining room has huge French doors that open into a front room that's even more elegantly furnished than the one on the other side of the foyer. A large, leaded-glass bay window opens to the front garden, with half-moon-shaped, stained-glass windows above.

"Well, that's the main floor," Gray says. "Maybe we should have a party sometime, so I can actually use it." He smiles back at Rock and me. "What do you think, roomies?"

Rock's hold on my hand tightens.

"Once Xavier's dead, of course." Gray goes back into the foyer and I notice the massive chandelier hanging there, too.

It's even more intricate than the ones in the dining room, with sculpted glass arches and more crystals than I could ever count.

Gray heads up the stairs, six at a time, and I drag my hand along the polished oak banister as Rock and I follow.

He turns to the left, into the farthest bedroom. My insides pulse as I see the big bed, wanting both of these men at the same time. My cheeks flush at the notion and I remember my erotic dream.

In my dream Pike had five or six hands—at least. What would it be like to be with more than one man at the same time? To be pleasured in so many ways at once? Pleasured by men I love?

I shake my head. Rock might tolerate Gray as my lover, but there's no way they'd ever make love to me together. At least, I don't think…

"Princess?" Gray wakes me from my lustful daydream.

"Sorry?" I shake my head. "What did you ask? I was distracted."

"I could tell." His grin is full of heat.

I look away and lean into Rock's chest.

"I was saying that the bed in here is the biggest. Might work for you two?"

Gray is assuming that Rock and I will share a bed while under his roof, and it makes me feel safe and respected, but also hurts. If I ever needed proof that Gray doesn't love me, that he's my lover but nothing else, this is it.

"Do you like this room?" I ask Rock as I come back from peeking into the bathroom. "The shower in the en suite is huge. I think it would work for you."

"Let's see the other rooms," Rock says. "You need to be in the one that's safest. I don't like the idea of those windows." He gestures around the room. "You'd be safer at my place."

"I'm not going to sleep in a dungeon again."

My words hit him like a punch.

"I didn't mean that." I shake my head. "No, sorry. Maybe I did mean it a little. I don't want to live underground. I'll feel trapped. I can't—"

"Acushla, it's okay." Rock gathers me into his arms. "I understand. I will stay here too and keep you safe."

CHAPTER 9

Selina

The girl fumbles with her phone as she staggers down the alley, zigzagging, doing the unmistakable dance of the drunken club girl. Her hair is brassy—the way dark brown hair turns with DIY bleach jobs, her shoes too high and her skirt too short.

Hatred builds inside me as I follow her down the alley, hatred I don't understand. I don't even know this young woman.

I feel strange, inside and outside my body at the same time. My surroundings grow fuzzy at the edges, blurred, even though my focus on the woman is crystal clear.

Her ankle turns as her stupidly high-heeled shoe tips to the side. Her phone clatters to the pavement, and she follows it down hard, landing on her knee. I can instantly smell the blood from her scraped skin.

Sitting, she sways forward and back like she's not really certain what happened, and then she reaches for her phone.

Stepping up beside her, I offer my hand. She looks up. Her

Chinese ethnicity is disguised under heavily contoured makeup that makes her look like a Kardashian, and her mouth moves like she's speaking, but I don't hear any words. All I hear is the sound of her blood.

She takes my hand. I pull her up quickly and then plunge my fangs into her neck.

I wake, thrashing, my heart rate soaring, and I have no idea where I am.

Quickly I remember. I'm not in the alley location of my dream, nor am I trapped underground by Pike. I'm safe at Gray's house and in bed with Rock.

Propping myself up on the bed, I watch Rock sleep, his blond eyelashes fluttering slightly against his skin, his breaths slow and deep. He looks so peaceful like this, but the solid expanse of his body and the rise and fall of his chest allude to the power of Rock. Even though we're not touching, heat emanates from him like a furnace and I know that with him I will never be cold or afraid.

And I have to believe that he'll get over whatever is holding him back from making love to me. If it turns out we're incompatible, fine, but at least we should try. I slide my legs together, my sex pulsing with renewed need. A deep need that has been nagging at me since I fed from that human, since my erotic dream about Pike.

Early this morning when Gray showed us the bedrooms—all except one, which he claimed was his *private space* and then quickly added that it was too messy—it was obvious Rock needed sleep. Me? I needed something else—and still do.

My desire for Rock must have brought on my vivid, feeding dream, although I'd expect this current hunger more likely to bring on a *sex* dream.

I could go to Gray now and get what my body craves.

With less than subtle hints, the vampire made it clear where I could find him if I wanted. But as much as my body needs sex, I long to be next to Rock more. Maybe he'll be in the mood when he wakes.

Rock stirs, his huge body shifting, moving the mattress between us. His eyes slowly open, and when he sees me he smiles and pulls me down for a kiss. Hallelujah!

"Acushla," he says while taking a breath. "I dreamed that I'd lost you again."

"Never." I kiss his nose, the edges of his mouth. "I had a bad dream too, but you'll never lose me. I plan to stay glued to your side."

He sits, and the massive wooden headboard creaks as he leans against it. "All joking aside, I'm not letting you out of my sight, you know. Never again." He shakes his head. "Shite. The bar. I can sell it, but I need to go in tonight—before dark." He glances at his watch. "My liquor vendor needs to be paid, and it's Kevin's night off, so I should at least handle the open and close…." He shifts his arm around me and I lean into his warm chest. His fingers dance on my upper arm, and even that light contact fuels sparks inside me.

"It's fine, Rock." I nestle in, stroking his chest, lightly dusted with thick blond hairs. "Go to work. And don't sell your bar. Not on my account. You love that place. I'll come over as soon as it's dark."

He shakes his head. "It's not safe. Stay inside. I'll make sure Gray stays with you. And Astrid can assign a team to watch the house."

My body tenses and air locks inside my chest. "Don't you think that's a bit over the top?"

He squeezes me in more tightly. "No. It's not. You

insisted on moving out of my basement, but you've got to stay inside here, where it's safe."

"Rock." I try to fight my irritation. "I need *some* freedom. I need to go outside. I need to live a normal life."

"Acushla. That's not possible. Not until Xavier's dead."

"So, you want me to stay in the house—all the time?"

"Of course."

I push back from him. "No. Rock, I can't bear the thought of being trapped here. If you insist on that you're no better than Pike."

He pulls back. "How's that, now?"

"Pike claimed he was holding me captive to keep me safe. I won't let you and Gray do that to me too."

He frowns. "I guess I can understand that." He sighs. "I actually understand more than you know, but Xavier's Guard found us at the warehouse. What if they know about my bar, too?"

"Then you'll be there to protect me." I do get that my life's at risk, but I also know being a prisoner feels like another kind of death. Even if I choose to stay here in Gray's house all night, it needs to be my choice.

His fingers stroke high on my chest. "You know, there's another reason you should stay away from O'Malley's."

"What's that?" I trace my hand up this thigh, my mind back on sex. I want to coax Rock into at least letting me give him some pleasure.

It's working, because he groans, but he catches my wrist before my fingers land where I want. "That cop," he says huskily. "He's been hanging out at the bar."

"What cop?" I ask, although I know who he means. He means Colton, that handsome blond man who looks like the quarterback character from a Hollywood movie.

"The one who was pumping Chelle for information about vampires." Rock pulls my hand away from his thigh, up to his chest, and holds it there, warm under his.

"Maybe the cop just likes your bar," I say. "Maybe he likes a beer after work."

Rock draws a long breath and I love how his chest expands beneath my hand. "At least where he's concerned I know I can protect you."

"My hero." I rise up on one knee to kiss him. "My big, brave hero."

"Don't mock me, Acushla."

"I would never." I grin mischievously and slide my other hand toward the massive bulge under his pajama bottoms.

He shifts to the side. "None of that. I really do need to go to work."

"Do you?" I straddle his body and slide against him. "Do you really?"

He puts his hands on my waist and lifts me, like he plans to toss me to the mattress, but before he can, I kiss him. Instantly, his hold on me changes, pulling our chests together and deepening the kiss.

Swept up in the taste of him, at the pleasure of his thick tongue probing my mouth, I grow even wetter at the memory of the other things Rock did to me with his tongue. That night was amazing. Mind blowing, in fact. I want that again. I want to feel his tongue stroking and plunging inside me, but it won't be enough—I want so much more from Rock.

I want him to join our bodies together. I want to feel part of him. Him part of me. I want, I *need* to feel him penetrating my body, and no matter Rock's size, I long to feel him buried deep and moving inside me. Both of us deriving pleasure from the act of love.

I move my kisses to the morning stubble on his chin and neck as my hands stroke his torso, skimming over his nipples. He's holding me against his chest, but up off his lap, and while the heat of his torso, the ridges of his abs, are delicious against my splayed legs and what lies between, I long to drop lower.

His breathing rate quickens and a moan rumbles under me, driving me on, making my body undulate against him. I want Rock. I *need* him. I've never wanted anything so badly.

I wiggle looser in his hold and slide down his body, longing to make contact with his cock—with any part of my body. I want to make him want me as much as I want him. I'll prove to him that we're compatible. If he makes me feel this way, how could we not be?

My inner thigh finds the waistband of his pajama pants and I reach down to stroke my fingers low on his stomach. As I glide along the edge of the fabric, hair tickles my fingers and another moan rumbles from his lips into mine. Emboldened I let my fingers slip under the waistband.

Before moving toward my target, I discover a strap that feels like leather. Is he wearing a jock strap? A leather thong? To bed?

I slide my fingers lower to investigate.

"No." His body tenses. "Acushla, I told you. We can't."

"I don't like the word can't." I rub my body against his.

"But do you *understand* the word *no*?"

No I do understand.

I slip off him onto the mattress, leaving one leg draped over his thighs. His hardness bulges under his pajamas, pulsing, the massive shape almost like a melon, or a football, and for the first time I wonder if he's right about our incompatibility. But even if those parts of us won't fit together in the conventional way, I want to make him feel good. Just like he made me feel good—so, so good.

I graze my fingers over his bulge.

"No." He grabs my wrist. "Too much." His voice is strained, like he's in pain.

"What are you wearing?" I accidentally graze the huge package again.

He groans, but it's more in pain than pleasure. "Nothing." Veins pop on his face and he grimaces.

"Rock. Tell me, please. What is it?"

"Something to protect you."

"*Protect* me?"

He's breathing very heavily now, his tight stomach rolling with each quick breath, and sweat rises on his chest and face.

I kneel next to him on the bed. "Rock. What is it? Show me."

He shakes his head.

"Please."

He turns away from me. "Don't look at me."

I grab his shoulder and tug back. "I won't touch you. Not if you don't want me to. I promise. But whatever you're wearing, it's *hurting* you. Show me, or take it off. Better yet, both."

Still facing away from me, he shakes his head. He tries to move his legs off the bed, but winces in obvious intense pain and stops.

"Rock." I clear my throat to swallow my sadness and concern. I need to sound firm. "Show me what you're wearing. Take it off, right now, or I'll never share your bed again."

He doesn't move.

"I'll ask Gray to kick you out of his home."

He turns back to face me.

As we make eye contact, I fight to show him I mean my threats. But we both know I could never go through with them. Still, in this moment I'm serious, and try to convey that with my eyes. I can't let him hurt himself. Especially not for my so-called protection.

He winces as he loosens the tie at the waist of his pajama bottoms. I reach forward to help him, but he shakes his head.

In one violent movement, he lifts his hips and slides the pants down to his knees.

I gasp. His penis and balls are strapped down by some sort of leather binding. Dark red flesh presses out between the straps of the cage-like contraption, and the organ itself is bent at what must be a painful angle. It's pretty much doubled over. No wonder the bulge looked like a melon.

"Rock…" I can barely make my voice work. "What? Why?"

His eyes fill with shame and he looks away.

"Take it off. Please." My voice breaks as I choke out the words. "It's hurting you. I can't stand to see you in pain." If I still had tears, they'd be streaming down my cheeks.

"Get away from me," he says.

"Rock…"

"Please. If you won't leave the room, move away from me. You're making it worse. If you care about me at all, you will do this for me."

"Care about you? Rock. I *love* you."

He turns to face me. Joy flashes for a brief second, striking away the pain, but the moment passes and the look on his face rips through me—agony and…and shame. Rock's pain is so much more than physical.

I shift back, backing away from him until I'm off the bed.

He undoes a buckle over his left hip. The instant the buckle's released, the contraption shifts like a coil's been released. His penis lifts away from his body, but it's still tightly wrapped and distorted at a bent angle. At least, I assume it's distorted.

When he said we weren't compatible, I figured he meant his size. Could it be more than that?

But right now, none of that matters. All that matters is that Rock is clearly in pain. Pain he inflicted on himself—because of me.

Hissing, he unties a knot securing a leather lace at the base of his cock, but before he gets the knot fully open, he tugs at the thin leather strap. It tightens, instead of loosening, and he roars, his back arching off the bed, his face turning red.

I lunge toward him, wanting to comfort him, to help, but I stop myself before I get there. I don't want to make it worse, or take the risk he'll change his mind about taking that thing off.

He adjusts the knot at the base, then slowly starts to loosen the tie that's laced along his cock and holding together the rings of leather that constrain him.

"Let me help."

He shakes his head, closing his eyes as he continues to loosen the laces. The rings of leather wrapped around him remain tight and flesh pushes over their sides.

Finally, the bend in his appendage starts to unfurl. He

tugs at the edges of the lacing and I realize that the leather ties loop from the top back down to the base. Not only is his cock tightly bound, the head was purposefully bent back toward his balls, while the strap around his waist held the entire business hard against his body.

I try to imagine how this looked when he did it, presumably while his penis was flaccid. Because he's aroused, the leather cage doesn't come close to fitting and the pain must be blinding.

He continues to loosen the lacing, working his way back down the other side, and it's so elaborate, so cruel. Who does something like this—to himself?

I want to know why he did this. What kind of pain he feels inside that would drive him to inflict so much self-damage.

He stops for a moment, panting, moaning.

"Are you okay?" I ask softly.

Without looking at me, he nods, then slowly he starts to nudge the rings of leather up. As he forces the first one over the head of his penis, he cries out, his entire body contracting then relaxing.

One by one, he works the rings up to the tip and off the end.

The process gets easier because the rings lower on his member are larger in diameter, but only slightly, and I can't stop staring at the engorged red flesh as it's released, as the blood flow fully returns, as his veins rise and pulse. His balls, too, are encased in leather sacks—at least, I assume that's not his actual skin.

His erect member must be three and a half or four inches in diameter and it's more than a foot long. There's no wonder I first thought it was part of his thigh.

When the last ring slides off the head, he slumps back,

but his erection stands straight, the weight and size of it defying the laws of logic and gravity. His body's slack now, unmoving against the mattress except for his breathing, and his chest and belly rise as he fights to slow his hearts' rates down.

I watch, mesmerized, my mouth dry. All I did was observe, but I feel like I've run a marathon. I'm both spent and out of breath. And in spite of observing this horrific scene, still turned on.

He reaches down to his package and my insides contract, thinking he's going to stroke himself, something I'd love to witness. But instead he undoes a lace at the base and, as I suspected, the sacks covering his balls slide off. That part of him is large too, like two encased peaches.

I take a small step forward. "Rock."

He half sits and holds up his palm toward me. "Don't come any closer."

"Please, Rock. Let me help you." I might not be able to get that inside me, but I can stroke it, lick it, suck on the head if I can open my mouth that wide. The heat and wetness inside intensify. I can barely keep still.

He shakes his head. "Stay there. I need to get ready for work. I can't go in like this." He grunts.

"Then you *definitely* need my help." I smile, hoping to lighten the mood, but instead his mood seems to sink under a hundred-ton weight.

"I'll take care of it in the shower." He swings off the bed to stand. His erection bounces and, as he takes it in his hand, he hangs his head as if ashamed.

"Let me watch you," I say, my voice unusually husky.

He crosses to the en suite in two long strides, but he leaves the door open. Is that an invitation?

I hear the sound of the shower and slowly approach the bathroom door and step through.

Leaning against the back wall of the stall, away from the controls, he holds his massive cock in one hand as the other rests against the tiles. The water sprays on his back, and his chest heaves as he draws long hard breaths, as if fighting to gain control over his body.

I sit on the edge of the large, freestanding bathtub. I should make sure he knows that I'm in here. It's an invasion of privacy. But my desire to alert him is overwritten by my fear that he'll make me leave.

Even his large hand can barely encircle his member as he strokes, gently, against what must be unbelievably sensitive skin after that constriction.

His head turns. He sees me. His hand stops as his eyes open wider. But instead of stopping, he turns away again and continues to rub himself—hard.

His grip tightens and the speed of his strokes increases, his head resting on his forearm against the glass wall of the shower as he uses the other hand to vigorously pleasure himself, pulling and tugging so hard I fear that he's causing more pain than pleasure.

Still, even with the hint of punishment in the action, watching Rock jerk off is the hottest thing I have ever seen, and I squirm on the edge of the tub, my insides throbbing with heat and desire.

I come. A massive orgasm, without so much as touching myself, and my insides contract as I squeeze my legs together and watch him.

Rock shouts, more like roars, and his arm slams against the shower wall so hard I fear he'll break it, and then his come paints the glass, spurting out of him over and over as his hips convulse.

I come again. My body has never felt so responsive, so orgasmic.

He drops his spent cock and slumps against the back wall of the shower, recovering and letting the jets of water clean the sweat and semen off his body.

His eyes open. But the expression I see isn't lust or relief—it's sadness and shame.

"Thank you," I say, hoping my voice carries over the sound of the shower. "For letting me watch. That was… amazing, erotic, beautiful."

Shaking his head, he looks down. He grabs a bath sheet that's hanging at the far end of the shower, wraps it tightly around his waist, then steps out onto the bathmat.

I push up off the tub, moving toward him. "Rock—"

He lifts a palm toward me. "I don't want to talk about it." His voice is sharp, his expression hard. He glances up at me, then down at the floor again. "I'm sorry, Selina." His tone has softened but he still won't look at me. "I can't."

CHAPTER 10

Selina

Rock refuses to look at me as he gets ready for work. Worse, we barely say two words to each other. He made it clear that he doesn't want to talk about that strange chastity belt, or whatever you call what he was wearing, and he *really* doesn't want to talk about his reaction to my seeing him jerk off in the shower. But those things completely occupy my brain, leaving no space for anything else.

The weather. Maybe we could talk about the weather?

I follow him down the stairs to Gray's huge foyer, staying a few feet back as he heads for the door.

"I'll come to the bar as soon as it's dark," I tell him when he's got his hand on the brass doorknob.

His back expands, growing by what looks like several inches, as he inhales. "Only come if Grayson can come with you."

"Rock, I—"

"*Please.*" He turns back toward me, but keeps his gaze

down. "I get that you don't want to feel trapped, but promise you won't go anywhere without Grayson."

"I can take care of myself." Nerves squirm inside me. I'm not sure why I'm arguing about this with Rock—arguing about anything, given what happened.

Still shaken, I have zero desire to go out into the city on my own. But I don't want to spend the entire night inside, either.

"Pike released you," he continues. "But we don't know why, or if he'll try to take you again. Not to mention Xavier himself."

I shift my weight back and forth, feeling restless. "Astrid's informant said Xavier won't take another shot at me, not for a while." I wish I felt as safe as I'm pretending to be.

Rock shakes his head, still refusing eye contact. "Better safe than sorry."

"Fine," I say a little more sharply than I mean to. "I won't come to the bar unless Gray can come too."

He nods, then turns back to the door. When he's about to close it behind him, he turns toward me again.

"I'm sorry about before."

"No, *I'm* sorry." I step forward.

He shakes his head. "You didn't do anything wrong. It's just—"

For a split second, his gaze lifts to meet mine, and the eye contact makes my heart stutter, my insides squeeze.

"None of it is about you," he says, with so much pain in his voice. "It's my problem. Mine alone."

"It's okay, Rock. We can talk about it later." My chest tightens as another fear springs to mind. "Will you come back here tonight—tomorrow morning, I mean—when the bar closes?"

What if Rock decides to move back to his apartment? And what if Gray *can't* go over to the bar with me tonight? It could be more than twenty-four hours before I see Rock again.

The thought makes me panic, and my breaths come too fast. Pike kept me from Rock's bed for two nights and I'm not going to miss another one. "Please come back here after work?"

"I need to pick up some things at home," he says softly. "But I will come. Four o'clock at the latest."

"Thank you." I exhale, hard.

"I'll see you then."

"If not before," I add.

He nods slightly, then closes the door behind him.

"What in the holy hell is going on with you two?" Gray's voice comes from above.

I turn to see him standing in the upstairs hall. He jumps over the railing and lands on the floor beside me.

"Walking down a set of stairs too much effort?" I smile as I shake my head at him.

"Anything to get to you more quickly." Kissing me hard, he slides his hands down, squeezes my butt and pulls me against him.

Desire erupts like a volcano inside me, but I push away. After what happened with Rock, this feels disloyal. Strange.

"Come on then." Gray looks at me with unexpected compassion in his eyes. "Let's talk this out."

He leads me into the smaller of the two sitting rooms, plops down on a plush velvet sofa and pulls me down next to him. I curl my legs up to the side and lean into his chest as he wraps his arm around my shoulders.

"Trouble in paradise?" Gray asks. "Why did Rock need to apologize?"

I chew my bottom lip, trying to decide how to respond.

"Did he hurt you?" Gray's expression hardens. "I heard some mighty roars earlier."

I shake my head. "He didn't hurt me. He would never."

Gray nods, then beckons for me to continue.

I don't want to embarrass Rock further by sharing the intimate details, but I do need to talk to *someone* about this, and a man might have a better understanding of what happened.

"First," I say firmly, "you've got to promise that you won't tell Rock we talked about him."

His fingers guide my chin around so we can look into each other's eyes. His expression is fierce. "You sure Rock didn't hurt you?"

"He didn't." I shake my head vigorously. "Not physically..."

"Good. Because, princess, if he did, or ever does, I will rip him limb from limb."

I pat his chest and lean back. "Hey, if the three of us are going to live here together, there will be no limb ripping, okay?"

"I'll do my best." He winks. "No promises." His expression has turned mischievous now, and I settle my head back against his chest.

"Now tell me what happened," he says.

"Rock, he..." I decide to just blurt it out. "We were fooling around, kissing." It sounds so trivial put like that. "And I discovered...he was wearing some kind of binding or cage on his...on his..."

Gray pulls my hand over his erection.

"Yes." I pull my hand back.

"Kinky."

I slap Gray's chest.

"Okay. And why did it make you so upset?" he asks more seriously. "Too weird?"

"It was hurting him. It was very tight and clearly painful. Like some kind of torture device. It must have been painful even before…"

"Before he got hard."

I nod against Gray's chest.

"Did he tell you *why* he was wearing it? I mean, I have noticed that he seems, um, well contained when we train, but I sometimes wear a cup, too."

"This wasn't a cup. It was leather rings and straps that bent back and twisted his penis and…" I can't really describe it. I don't want to. "He said he wears it for my safety."

"What the hell? Sorry." Gray squeezes my shoulder. "It's just… Safety from what? I mean, when you guys fuck—"

"We don't." I shake my head against Gray's chest.

"You're kidding." He rubs my back. "Oh, you're *not* kidding. Shit. Princess. Really?"

"He says we aren't compatible sexually." A lump of emotion rises in my throat. "He is big. I mean *really* big—"

"You're making me feel inadequate here."

I chuckle against Gray's chest. "Never." I bend over and kiss his erection through his slacks.

"Holy shit, princess. Do that again and I won't be able to contain that little fellow."

"He's not in the least bit little." Worried I hurt Gray's

feelings, I sit up to look into his eyes, and I'm relieved to find him grinning—through obvious desire. I should have known he was confident in that department.

I kiss his lips lightly, then settle back down, trying to tame my own growing arousal. I've been desperate for sex since I got free from Pike, even before I was free if I'm honest, but after what happened upstairs with Rock, sex with Gray right now feels wrong, even though the more I think about it, I'm not sure why. Rock knows I've had sex with Gray.

"Big guy's probably worried he'll hurt you," Rock says quietly. "If his dick is, like, elephant-sized or something, then he's probably scared he'll tear you."

I nod. "I get that, but like I've told him, even if that *does* happen—and we don't know that it will—I'll heal. I mean—I'm a vampire. And I want him so badly." I press my legs together and shift my position, barely able to contain my rising lust. Being this horny when I'm sitting next to Gray is difficult enough, but now that I'm thinking about Rock's huge cock stretching me, filling me past capacity, thrusting inside me as his climax builds…

"Can we talk about Pike for a minute?" Gray asks softly, bringing me back to the moment.

"What about him?"

"While he had you captive. Did he hurt you? Rape you?" Gray's voice breaks.

"No." I shake my head. "In fact, he was gentle with me. The only pain I had the whole time was self-inflicted when I tried to escape. Pike even *fed* me."

Gray tenses. "You took his vein?"

I shake my head. "No. He did offer his blood, his wrist, but I wouldn't take it. He brought me a human."

"Really?"

"Yeah. It's strange but the more I think through my kidnapping, the more I realize that Pike did everything he could to make me comfortable. If I ignore the chains and shackles, at least." And really, while they weren't exactly *comfortable*, the shackles didn't hurt until I tried to break them.

"After you fed…did you fuck Pike?" Gray's voice lowers to a near growl.

I can't tell whether he's jealous or turned on by the idea. I shake my head.

"So you haven't…" He sucks in a sharp breath and squeezes me against him. "You haven't fucked since you fed?"

"No. This morning with Rock…I was so turned on I…I know Rock has boundaries but I crossed them, anyway."

Gray's hand slips between my legs. "You know, anytime you're feeling needy, you can always count on me for help. Always willing to take one for the team." His finger flicks over my panties.

I suck in a gasp. "How noble of you."

His eyes darken as he looks into mine, and his fingers stroke over my underwear, worn under the big T-shirt I found and threw on upstairs. Gray guides one of my legs over his lap to straddle him, but I pause there, trapping his hand between my body and his.

"Why haven't you ever taken a mate?" I ask, wanting to understand this man better before having sex with him again.

"Let's say staying single's in my job description."

"I'm serious, Gray." My hips pulse involuntarily, moving my sex against his trapped hand. This conversation isn't going to last long.

"Well, I'm serious too." He strokes my back with his free hand. "Serious about wanting to fuck you." His hand underneath me pushes up and his fingers make rapid strokes against my panties.

My breath catches. "Don't you ever talk about yourself?" I ask, trying to contain the obvious lust in my voice. "I'm starting to feel like a sex object."

"Princess," he says, "if there's one thing you're not, it's an object."

In one swift motion, he lifts me off his lap, tears down my panties and lays me back on the sofa.

Leaving one foot on the floor, he thrusts into my body, hard and fast. The entire thing happens in a second and I don't know when or how he even got his cock out.

And speaking of fast…

Gray slams into me like a piston. His hips drive so fast and hard I can barely breathe and don't really care.

Then, without warning, he pulls out, flips me over onto my belly and pushes into me from behind. After a few minutes of thrusting, which steals my breath and has my body pressing deep into the sofa cushions, he shifts again.

Lifting me to stand on the carpet, facing away from him, he moves his hands to my breasts as he penetrates me again, driving into me from behind and lifting me up onto my toes.

Pulling me back, he sits back on the sofa and adjusts my legs so I'm kneeling on top of him, facing away.

His hands fondle my breasts and tug at my nipples as he thrusts into me, and I start to bounce, our combined forces working in tandem, and each drive hits so deeply inside me I gasp, over and over. He pinches my nipples with each thrust, further heightening the mind-blowing combination of pleasure and pain.

This is exactly what I needed tonight. What my body craved. I do wish that Gray would open up more, because my feelings for him grow every day, but *this* feeling, now, the feeling of him pounding deep inside me while he fondles my breasts, this feeling is so wonderful it almost makes up for his lack of emotional connection.

I know Gray cares on some level. He's clearly sexually attracted, and it's just as clear that he wants to protect me from harm, but call me greedy—I want more. Just as I wish Rock would give me more sexually, I wish Gray would give me more emotionally.

Releasing one of my nipples, his hand slides down my torso and his finger lands on my clit.

My pleasure peaks.

I bounce as Gray thrusts and his finger rubs my sensitive bud—and I completely forget any worries about emotions or Gray holding back. In fact, I forget everything else in the world. All that exists is my body and Gray's cock and the multitude of explosions inside me.

CHAPTER 11

Colton

Another murder at the hands—or more accurately the fangs—of a vampire.

I maneuver my way through the crowd of morbidly curious citizens gathered at the alley entrance.

"Police. Coming through. Police." I pass a woman, dressed for the clubs in a skimpy dress and high heels, and shivering in the cool night air. She scowls at me like I'm butting in line for whatever club she undoubtedly came from.

Reaching the police tape, I flash my badge at the constables guarding the alley.

"Task force only," one tells me.

I point to the Vampire Task Force card opposite my badge. She nods and lets me pass. It's twisted enough that all these civilians want to crash these horrific murder scenes, but it turns my stomach that so many fellow cops want to witness these horror shows for themselves.

That's the main reason we VTF members need to carry special cards. Without restricting access to other cops, this alley would be so mobbed that no one would be able to work—the evidence would be compromised or the victim trampled.

When I think of my sister Shelly, lying lifeless in that cold dark alley, winter coat tossed aside, snow accumulating on her cold, dead body…

Grief catches at the base of my throat.

I swallow it down. Now isn't the time for sadness. I need to know whether this victim was killed by the same bloodsucker that killed Shelly, the one that's been terrorizing this city for the past ten years—at least.

"Colton." Sanjay, my partner beckons me over. "What took you so long?"

"I was on the other side of town."

Off duty tonight, I was at O'Malley's—again. I told myself that it was because of the anonymous tip. But if I'm honest, I went hoping to run into that mysterious lavender-haired beauty again.

She wasn't there tonight, or the night before. And neither was the massive Viking-like owner. The whole staff seemed on edge, like something was off. I tried to get the biker-chick waitress to tell me what was going on, but although she kept flirting, I couldn't get her to give up a thing.

I step around my partner to get a full view of the crime scene. Female, the victim is young—almost looks like she could be in her teens. Her dark brown eyes are open and lifeless, reflecting the red light from a sign above a metal door in the alley.

Her too-blond-to-be-natural hair is fanned around her

on the pavement, and although her skin tone is falsely even and colored—either a spray tan or way too much makeup—it's clear that she's drained of blood.

"We know who she is?" I ask Sanjay.

"No purse found yet, but Wilson's still checking the body for evidence."

Wilson, the forensic examiner, dons fresh gloves, then crouches beside the body. She checks the victim's bra first, carefully pulling back the clothes. Finding nothing on the right, she scores some of the evidence we're seeking tucked next to the victim's left breast—a credit card, driver's license and phone.

The victim's breasts are disproportionately large compared to her body and I wonder where women at clubs stash their ID and phones if they don't have huge boobs to disguise them. I've never been into the club scene, only ever seeing inside the places the few times I've moonlighted as security. Something I no longer have time for since I joined the task force.

"Karen Chiu." Wilson reads the woman's license aloud. "According to this, she's thirty-two." Wilson shakes her head, one side of her mouth quirked up, not buying the age for a second. She shines a flashlight on the driver's license and moves it under the light. "Fake, but the credit card looks real. It's in the name of Henry Chiu. Father perhaps? Phone's locked."

One of her staff holds out an evidence bag, and Wilson drops the items inside.

"Does she have any unusual cuts or marks?" I ask.

"Give me a second," Wilson says. "Let me work."

Impatience crawls under my skin as I let the forensics expert do her thing. At least I know that Wilson will check for the mark while we're here in the alley instead of waiting for the coroner. I'm lucky it's her tonight and not Falzone. He's more by the book and I'd have to wait ages to know if the victim's marked.

I'm the one who first discovered the symbol so many victims have in common, solidifying the serial vamp-killer theory. Hard to believe it had been missed for so many years, but I'm more motivated than the average cop.

All cops hate vampires; in fact, any human who doesn't hate vamps is a total deviant, but since I've got a personal connection, it drives me to look harder, to turn over every stone and see what might slither out of the darkness.

Scouring the files on my own time, I found the connection between all these cases, and convinced the commissioner he should let me onto the task force—the youngest member of the team and the only one who's yet to qualify as detective.

Poring over the details of more than fifty files, covering two decades, I discovered in the past ten years sixteen of the bloodsucker victims had the same markings as the one that marred Shelly. In fact, the wounds were so similar they had to have been made by the same vamp.

"Here." Holding up the hem of the victim's skirt to expose her pelvis, Wilson shines her light there.

The image of my dead sister flashes before my eyes, and my stomach flips. The mark was on my sister's lower back, not her hip, but the symbol carved into the victim is unmistakable. Two parallel lines with a circle and a zigzag pattern bisecting the cuts at the top.

Like the others, the blood around the wound proves the victim was mutilated before death, carved while she still had blood in her body.

I turn away to make sure none of the others witness my emotions. This monster is not only killing these girls, he's torturing his victims, inflicting intense pain before sucking them dry.

I will find and kill this monster, even if it means staking every last vampire on the planet.

CHAPTER 12

Selina

Seventies R & B music pulses through O'Malley's, harmonizing with the soft chatter from the dozen or so customers tonight. After we had sex, Gray insisted that I do more combat training before we headed over here, but it's nearly 2:00 a.m., we've been here for nearly four hours and Rock still hasn't talked to me. Not really.

At the bar, he pours a glass of ale for a customer, and grins as he hands it to the hipster man. Rock glances toward me, and I smile, but he quickly looks down, away from me, like he's embarrassed to make eye contact.

We've got to fix this awkwardness between us.

There's no question in my mind that it's fixable. Logic tells me that Rock and I will be solid again and soon, but my stomach tightens, seemingly less confident. What if I ruined everything with Rock?

Gray shifts on the bench across from me. He's barely touched his glass of chardonnay.

"What's wrong?" Under the table, I slide my foot up his calf.

"What makes you think something's wrong?" He leans forward. Reaching his long arm under the table, his hand finds my upper thigh. "Want to go downstairs for a fuck?"

His words are crass, but lust flavors his English accent so richly, I can almost taste his question. His delivery is so elegant he might be asking me to dance at a royal ball.

Gray exudes confidence and sophistication—as always—but he's not his usual self tonight. He seems tired, and I've never known Gray to look or act tired. Maybe our training session took more out of him than usual? Or the sex?

"You're pale." I cup his cheek. "Your skin's cooler than normal and drier, I think?"

"I'll wager you're not dry." His long fingers find their way between my legs and stroke over my jeans.

I gasp, then squeeze my legs together to trap his hand.

He grins, and clearly taking the trap as a challenge, not a deterrent, his fingers rub the denim seam so hard and fast the heat threatens to burn through the fabric.

"Stop it." I shake my head. "People are watching."

He pulls back his hand and slumps against the bench. "That *cop's* watching, you mean."

"Who?" I feel a blush rise on my cheeks.

"Princess." He shakes his head. "You know exactly who I mean."

I glance over, and sure enough, the blond cop's eyes are focused on me.

He smiles and nods.

I look back to Gray. "What do you think he wants?"

"To fuck you."

"Oh, really?" I grin. "I hope you're right."

"My lady." Gray clasps his hands to his heart in a melodramatic gesture. "You wound me."

"As if." I shake my head.

Gray's pretending to be hurt by the idea of my attraction to the cop. His indifference hurts, even if it shouldn't. It's not like Gray and I have any kind of commitment. Astrid warned me about Gray's reputation with women—and Gray's made it very clear he has no plans to settle down with a mate—but when I think about it, I have no idea whether or not he's been with other women since we met.

I tell myself I don't care. I can't lay exclusive claim to Gray's body, even if I truly love when he drives it inside me. My insides clench at that thought. Taking Gray up on his suggestion to head downstairs suddenly sounds more tempting.

Gray sips his wine, and his nose wrinkles.

"The wine bad?" I ask.

Shaking his head, he sets the glass down. "No. But wine's not what I want right now."

"Then order something else." I look around for Chelle, but she's waiting on another customer.

"You need to feed tonight?" Gray asks.

I shake my head. Gray taps his long fingers on the table and the subtext of his question dawns on me.

"*You're* hungry. Gray, you need to feed. Go."

He shakes his head. "I'm fine."

"When did you last eat?" I ask him.

He shrugs. "Can't say."

"Then it's been too long." He's been spending too much of his time with me. With the exception of my captivity, since we met, he's barely been out of my sight during nighttime hours, not to mention the indoor training during daylight hours. "Gray. Don't you have a job?"

"A job?" He tips his head to the side. "Technically, I guess I have two jobs."

"Then go. Do your work. And go feed. Take care of yourself."

"I'd rather take care of you." Raising his eyebrows, he shoots me a lustful look that I feel between my legs.

"I'm serious, Gray. What do they say on planes? Put on your own oxygen first?" Not that I've ever been on a plane—another experience I'll never have now I'm a vampire. "I don't need a 24/7 babysitter."

"Work can wait. You're my priority, princess."

"You should at least feed. But be careful about it." I tip my head toward the nearby cop and catch him looking at us again. "Remember, if he's here there could be more hanging around."

Gray licks his lips. "Tonight, it's not human blood I need."

"Oh." I suck in a breath of realization. I wish I knew better how all these things worked. Not having been taught by my Maker, and then being held captive for the majority of time since I turned, there's so much I still have to learn. "Do you want…" I touch my throat. "I mean you can…"

Desire fills his eyes, along with a palpable deep hunger, but then he casts his gaze down toward the table. "That, princess, would be a very, *very* bad idea."

"Why?" I reach across the table. "I fed from you the night we met. Let me return the favor." He almost fed from me that night, too. "Don't you want my blood?" I ask, knowing that he does. His desire is beyond obvious.

He takes my hand and looks up into my eyes. "It's not

a question of *want*." His thumb strokes my palm, multiplying the need between my legs. It's all I can do not to crawl over the table and kiss him.

I glance over at Rock, but he quickly looks away. It stabs my heart.

"Gray." I lean across the table. "Rock's here. I'll be fine. Go. Feed. I'll see you at home."

"Home." He smiles. "I like the sound of that."

"Me, too." And I do. I can't believe I'm now sharing a home with these two wonderful men, one giant, one vampire. I only hope the former will share a bed with me again tonight.

Standing, Gray leans across the table and kisses me. It's a relatively chaste kiss for Gray, but it almost makes me come. My attraction to Gray is… Using the word *attraction* could never be enough, even adding the most powerful modifier. There must be stronger word to describe the connection between us. In its own way, it's as intense as my love for Rock.

Gray crosses to the bar and talks to Rock. My heart wants both men, but my body…my body wants Rock, but craves Grayson, like it needs him to survive. Maybe that's because I've already had a taste of Gray?

I look down at the table. I'm fooling myself with that overly simple explanation. My need for Gray is far too intense to be explained solely by the quest for pleasure or my near-animalistic desire—even if there is plenty of that.

"Can I buy you a drink?"

A male voice draws my attention from my confused haze, and I look up to see the cop is standing next to my table.

"I hope it's okay that I came over." He brushes his hand over his short blond hair. "It's just that I noticed your glass was empty and thought I'd offer some assistance with that." He grins, and it lights up his eyes—the most intense shade of green.

Rock's eyes are an aqua blue, like the ocean, but this cop's eyes look like grass after the rain and they're so focused on me I feel like he's seeing my soul. I hope he's not. If he figures out what I am he'll pull out a stake.

"I'm Colton, by the way." He extends his hand to shake. "What are you drinking?"

"Selina." I shake his hand, wondering immediately if I should have given a false name. But I don't know why.

It's not like anyone's ever reported me missing. If my mom had, if she'd ever wanted me back, I'd have been with her years ago.

There's no reason to keep my name from the police, but my adolescent habit of hiding from the authorities, or anyone who might report me to them, looms large.

"Irish whiskey." I touch the rim of my empty glass. "But I really don't need another."

"Come on." His infectious, boyish smile is so genuine. "You're not going to make me drink alone, are you?"

"You've been drinking alone the past two hours." I try to suppress my smile.

"That's okay. I forgive you."

I laugh. A little company wouldn't be a bad thing. I'll just have to be very careful about what I say.

He leans on the table. "If you want to be alone, that's fine, but I couldn't forgive myself if I didn't offer my company after your boyfriend left."

"He's not—" I stop myself. Boyfriend doesn't seem like the right word to describe who Gray is to me, but I have no idea what word to substitute.

"Not your boyfriend." He pumps his fist in the air. "So I've got a chance." He beckons Chelle over.

She arrives in seconds. Turns out Chelle can see this booth better when an attractive man's here.

"Another round for me and my friend here," he tells her.

Looking at me, Chelle raises her eyebrow. She clearly doesn't approve of this situation, and there are so many valid reasons for her concern that I can't pick out just one.

"Another double?" she asks me.

"Why not?" I answer. If I'm going to have a drink with this hunk of a man, I might as well enjoy it.

Colton slides into the booth opposite me, claiming the space Gray vacated but filling it with a totally different energy. My body's charged with a different energy too. One I don't fully recognize—both shy and excited that this clean-cut, good-looking hunk is paying attention to me.

I barely went to high school, never mind college, but based on Hollywood movies, Colton's the big man on campus type, whereas I'm the weird, art-student girl everyone makes fun of, and the dynamic makes me feel shy. But what I should be feeling instead of shyness is caution. I need to remember that he's a cop.

"You live around here?" he asks.

I lean back. "Why?"

"Sorry." He raises his palms toward me. "Just making conversation."

"No, *I'm* sorry. I didn't mean to sound rude, it's just—"

"A beautiful woman like you has to be careful." He finishes my sentence with his assumption. "I get it. But you're safe with me." He pulls out his badge and shows it to me. "I'm a cop."

Opposite the official police force badge is a card that makes my insides freeze. Vampire Task Force. Whatever that is, it doesn't sound good, especially for me.

"You're a vampire killer?" I wish I could hide the fear in my voice.

"Killer?" He tips his head to the side. "Exterminator is a more accurate word. The VTF is ridding this city of the vampire menace for good. His chest fills with pride as his large hand palms his nearly empty pint glass. "You'll always be safe next to me."

"Oh, I will, will I?"

His cheeks flush. "I only meant…"

Chelle shows up with our drinks and places them on the table.

"Thanks," I tell her.

"Yes, thanks, Chelle," Colton says. "Put them on my tab."

"No need," she replies. "They're on the house. On *Rock*." She looks at me as she says his name, and I nod.

Who knows what Chelle thinks is going on here, but Rock is right across the room so if he has a problem with my sharing a drink with this man, he can just come over and tell me. It's not like I'm hiding anything. In fact, I hope it motivates Rock to talk to me so we can banish the residual awkwardness between us.

But beyond my petty idea that talking to Colton might make Rock jealous, it seems smart to talk to this cop and find out what he wants. I've caught him staring at me numerous times, and need to know if his curiosity is of the man-to-woman variety or the way more dangerous cop-to-vampire kind.

With Chelle gone, I might as well cut to the chase. "Why do you keep staring at me?"

His cheek flush intensifies. "Staring? I…I haven't…" Grinning sheepishly, he shakes his head. "Okay. Guilty as charged." He reaches both hands across the table. "Cuff me."

"Maybe I will." I wink.

His neck joins in on the blushing, and I'm fairly certain I'm blushing now too. Sexual innuendo is outside my normal wheelhouse—so is flirting for that matter. While human, I avoided men like the plague. I was held prisoner for the first fourteen months after my transition, and this overwhelming desire to attract the attention of the opposite sex, to *enjoy* male attention, is new.

He takes a long drink of his beer. "I'm sorry for staring. It's just that…" He clears his throat and looks like he's gathering courage. "I've never seen such a beautiful woman."

I make a face. "I doubt that."

I'm not one of those girls who pretends she doesn't know that she's pretty. I know that men find me attractive —they always have, even before my transition eliminated things like bad hair days and pimples. Since I turned, my face looks like it's always made up, but in a natural way.

But my looks are what drew Xavier to me, and Pike. His scarred face and body flash through my mind and I shiver.

"Are you okay?" Colton asks.

I nod.

"You look like you saw a ghost or something." He turns to scan the room. "Or worse, a vampire." He frowns, then gets up. "Is it okay if I sit beside you? I feel better if I can see the entrance. I did promise you'd be safe around me."

"Okay," I say carefully. "I wouldn't want you to break any promises."

He slides onto the bench next to me. At least his angle for staking me is more awkward now that he's right next to me.

"I'll keep my hands to myself," he says. "Unlike some people," he adds under his breath.

"Thanks." Although I'm not sure *I'll* be able to keep my hands to myself.

Colton's scent overwhelms my senses. Clean and citrusy, the man smells so good I want to lick him, taste him. And although I told Gray I didn't need to feed, I'm suddenly hungry as I listen to the blood coursing through his veins.

I take a sip of my whiskey to drown the urge to dig my fangs into Colton's neck and taste his warm nectar. "So," I say, hoping to change the subject. "What's a vampire-exterminator like you, doing in a gin joint like this?"

"Gin joint?"

I shake my head. "Old movie reference. Not a good one."

"Bad movie?"

"No, a good movie—*Casablanca*—just not a good reference. Not even close to the actual quote."

"Movies. Is that what you're into?" His eyes light up with interest as he turns toward me.

I shrug. "I used to be."

"Why not anymore?"

"Since you're a cop, I shouldn't tell you this..."

"Off the record." He grins.

I smile from the inside out. "When I was in my teens, my friend Lark and I used to spend entire days in multiplexes."

"That's not illegal."

"It is if you don't buy tickets."

His eyebrows rise a little, then his expression softens. "You were just a kid."

"Yeah." And movie theaters were a way to keep warm. Memories of Lark flood in, and sadness steals my voice. On lucky days, she and I would score the magic combo of discarded ticket stubs *and* a lazy teenage ticket taker—usually a guy Lark flirted with so he wouldn't look at our tickets too closely.

Then, once we got inside, we'd stay until the last movie ended. Tons of free food, too. It's shocking what people leave under seats.

"Why so much time in movie theaters?" he asks softly. "Do you want to talk about it?"

Looking at the table, I shake my head.

"New topic then." His voice brightens. "What are you into now? Besides hanging out in this bar, I mean." He gestures toward Rock with his head. "You know the owner I take it?"

Rock is looking toward us, concern in his eyes. At least he's made eye contact with me, and I smile softly to tell him I'm okay, then turn back toward Colton. I can't lose sight of the fact that this conversation is my chance to find out whether his presence here poses a danger. I got caught up in his attention.

"You never answered my question," I say.

"What question is that?"

"Why is a cop, a *vampire killer cop*, hanging out at O'Malley's?" Nerves scatter through me the second my question's out there. I fear his answer as much as I want to hear it.

My instincts say I can trust Colton, but my better

judgment says he could put a stake through my heart at any second. He's got at least two tucked into the lining of his jacket, and given his job he probably has more concealed.

"I'm here—" his eyes narrow and his jaw hardens "—because we got an anonymous tip that this place shelters vampires."

I clasp my glass of whiskey to steady my shaking hand.

He touches my forearm. "Don't be afraid, Selina. I haven't seen any bloodsuckers here, and if one *does* come in, I'm here to protect you."

I nod, my mouth so dry I can't begin to speak.

"If one of those monsters comes anywhere near you, it's dead." His grip on my arm tightens and the hate in his eyes turns intense.

"I feel safe here. Thank you." My voice comes out softer than I'd like, but clearly he's interpreting my fear to be a fear of vampires, rather than what it is—a fear of him.

"How did you get into the vampire killing business?" I ask, hoping to sound casual.

"It's not a *business*," he says in a serious tone. "I'm a police constable."

"But there's more to it for you, isn't there. Something personal?" Every instinct inside me says that I'm right, and even if I'm not, I hope my question will get him talking again.

His grip on my arm softens, but he leaves his hand there and I don't ask him to move it.

I tell myself that I'm letting him flirt to keep him distracted from discovering what I am, but if I'm honest, I like the physical contact and flirting. His palm is warm and comforting—the connection electric—and there's no denying that Colton's attractive. No denying our natural chemistry.

I look into his eyes, and it seems corny but sparks fly between us—almost literally. When we look into each other's eyes I imagine pulses of light, laser beams joining our eyes. I giggle.

"What's funny?" he asks.

I shake my head. "Nothing. I just had a funny image run through my mind."

"What?"

My teeth scrape the corner of my lower lip as I consider whether or not to answer honestly. "Laser eyes."

His eyes widen. "You felt it too?"

"Felt what?"

He moves an inch closer, his hand slides down my forearm, and we entwine our fingers.

Holding hands with Colton is the most intimate moment I've had with anyone other than Rock, even more intimate than sex with Gray. It should feel wrong, holding hands with this man, but it doesn't. It feels right—perfect.

"The attraction between us." His voice is lower now, softer and deeper, and it strokes me like velvet. "You feel it too. Don't you."

I lick my lips. "I don't know what you mean."

He leans forward. "I think that you do."

He is going to kiss me.

Our mouths are only a few delicious inches apart, and I'm trapped by his gaze, caught in the grass-green gorgeousness of his eyes, in the pools of his dimples, in the draw of the lush pillows that form his pink lips.

He straightens, pulling back from me.

The space between us widens, but the connection doesn't break. "Sorry." He shakes his head.

"For what?"

"For coming on so strong." He clears his throat. "And for lying."

My chest tightens. "What did you lie about?"

"When I told you I came to the bar looking for vampires." His thumb strokes my index finger as he holds my hand. "The tip is what brought me in here the *first* time, and the second, but the lead didn't check out."

"It didn't?" My heart thumps.

He shakes his head.

"So, I guess you came back for the Motown and free peanuts?" My voice is thready as I anticipate his answer.

"Sure, the peanuts are great." He smiles softly. "But that's not why I keep coming back here."

"It's not?" I can barely breathe now.

"I've come here every night, hoping to get a chance to meet you."

Warmth spreads inside me. On the surface, his words sound like a pickup line, but they didn't come across that way—at all. They came across as...confessional.

He shifts on the bench. "I'm not a stalker, honest. But the moment I first saw you..." He looks away for a moment. "Ever since then, Selina, you're all I can think about. From the first second I saw you, I wanted to meet you, to get to know you."

"Wow." I'm not sure what else to say.

"I've never felt so immediately drawn to anyone," he continues. "Never been so attracted to someone, especially since—" He stops himself, pausing so long I almost interject, but then he adds, "Do you believe in love at first sight?"

I suck in a sharp breath. "You're saying you're *in love* with me?"

"All I know is..." He blinks hard. "My heart is racing a million miles an hour and my stomach is fluttering, and I know it's crazy." He shakes his head. "I know it could just be infatuation, but I *am* falling—and falling hard."

He rakes his hand through his short blond hair. "I don't know what's going on between you and the bar owner, or that sharp-dressing dude who left you sitting here all alone." His expression fills with a palpable longing, combined with pain or possibly sadness. "But if you're available, or can make yourself available, I'd very much like to date you."

"Date me?" I've never been on a date in my life.

"I'm just going to put everything all out there." He clears his throat. "Selina, I feel like we're meant to be together. I feel like we'd be missing out on something great if we don't at least give it a shot."

His words are so candid and honest and raw that I'm taken aback, floored by how directly, and quickly, he put all his cards on the table.

It's almost like Colton just bared his throat and exposed his vein for me. He metaphorically gave me an opening to slash him down, to bleed him dry with a few cutting words.

"I'm very flattered." I draw a long breath. "But I'm not sure whether or not I believe in it—love at first sight."

Although it didn't take long for me to fall in love with Rock—or in lust with Gray—and while love isn't a word I'd use at this moment about Colton, I can't deny the chemistry and attraction.

And there is something beyond the physical between us, too. The connection is unmistakable. I feel safe next to Colton, which is crazy, because I know that if I let my guard down—if I revealed myself with the same vulnerable honesty he just showed me—Colton would kill me.

Drawing a long breath, I regain my sanity. This is a human man. Not only is he human, he's a cop. And not only a cop, one who *specializes* in hunting down and killing vampires. This is way too dangerous. I need to shut it down. But carefully. The last thing I need is a vampire hunter for an enemy.

"You're too funny." Grinning, I mock slap his chest. "You almost had me going there for a second. Does that line work on most women?"

"It wasn't a line." He looks ill.

"Come on." I pull my hand from his and take a sip of my whiskey. "We're *meant to be together*? We've known each other for what, thirty minutes? Forty?"

He opens his mouth to respond, but I keep going. "Message received. You want to get me into bed. But even you've got to admit that your pickup lines were a bit over the top."

CHAPTER 13

Colton

Selina's words hit like a slam to my solar plexus. I can barely breathe.

What did I expect? I came on way too strong. My inexperience with women is showing, big time, but I meant every word.

Honesty is always the best policy, and even if she doesn't believe that my feelings are genuine—it's hard for *me* to believe the power of what I'm feeling so fast—at least she didn't reject me. Not yet. And even better, it doesn't sound like she's committed to either of those two men.

Until she tells me to leave her alone, I've still got a shot.

"Want another drink?" I ask, my voice hoarse, like I just woke from a long sleep.

"No thanks." Lifting her glass, she looks surprised to find it empty. "But you go ahead and order another."

Selina handles her liquor well, especially for such a

petite person. I palm my glass, enjoying the cold on my overheated body. "I've still got most of the last beer."

Her smile brightens my heart. In high school I never went for the artsy types, the ones who dyed their hair unnatural colors, got tattoos or pierced anything beyond their earlobes, but Selina is different.

Her light purple hair suits her so well it's like she was born with that shade, and her skin is so delicate it must be so, so soft. It's all I can do to keep from touching her cheek, kissing her lips to find out.

But I already moved too fast with my words. I'm not going to do that with my actions. I can be patient. Selina is worth it.

"Did you grow up around here?" I ask, hoping she'll open up more.

She shakes her head. "I moved to the city in my teens. How about you?"

"Toronto born and bred. Although, to be honest, I grew up in the burbs. Ajax. I didn't move downtown until I started with the police service."

"Are your parents in the city, too?" she asks. "Brothers and sisters?"

I shudder as her question draws grief from the deep place where I store it, and I can't form an answer.

"What's wrong?" She takes my hand. "What did I say?"

I force a smile through my sadness. "I had a sister. She died."

"Oh, I'm so sorry." She shifts on the bench beside me, her arm moves like she might give me a hug, and my entire body tingles with the anticipation of comfort and contact, but the hug doesn't come.

"My sister was murdered," I tell her.

"That's terrible."

"Viciously attacked by a vampire. The same one who's on a killing spree now." Rage shoves my sadness down, and I realize I raised my voice. Selina looks terrified.

"Sorry." I give her an apologetic smile. "It just makes me so angry. These monsters—"

"How do you know it's the same vampire?" Her voice shakes.

I turn on the bench to fully face her. The answer's confidential, no matter how badly I want to tell her I shouldn't. But I want Selina to know *everything* about me, my life, my work. "You're not a reporter, are you?"

"No, why?"

"The information isn't public."

"I'm good with secrets." Her shaking hand, her wide eyes, betray her attempt at courage. She might be interested, but she's terrified.

"Don't worry," I tell her. "We're going to catch him."

"You know it's a him?" Her shoulders relax a little, and I'm glad that I've been able to calm her fears—at least a little.

"Logic and probabilities tell us the killer is male," I tell her.

"Probabilities?" She tips her head to the side and her shiny purple hair brushes her shoulder. "What do you mean?"

"Female vampires are rare."

Her head straightens quickly. "They are?"

I nod.

"How do you know that?" Pushing through her fear, she seems eager to know more.

"We believe it's harder for women to survive the transition process." I shrug. That's what they taught us, and it makes sense to me. "But even if the numbers were even, females are less likely to kill, even human women."

She nods, her eyes showing genuine interest, and my feelings for Selina expand. I rarely date, and the few times I've brought up my work with women they've shut me down or run the other direction.

Selina must hate vampires as much as I do, and I'm so glad I've discovered a shared interest. If she likes football, that clinches it. Selina's my soul mate.

"What are you thinking?" I ask her. "You look like you've got more questions. I'll answer all the ones that I can." I feel like my entire body is smiling and I want to tell her everything. I want to know her thoughts and for her to know all of mine.

"You said women are less likely to kill, but most *men* don't kill either, so why do you assume most vampires do?"

I hold back my laugh, trying to figure out if she's joking. "It's not an assumption," I say when I realize she's not. "They *all* kill. That's what vampires do. It's how they live."

She looks skeptical now. Like I'm telling a fairy tale. "Can you prove that any of the vampires you've staked killed humans?"

Instead of blurting out the pat answer my boss would want me to, I pause. Selina isn't just some random member of the public, she's the woman I'm falling in love with. I've got to be honest.

"If I'm keeping it totally one hundred," I answer carefully. "We rarely have irrefutable proof to tie an individual vampire to a specific murder. But killing is in vampires' nature. They prey on humans and suck them dry."

"How often to vampires commit murder?" Her

knuckles turn white as she presses her hand against the table.

"The city is getting safer. Our methods work."

"What methods are those?" Her voice is flatter now, colder.

"Our methods are dangerous, but simple and effective. Strike first. Kill every vampire we find. It works."

She looks horrified. "How do you know it works?"

"Because after we've done a sweep, there are no vampire killings in that area."

"But…" Her eyes narrow and her hand trembles. "You just admitted you don't have evidence of vampire killings *before* your sweeps, either."

I shake my head. "I misspoke before. Vampire murders exist. We find victims drained of blood." Sometimes their throats ripped out. But I want to spare her the gory details.

She remains quiet, so I continue. "Just the other night we found a victim in Forest Hill. We're sweeping that neighborhood this week and all the surrounding ones. Searching every place bloodsuckers might be hiding. Staking every vamp we find."

"How can you tell when you've found a vampire?" she asks, her voice trembling.

I hate that I've scared her, but if I stop answering her questions now, I'll just make things worse. "We have ways of identifying the monsters."

"How?"

"It's confidential."

She tips her head to the side. "Okay, let's say you've identified someone as a vampire, how do you know that vampire has killed the victim you found?"

"They're *all* killers."

"So you just stake them all, hoping you got the right one?"

I nod.

She leans back from me. "What if you took that same approach with human suspects?"

"Selina." I take her hand. "You've got a soft heart, and I love that. But you know it's not the same. Vampires, they're murderers. Monsters."

She looks down. "Even wild animals get treated better than that."

"I suppose you're right, but wild animals are innocent. They don't know any better. Vampires are vicious murderers. Monsters who can masquerade as human." She's got to understand.

She pulls her hand out of mine and lifts her glass to her lips. Realizing it's empty she sets it down. "Maybe I will have another whiskey."

I get the attention of Chelle and signal to her that Selina wants another round. Chelle brings the drink quickly.

"Thank you," Selina says.

Chelle grunts and walks away quickly. I take a long draft of the beer I've barely touched, quenching a strong thirst. Talking about this with Selina rattled my nerves, because I care so much what she thinks and I need her to understand.

Selina sips her whiskey, quiet for what feels like a very long time, and I wonder if I've blown it. A sick feeling invades my happiness. Maybe I was wrong about her. I feel so connected to her already, but if she's a member of one of those crazy, vampire rights groups… If she is, I need to make her sees she's wrong, because I'm not going to quit the VTF until every vampire in the city has a stake through its heart.

"The vampire killer we're hunting now," I tell her softly, so no one can overhear, "has a calling card. We know the murders are connected."

"A calling card?" She looks up at me expectantly. "What is it?"

I pause. "Are you squeamish—about blood?"

"Not really." She looks up and to the side, making me wonder if she's telling the truth, but in spite of her fear and her soft-heartedness, she still seems more interested than repulsed, so I continue.

"Before sucking them dry, the monster carves a symbol into his victims."

"A symbol?" Her voice comes out low and breathy, then she looks up into my eyes.

"Yes. And the monster carves it into the victims while they're still alive."

"How do you know that?" Her voice is shaky.

"Because the wounds bleed."

She cringes. "The symbol. What does it look like?"

It's confidential, but if I want her to trust me, I need to trust her, too.

Using the condensation from the side of my beer glass, I sketch a diagram on the wooden table. "It's two lines, like this. Then a circle up here through the lines, and then this pointy thing on top of that."

"A crown."

I turn to her, smiling. "Yes. Exactly. It looks like a crown."

She shrinks back, almost collapsing into herself.

I went too far. "I'm sorry," I tell her. "TMI. I sometimes forget that not everyone I talk to is a cop or medical examiner. I'm sorry if I upset you." I reach for her hand and to my relief she lets me take it again. But her fingers are trembling.

"Don't be afraid, Selina. You're safe with me." If she lets me, I'll protect her from vampire attacks, from everything, for the rest of her life. "You'll always be safe with me."

"Thanks." She shakes out her body, as if trying to reset, then smiles softly. The sight of her upturned lips and sparkling eyes sends ripples of joy racing through me. Ripples of desire too. I shift on the bench, hoping to hide that particular reaction.

"Enough about me and my work. Let's talk about something else," I suggest lightly. "What do you do for a living?"

"Your job's way more interesting." She's recovered and I'm drawn to her inner strength. "Have all the bodies you've found been marked with that symbol?"

"Most of them. A very significant percentage of the murders in the past decade, anyway. My sister had the mark—" My voice catches. "That's how I put it all together."

"*You* put it together?" She's clearly impressed.

"Yup. I spent hours, on my own time, going over the files for every vampire murder since they've been recorded. Not all the files had enough detail to be certain, though."

"How come some files aren't complete?"

"For vamp killings, especially in the past, some cops didn't bother with all the paperwork. No trial to prepare for."

She nods, a little stiffly.

"But even with that limitation, I discovered that several of the victims had the mark. Plus, some clearly *didn't* have the mark, and there are no reports of it in other locations around the world, so we know carving the symbol isn't something all vampires do."

"How will you find this vampire?" she asks. "Do you have leads?"

"Want anything for last call?" A deep male voice asks.

I turn to find the owner glaring down at me.

"We're good here." I turn my back to him, but it doesn't take detective skills to figure out he hasn't left. Selina continues to look past me toward him.

"Colton," she says softly. "It's been really nice meeting you, but I need to talk to Rock."

"Oh." My chest deflates. "Sure." Then a little bit of hope reinflates it. Maybe she wants to break up with him. Maybe that's why they need to talk. "When can I see you again?" I ask her.

"Soon." She smiles. "I want to hear more about your work. It's fascinating."

My chest fully inflates, expanding by three inches if I had to guess, and I slide out of the booth. "Tomorrow night?" I ask hopefully, then grin. "I guess that's tonight, at this point." Although even as I say it, I remember that tonight is my only night off this week. With the intensified sweeps, everyone on the VTF will be required for duty from sunset to dawn.

She looks toward Rock before answering, and that breaks my heart just a little.

"I'm not sure about tonight," she says. "But soon."

"Great. I'll hold you to that." I walk away, my body buzzing from our time together, and I miss her before I get halfway across the room.

I wish I knew which one of those men was my main rival, the bar owner or that tall, elegant dude. It's not surprising that she's got multiple men in pursuit, but she doesn't seem the type to lead men on.

I have to believe I'll be the one that she chooses. If she doesn't, I don't know what I'll do. Meeting her in person was even better than my fantasy of her, and my heart will be pulverized if she doesn't feel the same way.

When I reach the door, I turn back. The owner's arm is draped over her shoulders, but she rewards me with a quick smile.

Whatever's going on between those two, she hasn't shut the door on me, on us, and I plan to keep my foot firmly planted in that door until she opens it wide or locks it shut.

CHAPTER 14

Selina

"What was that all about?" Rock's heavy arm draped over my shoulders, his fingers stroke my arm, sending tingles through me. Tingles that started while I was talking to Colton if I'm honest.

"It's nothing. He was just flirting."

"Selina." Rock frowns. "That man is a cop. A cop who's been asking around about *vampires*. Stay away from him."

"I thought the line was—keep your friends close and your enemies closer?"

He pulls me more tightly against him. "I just want to keep you safe."

"So does Colton. He promised to protect me from *vampires*."

"Ha." Rock's laugh rumbles through me.

I touch his hard chest. "Colton's a good guy, Rock. I don't trust people easily, especially not men, but for some reason I trust him." And it's true. I do. I know I can't let my guard down around Colton. He's incredibly prejudiced against vampires, and he'd stake me the second he found out what I am, but still, I want to see him again.

In fact, I need to see him again, because Colton can help me find my Maker.

I think he can help me find my Maker, because I know the symbol he showed me.

I've got that same symbol carved on me.

Gray walks into the bar. Several sets of female eyes turn toward him as he crosses to join us. How can I blame them? He slides into the booth, then partially rises to lean across the table and kiss me, his tongue flicking my lips like a vibrator. Rock's arm stays around me the whole time.

"Feeling better, I take it?" Rock asks him gruffly.

Gray sits down, then, keeping eye contact with me, not Rock, Gray answers, "Much better. Thank you, mate."

His teeth scrape his lower lip and his eyes are so full of lust I feel naked, almost violated, as if his gaze is stroking and probing my body in front of everyone in the bar, in front of Rock.

"You ready to go home?" he asks.

"You two go." Rock kisses the top of my head and slides his arm out from around me. "I've got a lot to do here."

I grab Rock's hand before he rises. "But you will come to Gray's, right? We still need to talk."

He looks at Gray quickly, then nods.

"Don't worry, big guy," Gray says. "I'll escort Selina home."

Gray's sitting with perfect posture, the picture of the consummate gentleman, but his eyes tell a different story.

No gentleman would ever consider what he clearly hopes to do to me tonight.

Anticipation pulses through me, turning me instantly slick.

The three of us have barely talked over the logistics of living under the same roof. For all I know the two of them have talked it out and arranged some kind of time-share, giving the other alone time with me.

The idea of them discussing me behind my back makes me squirm but I don't feel ready to be involved in the potentially awkward conversation. Not right now. For the moment, I'm grateful that they don't want to kill each other, that they're friends. Because I can't bear the thought of living without them, either of them.

"Keep her safe." Rock nods toward Gray. "That cop was hanging around, bothering her."

"His name is Colton," I interject. "And he wasn't bothering me. I willingly talked to him the whole time you were gone." I don't want to keep secrets from Gray.

Gray's eyes widen and he takes my hands. "Tell me he doesn't suspect what you are."

"Not a chance." I am certain of that.

"Good." Gray stands and slides out of the booth. "Shall we go, my lady?"

I take his offered hand.

"See you later." Rock kisses me lightly on the lips and I head out of the bar with Gray. I still want to talk with Rock about what happened, but at least some of the awkwardness has broken down. We'll talk when he gets home.

The night air is clear and cool, and it fills my lungs as soon as we get outside. Gray takes my hand and tugs me into a dark alley nearby. In a flash, his lips are on mine, his hand between my legs.

I squirm against him. Can't he wait until we get home? My body doesn't want him to stop though, and his hand strokes over my jeans as his tongue slides into my mouth. The rest of the world incinerates in the fire we generate.

He unbuttons my fly, and his hand slides under the denim.

I grab his wrist. "Gray. Let's go home."

"I need you. Now." His voice is a near growl, the last word delivered against my throat. "I need to be inside you." He licks the skin over my vein and I almost come.

"I need you too, Gray." Each of my words comes out on its own exhale as he strokes between my legs. "But it's dangerous out here. They're doing a vampire sweep. I'll enjoy it more if we go home."

His erection presses against my stomach and his hips pulse as he dry humps me against the wall. He groans, and I've never seen Gray so out of control.

"Not here. Please. What if someone's watching? What if Colton *does* suspect what I am? What you are."

He pulls his hand from my pants and sighs as I do up my jeans. And then with his arm draped over my shoulders we head toward his house.

"Was it the feeding?" I ask.

"Was what the feeding?"

"I've never seen you so, so—"

"Randy?"

"Who's Randy?"

"No." He chuckles. "It's British slang for horny."

"Oh. Yeah. That's what I meant."

"It doesn't take a feeding to get me up for you." He licks his lips. "Do I sometimes make you feel unwanted, princess? Have I ever refused you?" His fingers graze my breast from the side.

I shake my head. "You know you haven't…but tonight. In the alley. That felt…different."

"Yes." He adjusts his slacks as we walk. "Tonight I do have a particularly strong need for you."

"Because of the feeding."

"Yes, while I fed…"

"What, Gray?" I'm not sure I want to hear, but I need to.

"I didn't fuck while I fed like I normally would."

"Oh." The frank admission raises so many questions. Questions I wish I could ask Astrid instead of Gray. But she's not here. "And you normally… Is that something…" I want to know everything about vampires and, even more, I want to know everything about Gray. Still, the topic makes me shy.

"Remember what happened when you fed from me?" he asks, his voice low.

"It made me want you." My throat feels thick, my entire body pulsing with desire. "It made me want you so badly I couldn't think of anything else. Just remembering it now makes me want you again."

He picks me up and presses me back against the trunk of a tree we're passing. "Princess, you've got me." His body parts my legs and he rubs himself against my sex.

I groan. "We're almost home."

He pulls back, sets me down on my feet, then he takes my hand as we walk.

"Is that typical?" I ask.

"What?"

"Do vampires always get turned on when they feed from other vampires?"

Gray nods. "Sex and feedings go together. It's a very sensual act to feed from another vampire's vein, very intimate. Wouldn't you agree?"

I nod. "So…when vampires feed from their Maker. Do they have sex?" An image of my Maker flashes through my mind, but there's nothing vaguely erotic about it. Especially now I suspect she might be the serial killer. How else can I explain my scar matching the symbols carved into the serial killer's victims?

He shakes his head. "The Maker/Progeny bond is different. Equally intimate, perhaps even more so, but the sharing of blood between Maker and Progeny forms a different kind of bond. A family bond. One that can never be broken, even after death."

"Is your Maker still alive?" I ask him.

"Yes."

"Then why aren't you with her?"

"It was time for me to leave the nest, find my own way, my own life," he says wistfully. "I haven't seen her in nearly fifty years, but still feel her with me. Always." His voice sounds sad as he says this and I want to know more.

"When you left her, you came here? To Toronto?"

He's quiet, not answering for what feels like a long time. "I was in Europe first. I came here about eighteen years ago."

"What brought you here?"

"Work."

"Does FJS have offices in Europe, too?"

"You, my princess, are very inquisitive tonight." We round the corner onto his block. "I've got a proposition for you. No more talking until after we fuck."

CHAPTER 15

Gray

I fumble with the keypad that secures my front door. Even though I've opened this door thousands of times before, while tired, drunk or horny—tonight, my entire body is shaking and my fingers refuse to work. My physical need for Selina is no joke, but it's more than just physical. If sex was all I needed, I would have fucked while I fed.

At the club, I purposefully chose a man for my feeding, an unattractive one at that, thinking it would lessen my desire for sex while I drank, but it didn't. I wanted to fuck the man the instant my fangs pierced his vein, and he wanted it, too.

But I couldn't bring myself to go through with it. As badly as my body wanted him during the act—wanted anyone—my mind only wanted Selina. I don't think I'll ever desire sex with anyone else ever again.

But this can't go on forever. I know it can't.

I can't bear the thought of telling her why we can

never be mates, but I also can't bear the idea of depriving myself, so the best I can do is be with her as much as possible while I still have the chance.

After we kill that Xavier asshole…that's when I'll do my duty and tell her the truth.

Her hand strokes down my back and over my ass, and my cock pulses under my trousers. A growl rumbles inside me.

"You okay?" she asks.

"Nothing a hard fuck won't fix." The keypad and my fingers finally cooperate.

I push open the huge oak door and the second one leading into the foyer, then slam the latter door closed behind us.

Turning Selina away from me, I bend her over the table in the center of the foyer.

She turns her head to the side, resting her cheek on the shiny wooden surface. "Gray?"

One hand on her upper back to hold her down, I stroke her heat through the denim of her jeans.

To make this easier, I'll fuck her here, from behind, and imagine she's some random bird in the club. I need to keep this as impersonal as possible, while I take care of my raging need.

I undo her jeans and plunge my fingers under her panties, quickly finding her wetness. She moans, pushing her ass back against me as I rub her clit.

"Holy shit," she says, her voice strained, and I realize she's already come.

Still reaching from behind, I plunge two fingers inside, and her orgasm contracts around them.

I didn't mean to make her climax so quickly, but it's for the best. Knowing she's already come gives me another excuse to ignore her needs as I take care of my own—and try ignore my heart.

Her body convulses with a few last aftershocks and then she relaxes against the table, her breaths coming quickly and leaving a trail of condensation on the table's surface.

While she's still recovering, I tug down her jeans and pull them off one ankle. I kick her legs apart, undo my waistband and fly, and then plunge my cock hard and deep inside her. The pleasure nearly steals my breath, my sight, my soul.

I tell myself that this intense pleasure is about biology—cock meets cunt—that my raging need could be satisfied by any tight, wet orifice, but I know it's a lie.

Resting inside her for a moment, I regain control over my body, then I start to pump. My hips and thighs drive like a piston, and heat builds inside her, surrounding my rock-hard rod. My entire body transforms until every part of me is involved in the pleasure.

Back when I was human, I tried heroin once. Up until now, I thought that was the best thing I'd felt or would ever feel, but this—moving my cock inside Selina not long after feeding—the only thing better would be drinking from her vein.

Bending over her body and tempting danger, I suck on her neck, scrape my fangs against her skin.

"Yes. Please. Oh, Gray. Take my vein."

Her voice snaps me out of my euphoric haze.

I can't risk it. If we do that, I'll literally die when I lose her.

Tucking my hands under her hips, I raise her up so she's forced to brace herself on her hands. Then I guide her knees onto the table and bend her into a position with her chest down between her spread knees.

I can't see her face like this, and hope it will make it easier for me to stay detached. Bracing one hand on her shoulder, one on her hip, I pound, my eyes closed, trying to forget who I'm fucking, hoping to come quickly so I can regain control of my mind and body—and most of all my emotions.

But the fresh vampire blood coursing through my veins has heightened my virility, and I can't come. Even if I could, I know coming once won't be enough. Not nearly enough.

And I realize this position must be uncomfortable for Selina.

I pull out. "Let's go upstairs."

She remains in the same position on the table, panting, her back rising and falling as she fights to catch her breath. I want to stroke her, to soothe her. I want to gather her into my arms and hold her against me, but I resist.

Her sex is swollen and glistening and I have to turn away to keep myself from burying my face there.

I hear her feet land on the floor behind me, and her hand slides up my back to my shoulder. "That was…intense."

"Did I hurt you?" I ask.

"No." She reaches from behind me and takes hold of my stiff rod.

Groaning, I remove her hand and lead her toward the stairs while I loosen my tie. I undo the buttons of my shirt as we climb, and with every step my cock grows harder and my need for her escalates. About four stairs from the top, I can't take another step.

I bend her forward, her hands fall to the landing,

shirting her into a sharp V position with her sex exposed. I leave one of my feet a few steps down and move the other to the step above her feet, then taking her hips in a tight grip, I drive back inside.

She cries out at the initial penetration, but I don't slow or stop and soon I'm moving so fast and hard it's hard to keep us balanced.

If I'm not careful, we'll tumble down the stairs and break our necks, and the extra concentration required to keep us on the stairs, distracts me from anything beyond the sex.

I try to focus only on not falling and on the sensation of her tight, slick pussy encasing my dick. And with each hard drive, my body slaps against hers—deeper inside her now than I thought possible given her small size.

"Gray?"

I pound harder, trying to ignore the magical sound of her voice.

"Gray, stop."

I pull out and stagger back a few stairs, grabbing onto the paneling to keep from falling.

She turns to sit on the landing and bends forward, hugging her legs.

I turn to face the wall, ashamed. My plan to fuck her dispassionately, like she's only a tool for my pleasure, was beyond selfish. My attempt to protect my heart ignored her feelings and risked hurting her—physically and emotionally.

She ended it. Rightfully so.

My boner's still raging, and at this point I'm not sure if it will ever go down. I might have to live out the rest of my life in this painful state of arousal.

I've never denied my body what it wanted during or

after a feeding—never denied my body's sexual desire at any time to be honest, and I'm in uncharted territory here. But I can't ask her to let me fuck her again.

"Which bedroom?" Her voice draws me through my self-pity.

I turn toward her. She's standing on the landing, hand reaching down toward me in clear invitation.

I am too weak to deny her—or myself. I have to finish what we've started no matter the cost to her, or to my heart.

CHAPTER 16

Selina

Gray stands on the staircase, so much pain in his eyes. "What's wrong?" I ask him.

"I'm sorry." His voice is hoarse and he casts his eyes down.

"Why are you sorry?" I descend a step, getting the impression that if I move toward him too quickly he'll run.

My sex is throbbing, hot and raw from how hard he took me against that table and then here on the stairs, but although he bruised me inside, my vampiric body is already healing. And even though my first orgasm came fast and hard, I want more—I don't just want Gray, I need him.

"Come," I say when he doesn't answer. "Let's go to your bedroom."

He looks at me, and I'm relieved to see something besides pain or regret in his expression. Something new.

Something tender and emotional that makes my breath catch in my throat.

He takes my extended hand, brings it to his lips and slowly kisses my knuckles, lingering to circle each one with his tongue.

Looking up into my eyes, he laves the joints on my hand, and as he does my need pulses between my legs, as if his mouth's down there and not on my knuckles.

We move to the landing together, but instead of taking me to his bedroom, which I still haven't seen, he leads me toward the room I've been using. The one I've shared with Rock.

"Let's go to *your* room," I suggest.

He pushes open the door to mine and heads to the huge bed.

I stop, letting my hand slip from his. "What if Rock comes home while we're..."

"Maybe he'll join us." Gray steps quickly toward me.

His fingers find my sex in an instant, two long fingers pushing inside me so hard and fast that I'm forced to rise onto my toes.

And at the same time, he captures my gasp with a kiss and soon his tongue and fingers are stroking in tandem. His other hand slides up under my T-shirt, pushing under the band of my bra to palm my breast and then squeeze my nipple.

The effect is electric and I'm transported back to the erotic dream I had about Pike. So many hands on and in and over all of my places at once.

"You like that, princess?" Gray asks against my lips. "You like when I pinch your tits?" He squeezes my nipple again as his fingers pump inside and his thumb strums my clit.

"Yessss." The word comes out of me like a long hiss, and he backs me to the end of the bed.

My legs strike the mattress, and I almost fall back.

Taking his fingers from inside me, he pulls off my T-shirt, then tears off his own. He gets rid of his pants almost as quickly, leaving them crumpled on the floor.

I reach for his shoulders, planning to kiss him, but he picks me up at the waist and tosses me onto the bed. I land on my back, and before I can recover from the shock, he tugs me down to the end of the mattress and spreads my legs wide.

Standing with one foot on the floor, the other securing my bent leg on the bed, he braces his arms on the mattress beside me and enters in one hard, deep stroke. The sudden penetration steals my breath.

Slowly he pumps inside of me, each drive long and deliberate, each giving me so much pleasure.

Resting his forearm next to my head, he kisses me tenderly while he moves inside me, and I feel like we're one. I feel like he's part of me, like I'm part of him. I need him so much, need every inch of him, and if my mouth weren't occupied by our kissing, I'm not sure I could hold myself back from telling him this—or from taking his vein.

Breaking our kiss, he looks into my eyes as he continues to move above me and inside me. I thought this act couldn't get any better than what I'd already experienced, but I was wrong. It just did.

The first time Gray was inside me was my first consensual sex, and that day I thought I'd discovered the most pleasure a woman could have. I thought that I'd finally figured out the true reason why humans, vampires—all species—make love, and I thought I'd never encounter anything more pleasurable than simply having Gray inside me.

But this—this now, with him looking into my eyes while his body slides slowly and deeply, filling me over and over—I've never felt so connected, so fulfilled, so joyous. And all that is on top of the intense physical pleasure.

"Gray."

"Princess." Driving faster for a few strokes, he groans.

"I think I'm falling in love with you."

He stops moving, his erection buried deep inside me.

As he looks into my eyes, I think he's going to tell me that he loves me too. I can see the words in his eyes, almost see them on his lips, but then his expression grows cold and he closes his eyes.

"No you're not." He grunts.

"Yes I—"

But I don't get to finish that sentence. He flips me over and positions me on all fours. Putting his knees between mine to hold them open, he plows into me from behind, landing each thrust deep and hard.

I want to object, but it feels too good.

Bending my upper body, he presses my forehead onto the duvet and uses the weight of his much taller body to trap me beneath him as he pumps.

The power and speed of each pounding stroke is beyond belief. I can't move. I don't want to.

As amazing as that brief intimate moment between us was, as much as I want to experience that again—and soon and over and over for the rest of our lives—there is no way I would ever want to put a stop to what he's doing to my body right now.

His hands land on my breasts and cover them, then, holding me there, he uses them to pull my body back to meet each of his thrusts. My nipples become scissored between his fingers, and he slides my sensitive nipples between his index and middle fingers as he grips my breasts, squeezing tightly, pinching my nipples with each stroke so hard that it hurts. But then it doesn't hurt anymore. It all becomes part of the intense pleasure that's flowing through every part of my body.

One of his hands drops from my breast to my clit. "Come for me, princess."

My orgasm overtakes me.

Unable to control it, not wanting to, I buck beneath him, and still he pumps, one hand on my nipple and the other on my clit as my insides pulse around his cock.

My contractions continue, building higher and stronger, so fierce I can barely breathe, and then he comes, too. His strokes grow erratic and he moans, shouting my name as his hot semen transfers from his body to mine and combines with my own juices to lubricate the final moments of our sex act.

My orgasm continues with sporadic aftershocks as he pulls out and flops facedown on the bed beside me. Even though I know he's withdrawn, I can still sense his hot hardness inside me. The sense memory of his punishing rod now lives in the cells that line my tragically empty tunnel.

The orgasmic contractions subside, but still my muscles squeeze, as if they're crying out to be massaged again by his thick cock.

I stretch out beside him and caress his back. I want to tell him again that I love him. I want him to respond, at least to know where we stand, but I'm so spent I'm not sure I can speak, plus I don't want to risk anything that might invade my euphoria.

He turns on his side to face me.

Smiling wickedly, he brushes stray hairs off my face, then caresses my body, his hands stroking over my throat and chest, then down the side of me until he reaches my wrist. He takes hold of my hand as I look into his eyes and he pulls it toward him, placing my fingers firmly around his sex.

I gasp. "You're still hard." And hot and wet from my juices.

"With you, princess, it seems I'm insatiable."

His words warm my heart. It's not like he said, *I love you*, but maybe *insatiable* is as close as I'm going to get to an admission of emotions from Gray, at least tonight.

"Ready to go again?" he asks huskily. "Can you take more?"

I stroke his cock. "With you, it seems I'm insatiable too."

In a flash, he pulls my leg over his hip and presses inside me.

I like this position, face-to-face, side-by-side, and looking into each other's eyes as he thrusts. But just as I gather the courage to express my love again, he flips me onto my hands and knees to take me from behind, faster and harder , more like the animalistic, athletic sex I've become used to.

But I'm not complaining. Each stroke elevates my pleasure to new heights.

He alters our position a few times, and with each change in angle, in depth of penetration, my excitement and pleasure build even higher. I feel like I'm going to explode, but I'm not sure my body is capable of another orgasm. I can't think, I'm barely aware of controlling my limbs as he moves me wherever he wants, as he touches me and takes me in any and every way.

With Gray, I'm a pliable toy, putty under his hands and around his cock.

And before long, I find myself with my feet on the floor beside the bed, hands on the mattress and Gray standing behind, using his powerful legs to help him drive, and his hands on my hips to pull me back hard against each stroke.

The force of each upward thrust lifts me off my toes, and his pelvis strikes my ass cheeks with wet slaps. I moan and cry out, not sure if my body can take more pleasure. My insides are on fire, my nerves so raw I can't distinguish between pleasure and pain.

How much longer can he last before coming? Can I take any more? On second thought, could I bear the loss if it stopped? Neither option seems possible. I want it to stop *and* to go on forever.

With a roar, Gray climaxes.

One of his hands moves up to my shoulder like he thinks the leverage will help him drive deeper, but deeper isn't possible. His balls slap against me each time he hits home.

His hot liquid shoots inside me, each jet first scalding then salving my raw pussy, and he slows his pace, sliding more slowly. His hands move to my breasts, then my throat.

Yes, I think. *Feed from me, Gray. Feed.*

Longing to make eye contact, I turn to look over my shoulder.

Rock is standing in the doorway.

"Gray," I call out. "Stop."

He pulls out and strokes my back. "What's wrong, princess?"

I scramble onto the mattress. "Rock's here. I told you we should have used another room."

"Sorry to interrupt," Rock says softly. "The door was open."

"Rock—" I cross my arms over my chest, suddenly feeling naked now there's someone fully clothed in the room.

Rock doesn't seem jealous or angry. Not even sad, and I'm not sure how I feel about that. He insists that he's okay with my having sex with Gray, but I still can't fully believe that witnessing the act doesn't bother him at all.

"Don't stop on my account." Rock leans against the doorframe.

Gray picks up his discarded clothes from the floor. "She's all yours, mate." He kisses my cheek. "Thank you, princess. That was lovely."

"Lovely?" Seems like an understatement.

"Fan-fucking-tastic." He raises his eyebrows. "For me, anyway, and if I were a gentleman, which clearly I am not, I'd make sure you finished again." He nods at Rock as he walks toward him. "Maybe you could take care of that?"

Gray turns back at the door and winks.

Rock steps inside the room to let Gray pass into the hall, and I sit on the bed, feeling uncertain, nervous. Rock and I still haven't talked since the episode in the shower and I didn't plan for a sex show to be the icebreaker.

Rock joins me, and the mattress sinks when he sits. "You love Grayson," he says softly.

Hand around Rock's neck, I slide onto his lap, straddling him as he sits on the edge of the bed. "I love *you.*"

"You love him too," Rock says. "It's okay." His huge

hands span my back and hold me securely. "It's natural for vampires to love more than one mate. Even humans sometimes have polyamorous relationships."

"And giants?"

He shrugs. "I wouldn't know."

I kiss him softly.

"Correction." His hand slides down to cup my ass. "I do know, because this giant has found himself in a polyamorous relationship."

"Is that what this is?"

"You tell me."

I shift my hips over the hardness resting under my thigh. "I'm not sure. I have no idea what Gray wants."

"He wants *you*, Acushla. That's pretty clear."

"For sex. Sure. But anything more?" I shake my head. "Tonight, he was so—so eager. But it was only because he didn't have sex when he fed."

Rock's eyes open wider.

"I don't think I should read anything into his lust tonight," I continue to explain to make sure Rock gets it. Gray's eagerness, his vigor, his passion tonight… "It was just a physical need."

"I reach the opposite conclusion," Rock says. "If Gray fed without having sex, that means he fought against his body's natural urges. To me that proves he not only *wants* you, it means that he *loves* you."

My chest warms even as I shake my head. "I'm not sure. I wish he'd let me in, just a little. Tell me what he's feeling."

Rock nods understandingly. "You'll always know where you stand with me."

"And where do I stand?" I rock against his hardness. "Or *sit* with you right now?"

He exhales deeply and lifts me a fraction of an inch to relieve the pressure on his erection.

"Where you stand is—I love you. I love you more than life. Your happiness begets my happiness. Your pleasure begets my pleasure." He stills my hips, preventing me from rubbing his cock. "And whether he loves you or not—and I think he does—I'm grateful you have Gray to fulfill your sexual needs."

"Rock." I squirm under his hold. "I could say the same thing. Your happiness means everything to me and so does *your* pleasure." I circle my hips, trying to build some friction, constrained by his tight grip.

He shifts me to kneel on the bed beside him.

"Rock." I caress his chest. "Can we talk about what happened? You seemed ashamed. Ashamed that you were wearing that contraption? Or ashamed that I saw you pleasure yourself? Help me understand."

He looks to the side.

"You pleasuring yourself was natural. Beautiful. Erotic." I glance down to the thickness under his jeans. "And your getting hard when you're with me—that's beautiful, too, and flattering. Seeing your reaction to me makes me very happy."

When he turns back toward me, there's hope in his eyes, but it's still tinged with sadness.

"That leather contraption you were wearing," I say softly. "Promise me you'll never cage yourself like that again."

"That's to protect you."

I shake my head. "I don't need to be protected—not from you."

"You're wrong." His voice is deep and he won't look me in the eye.

I slip back over his lap, my hand aiming for his crotch, but he slides me against him, and my hand lands trapped between our bellies instead.

"Acushla." He rests his forehead against mine. "The sex act. I can't. I will *not* do that to you."

"You said we weren't compatible, but I've seen you, Rock."

"So you understand."

"No, I don't." I take his face in my hands and force him to look at me. "In fact, I think a vampire might be your ideal sex partner." If he can't find a female giant, that is, and I don't want to put that thought in his mind if it's not already there.

"You're big, yes, but I can heal." I rock against him, trying to work my fingers lower, hoping to increase his need so that he'll give me what I most want.

He lifts me from his lap and lays me on my back on the bed.

He's very gentle about it, putting me down softly, and yet all the air leaves my chest. This is going to happen.

I want it to, I do, but I'm not as confident as I just sounded that it's going to work, that he'll fit. Or that I'll be able to hide my pain if he doesn't.

He stands at the side of the bed, his chest rising and falling with heavy breaths, and his jeans look like they're about to burst from the pressure of his bulge.

I lift one of my feet and press it softly against the hot ridge.

He grabs my ankle.

His hand stays on my ankle as I spread my legs for him, fully exposing my sex, and his gaze drops where I want it to. His pupils widen and his breaths grow even heavier.

Both of his hearts beat hard, one slightly faster than the other, as blood rushes from other parts of his body straight to his cock, like creeks feeding a river after a springtime rain.

His gaze rises to meet mine. "I would give you anything you desire, Selina. Anything. Everything that's within my power to give you is yours. But you must understand. I cannot give you that."

Dropping to his knees, he buries his face between my legs.

I want to object, to finish the conversation and convince him that we should at least *try* penetrative sex, but he presses a thick finger inside me and sucks on my clit.

My body arches like a bow and words are no longer possible. Words can wait.

CHAPTER 17

Pike

The muted sounds of Selina's pleasure drift through the night air to reach my ears, as I stand atop a twelve-story apartment building ten blocks away from her. My ability to track others using sound is acute compared to other vampires, and connecting directly to the frequency of Selina's voice is my best way to track her—the only reliable way.

If I'd done it from the day she left Xavier's dungeon, I could have kept her safe.

I shake my head. That would never have worked. Even if I'd made an auditory link when she first ran, I would have had to break it before the first threat of dawn. Just like I'll have to in a few hours from now.

Knowing I'll have to leave her unguarded yet again—find her tomorrow after dusk to redo the connection—shoots terror through my bloodstream. Hours and hours when I won't know where she is or if she's safe.

I'll stay here until the last possible moment, until I'm sure that she'll be inside Gray's house until dusk.

Xavier wants her to suffer. He wants her dead, but only after considerable pain. If I know anything about the vampire I used to call King, I know that.

But I tell myself she's not in danger tonight. Xavier lost at least five guards—almost every one he trusts to leave the palace compound.

With his team depleted, he risks losing control, leaving himself exposed to revolution.

As much as he wants Selina dead, he's not going to risk his own neck or his so-called kingdom.

Xavier needs time to rebuild before trying to capture her again, but on the slim chance I'm wrong, this vantage point has clear sight lines for every possible approach. If any of Xavier's Guard go anywhere near Selina, within seconds they'll be impaled on my stake.

Selina cries out in ecstasy, and I wish for a moment that I hadn't tuned my hearing so finely to her voice. I should break the connection now I know she's inside the house, but I can't stop myself.

And my eavesdropping has confirmed that I'm unlikely to ever win her heart. Not that I ever had a chance. Not really. But now it's clear. The big man *and* the vampire. She's fucking them both. She loves them both. Pain tightens my chest.

From what I got from her side of the conversation, the giant man refuses to fuck her, with his dick, anyway. I didn't hear his reasons, but I've heard her trying to change his mind, and it's clear the giant is filled with something I very well understand. Shame.

Selina's sex sounds escalate, her breaths come heavy

and shallow as the giant—I assume it's just the giant—gives her oral pleasure.

My cock throbs so hard I can barely stand it, and I shove my hands in my jacket pockets to stop myself from taking out my dick to relieve the pressure. Listening to her every word, her every sigh and breath, is intrusive. There's a fine line between protector and stalker, and I've crossed it tonight.

But jacking off while thinking of her is one line I refuse to cross. So since meeting her I haven't been able to give myself pleasure.

I find the razor blade in my pocket and dig it under my fingernail. For a moment, the sharp pain distracts me from my lust, but even as my pocket fills with blood, it's not enough to distract me from Selina.

Crying out, she calls the giant's name and tells him it's too much, then with the next exhale she changes her mind and asks him to continue whatever it is that he's doing to ravish her soft body parts.

I force the blade under the nail of the next finger and curse into the night. I would do anything for Selina. Anything. Pain is a small price.

CHAPTER 18

Selina

Astrid flips me onto my back on the floor of Gray's basement gymnasium and presses a steel training spike between my ribs. Her move was so unexpected, and the force of my landing so hard, I can't breathe.

"Never let down your guard." Astrid releases her pressure. "Because of your size, you can't rely on your weight in close combat. Not even against a human."

I roll over onto my back as my ability to breathe slowly returns. Astrid remains crouched beside me and I adjust my position to sit cross-legged beside her.

"Can we take a short break?" I ask while staring up at the ceiling. Gray's gym might be in a basement, but it's about five times the size of the one we were using under Rock's bar.

"Sure." Astrid mirrors my position, sitting across from me. "Don't get discouraged. You're doing well. You're a fast learner and gaining power more quickly than any baby vampire I've come across. Let me know if you ever want a job working security for FJS."

"Thanks." Pride swells inside me, although working security holds zero appeal. "It's hard to think of having a job or any kind of normal life again." I shake my head. "I've lived most of my life alternating between prisoner and fugitive."

"Don't worry." She rubs my arm. "We'll find Xavier. He's been on our radar for centuries."

"Centuries?"

She leans forward. "Xavier claims to have arrived in North America with the first explorers from France in 1534."

"That can't be true."

"Yeah." She shrugs. "I doubt he came with Jacques Cartier, like he claims. Hard to know for sure, but I do know that the first contingent from FJS came to what's now Québec in 1670, and Xavier was already here."

My insides tremble. The sadist who's after me suddenly looms so much larger, like he's invincible. "If you haven't been able to catch him for three hundred and fifty years…"

My throat closes and my chest caves like the ceiling is pressing down and the walls are closing in around me. "I need to go upstairs." I dash up from the basement.

Struggling to breathe, I pause at the top of the stairs at the door to Gray's bright kitchen. My instincts tell me the daylight streaming into the room isn't safe, even though I've been living inside of Gray's treated glass for nearly a week now.

I stagger into the room, crossing toward the sinks. Willing the tightness in my chest to release, I stare out the large double window above the sunken ceramic sinks and the sight seems like a miracle. The sunlight on green grass, on the leaves of trees, the brilliant white clouds floating through the blue sky… My chest opens enough to let me breathe again.

A butterfly flits past the window, and I lean forward to watch its path across Gray's yard. It's been so long since I've witnessed daylight. Resting my hands on the edge of the sink, I try to remember the feel of sunlight on my skin, the smell of fresh air in the daytime—but even the sight of sunlight feels good, beyond good.

"Selina." Astrid steps up beside me and rests her hand on my shoulder. "You're safe here at Gray's. I promise. And we will get Xavier."

I shake my head. "So many years…"

"We've never had grounds to go after him before," she says. "We knew about his false claim of royalty and suspected what went on in his court, but we've never had evidence to charge him with any crimes. We've never had a *witness.* Now we have two, maybe three."

"Is the third that vampire who was burned under the silver net?"

"He's not cooperating." She frowns. "He's been charged with attempted murder and kidnapping."

"And Kwana?"

"She's told us a lot." Astrid rests her fingers on the counter beside the sink. "But she claims not to know another way in."

"Do you think she's telling the truth?"

"She hasn't given us any reason not to trust her."

"And you can't find the door I escaped through downtown?"

Astrid shakes her head. "You haven't remembered anything more, have you?"

"No." I look down and clench my fists. "I hate that I can't remember where it was."

"You were starved, sun-burned, traumatized." Jumping up, she twists to sit on the counter next to the sink. "Trauma's probably affecting Kwana's memory, too. That night was the first time she'd been above ground as a vampire. She was turned in Xavier's court."

"Wow." I shake my head, but Kwana's story rings true. "I was blindfolded when I was taken to his court," I tell Astrid, "and while I knew none of Xavier's mates ever left the palace compound, it never occurred to me that *no one* ever left."

Astrid adjusts the elastic holding back her thick red mane. "According to Kwana, only a few of Xavier's most trusted Guard ever come up to the city."

A blue jay lands on the branch of a tree. Joy and regret flood through me at once. The bird seems like a sign of opportunity, of hope, but its freedom is a reminder that I'm caged. Even if my cage isn't Xavier's now—not directly.

I turn toward Astrid and lean against the edge of the sink. "Santos. The vampire who recruited me. *He* was allowed outside."

She nods. "Everyone on my team is searching for Santos too. Xavier uses him to find baby vampires—like you—and to lure humans to feed from or turn. That's what happened to Kwana. She was human when she was captured."

Astrid leans and rests her head on the cupboard next to the window. "There is one encouraging thing."

"What's that?"

"Kwana doesn't think Xavier will send anyone after you right away."

"Why not?"

"It would leave him exposed to an attack."

"An attack from—"

"His own so-called subjects and courtiers—maybe even his mates."

His mates would never turn against him. *Would they?*

I back away from the counter and lean back against the island, facing Astrid. "Xavier's mates love him." I think back to Jordina and Alexander, the vampires who bathed and dressed me before my last wedding attempt.

"If his mates don't love him," I say, "they sure convinced me that they do."

"Maybe so." Astrid tips her head to the side. "But Kwana believes most of the court would leave, given the opportunity."

My eyes narrow as I consider this. "Most of Xavier's subjects have free run of the palace from what I could tell."

Astrid shrugs. "That doesn't mean they aren't trapped."

I nod. Some might just be held captive by their own minds, fearing what's waiting on the surface. Especially if they've been down there a long time.

I try to let my fear pass out of my body. "So Xavier's not coming after me anymore?"

"That's not what I said." Her expression grows serious and she pushes off the counter to stand in front of me. "But there's a good chance we have a bit of time before he comes after you again."

"That's a relief, I guess." I should run away from here. Run as far away from Xavier as I can get.

If I hadn't made connections here, more connections than I've had in my entire life, I'd leave the city right now. Leave the country. The continent. But, if life as a lone vampire was hard in a place that I know, I can't imagine being a lone vamp on the run.

"We're still learning more from Kwana," Astrid says. "And then there's Pike."

I raise my gaze quickly to meet hers, my heart rate increasing again. "What about Pike?"

"Gray thinks he'd be willing to cooperate."

"Gray has *talked* to Pike?"

She shakes her head. "Not since he released you. Neither have we. My team's looking for him. We'd like to ask him some questions."

"Don't trust Pike," I blurt. "He's a monster." The words come out on instinct, but something deep in my gut disagrees with what I said.

"I hear you," she says. "When we find him we'll charge him with assault, at a minimum, and for your kidnapping on the night of the attack. But we can't ignore the fact that he *did* let you go—maybe twice. And he told Gray that he wants Xavier dead…"

"It could be a trick." But I'm shocked to realize that the mention of Pike woke an ache between my legs and—even stranger—one in my heart. I close my eyes to fight the unwanted feelings. *What is wrong with me?*

Clearly I've spent too much of my life as a prisoner or running from predators. My body no longer reacts to danger in a normal way. That's the only explanation for how I'm feeling right now.

And speaking of dangerous men, I haven't seen Colton since he told me about the symbol carved into the flesh of all those victims. Training so often, I've barely been to O'Malley's since the night Colton and I talked, but Rock told me the cop's been by a few times, although mostly before dark.

I need to talk to someone about what Colton told me, and Astrid's the closest thing I have to a friend.

"You know how that cop's been hanging out in Rock's bar?" I ask Astrid.

She nods. "Rock says he's asked about you. Best to steer clear of O'Malley's for a while."

Biting my lower lip, I shake my head. "I need to talk to him again."

"The cop?" Astrid's bright green eyes spark with shock. "Why?"

"He told me something about the serial killer—"

"You talked about *that*?" She turns toward me, eyes wide. "Why?"

I straighten. "He brought it up." Although to be honest, I'm no longer certain how the topic came up. "Colton, that's the cop's name, he's part of the task force that's hunting for the serial killer."

"All the more reason to stay away from him." Astrid tips her head to the side. "What if he suspects *you're* the killer?"

"Why would he think that?"

"Bad enough if he suspects you're a vampire."

I shake my head, but a shiver runs down my spine. "If he knew that, wouldn't I already be dead?"

She shrugs, conceding. "The serial killer's making life more dangerous for every vampire in the city. The police tactics are escalating. We're hunting him too."

"Not him." I take a deep breath. "Her."

"What?" Astrid leans forward. "Do the humans know the killer's female? Did the cop tell you that?"

I shake my head, then draw a long breath. "I know it. Or suspect it anyway. I think the serial killer is my Maker."

Astrid's head snaps back. "What in the world makes you think that?"

"Colton told me that all the killer's victims had the same wound."

"Sure," Astrid shrugs. "Most have unhealed fang marks on their necks. Although according to our sources, a few of them had their throats ripped out."

"Not that," I tell her. "A symbol. A symbol carved into the victims that matches this one." Turning, I pull up my hair and show her the scar at the back of my neck.

"What is that?" she asks.

"I don't know." I shake my head. "It appeared after I turned." I didn't mention it when I described my transition to Astrid, Malcolm and Rock.

"Fascinating." Moving behind me as I hold my hair up, she runs her finger over the mark. "It's very red. Somewhere between a scab and a scar. I've never seen anything like it on a vampire. Usually open sores heal during the transition process. Only fully formed scars stay."

I drop my hair and turn back to her.

"Has Gray seen it?" she asks.

"Probably." I shake my head. "I don't know. I haven't *shown* it to him. Why?"

She shrugs, but suddenly looks like she wishes she hadn't asked the question. "Your transition is still a mystery, and Gray knows more about that kind of thing."

"He's never mentioned my scar." It's small and hidden by my hair. Besides Gray doesn't spend a lot of time taking in the details of my body or letting me take in the details of his. We always get straight to the fucking, and as much as I enjoy the sex, physically, his detachment is starting to hurt my feelings.

Gray's put up a wall between us—more like a curtain

or sheet. Whatever it is that's hanging between us, it's like Gray fucks me through a hole in that barrier, taking and giving me pleasure while minimizing any kind of intimacy —or even skin contact.

"Did you show your scar to that cop?" Astrid brings me back to the present.

"No."

She exhales hard. "That's good. At least I think it's good. Or, maybe…" Her eyes narrow. "If you show him, do you think you could get him to tell you more about the serial killer case?"

"I don't know. Why?"

"FJS needs to catch this vampire before the humans do. Bring her to justice with a proper trial."

"I'm pretty sure I can get the cop to tell me more." Colton likes telling me about his work.

Astrid bites her lower lip. "On second thought. Don't show him the scar. If he thinks you're one of the killer's victims, he might want to take you in to file a police report—during daylight hours."

I nod. I don't really want to show Colton my scar, but I do know that I want to see him again. "Can you help me?"

"With what?" she asks.

"With Rock and Gray. They barely let me out of their sight. If I'm going to get the cop to talk, I need to get away from them for a while."

CHAPTER 19

Rock

I push a freshly poured beer across the bar.

"What's this?" the customer asks.

I look back at the short man with a beard, who's glancing between me and the glass like I just poured him a pint of cat piss.

"I ordered a Barking Squirrel IPA." The customer shoots me a look of scorn.

"Oh. Yeah. Sorry." I move the mild lager below the bar, grab a fresh glass and start to pull the right beer.

Across the room, Selina leans intimately toward the cop, and jealousy pounds inside me. Jealousy mixed with a strong dose of fear. What if he figures out what she is?

Beer washes over the top of the pint glass and splatters down onto my shoes. *Feck*! I shut off the tap, wipe the sides of the glass and hand it to my customer.

"About time," he says.

"It's on the house." The customer's a demanding git,

rude, but right now I just want him out of my face so I can keep my eyes on Selina.

The bell over the front door jangles, but I don't even look up to see who entered. Danger is already in the building.

The cop has two wooden stakes stashed in his jacket—two I can see—and I'm shocked that Selina's taking such a chance with her life. If I see one hint that he's figured out she's a vampire, I'll leap over the bar and kill him before one of those stakes goes anywhere near her heart.

"Earth to Rock."

I turn to see Astrid and Malcolm leaning against the bar. "Hey. Sorry. Didn't see you come in."

"We got that." Malcolm winks.

"Cocktails? Red wine? What's your pleasure tonight?"

"Red wine sounds great," Malcolm answers.

Astrid nods, and I grab two glasses, set them on the bar and turn away from Selina for a few seconds to snag an open bottle of the Cab Sauv that my vampire friends both favor.

I keep my eyes on Selina as I pour their wine. "What is she thinking, talking to that cop?"

"He has information she wants." Astrid lifts her wine glass, swirls the liquid inside, then looks over her shoulder toward Selina and the cop. "Information about her Maker."

"What? How?" *And why didn't she tell me?* I shake my head. The answer's obvious. She didn't mention it because I would have argued even more strongly against her coming to the bar tonight.

"Rock." Astrid draws my attention. "Selina can handle herself with a human. But if you like, I can keep an eye on her."

"I'm keeping an eye on her."

A customer beckons from the other end of the bar.

I deeply regret that I agreed to let Selina come in on Kev's night off. But as she very forcefully pointed out when I brought it up, she doesn't need my permission to do anything. And she's right.

I know that she's strong, and becomes more so every day, but I wish she'd make it easier for me to protect her.

The customer orders a Manhattan, and I curse under my breath as I prepare it. While I'm searching for maraschino cherries, not often used in this place, Chelle gives me an order for the party of six in the front booth.

I finish the Manhattan, then rush around pulling three beers, opening a bottle of Pinot Gris to pour a single glass. Then I make two margaritas, one with salt, one without. Don't these people realize this is a beer and peanuts kind of bar? And why is everyone choosing tonight to order drinks I have to do more than just pour?

After I put the last of the drinks on a tray for Chelle, I shift my attention back to Selina. I nearly leap over the bar.

Selina and the cop are walking toward the exit together, and I want to smash the obvious desire and adoration off the human male's face. But at least that's better than if he looked ready to stake her.

"Selina!" I call out.

She says something to the cop, and he pauses at the door.

I meet her at the end of the bar. "You just seeing him out?"

She smiles a smile that makes everything inside me go mushy. "No, I'm not just seeing him out."

"Then what?"

"We're going for a walk."

"What?"

Heads turn in the bar and I realize I raised my voice. Big time. I lean over the bar and speak more softly. "You're joking, right?"

She whispers in my ear. "Astrid is going to follow behind us, just in case. Don't worry. I'll be safe."

My hearts are thumping out of my chest. "Why would you take such a huge risk?"

"I need information from him," she says. "It's important. Trust me, please?" She looks into my eyes, pleading.

"Information about your Maker."

Her eyes open wider.

"Astrid told me."

"Oh." She draws a long breath. "I need to know more about who I am, and Rock, if anyone should understand my curiosity about this, it's you. What would you risk to know more about *your* people?"

My breath catches and anger flares inside me. It feels like a low blow for her to bring up how alone I am in the world, how I don't even know with certainty *what* I am, never mind who my parents were.

But she's right. I'd jump at any lead that would help find my family or *anyone* who knows about my life before that infernal circus.

At my long pause, her expression grows colder. She's angry.

"I'm going, Rock, whether you like it or not." She pushes back from the bar, and the cop's face lights up as she walks back to join him at the exit.

He holds open the door and his hand softly touches her back as she leaves. I want to kill him.

Astrid touches my hand. Braced for danger and caught up in my anger and fear, I almost strike her.

But I'm not nearly fast enough to strike a vampire. Astrid grabs my wrist, her tight grip stopping both the motion and my circulation, and reminding me just how strong my vampire friend is.

"I've got this, Rock," she says. "Don't worry. I won't let anything happen to your Selina."

And with that, Astrid follows them out the door.

Backing away from the bar I bend at the waist, trying not to hyperventilate, trying to keep from running after my love.

CHAPTER 20

Selina

"Such a nice night for a walk," Colton says from beside me.

He's holding my hand, and it's like I'm fourteen. Or how I imagine a fourteen-year-old girl would feel holding hands with a smoking-hot boy she's crushing on. Living on the streets by that age, I never got the chance to know for sure.

Right now, I can't stop smiling, my giddiness fueled by the energy that's transferring between us and the excitement of receiving attention from such a classically handsome man.

But I need to remind myself that this stroll has a purpose beyond fresh air, flirting and getting to know Colton better.

"Will you show me where the last murder happened?" I ask, once we're a block away from the bar.

"The actual crime scene?" Dropping my hand to step

ahead of me, he kicks a broken piece of glass from my path. "Why would you want to see that?"

"Is it gruesome?"

"No." He takes my hand again. "It's basically a park bench."

"I'm just curious." But I realize my request came off a bit strange. He's been happy to talk about his work, possibly thrilled that I'm interested, but I have no explanation for why I'd want to see the crime scene.

"Never mind." I stroke his thumb with mine.

Squeezing my hand in response, he smiles. "If you're that curious about the bloodsucker…" He stops midsentence. "No, never mind."

"What?"

"I've got copies of the files at home." He stops and turns toward me looking sheepish. "I'm sorry. That sounded like a line to get you into my apartment." He shifts his weight. "I don't mean any disrespect."

"I'd love to see the files." Excitement stirs inside me. This little stroll could turn out better than my wildest expectations.

Even if she's a killer, I need to know more about my Maker. *Especially* if she's a killer. I need to find out how I transitioned without the normal ritual. And if the police find her first, they'll stake her and I lose my chance.

I need to know everything the police do, both for myself and for Astrid. It's way better for me if Astrid is the one to capture her. Better for Astrid, too, which is why she agreed to help and is following us, I think… I still haven't developed the ability to sense when I'm being followed that Gray and even Rock seem to have.

"Do you live nearby?" I ask Colton.

He tips back his head. "A few blocks that way. On Evelyn. It's just a basement studio. Pretty crappy place."

"I'm sure it's lovely." I smile. "Let's go."

He tries to hide the joy that invades his face. "You sure?"

"Why wouldn't I be sure?" I exaggerate a shoulder shrug. "I mean, a man I barely know invited me into his basement apartment. Nothing dangerous about that. Nothing at all."

Taking both my hands, he faces me and his expression turns serious. "All joking aside, Selina. You have absolutely nothing to fear with me, but that said, I don't want you to do anything that makes you uncomfortable."

He really is a Boy Scout.

"I trust you. Let's go." We start walking again. "Besides, if you try anything, I can handle myself." I hip check him lightly.

"Oh, you can, can you?" An overhead streetlight captures a flash of white teeth as he smiles. "Remember, I *am* a cop. We have martial arts training, you know."

"Who says I haven't had martial arts training, too?"

"Really…" His grin widens, deepening his dimples. "What other secret skills are you hiding?"

"Oh, you have no idea."

"I can't wait to find out."

The flirty banter stirs desire and happiness inside me as we walk the rest of the way in silence, and the connection between our hands makes me feel like I've got a protective shield around me.

Protective, comforting and sensual.

Colton stops. "This is me." We're in front of a two-and-a-half-story brick house in a densely packed neighborhood.

"Nice," I say.

"I'm in the basement." He leads me through the gate of a chain-link fence and down the front path, but he turns right before the steps to the porch.

"My entrance is around back." He closes his eyes for a moment. "We've got to go down the breezeway between the houses. It's dark, but there's a motion detector light halfway."

"Okay." With anyone else, I might be alarmed about being led down a dark narrow passage between two houses, but Colton is like a golden retriever or something—athletic and powerful but nonthreatening unless threatened. I am safe with Colton as long as he doesn't figure out what I am. I've never been so certain of anything; plus, he doesn't realize I can see in the dark.

We enter the narrow space between the two buildings, and his wide shoulders brush the sides, forcing him to drop my hand. A light comes on almost immediately, and I follow until we're through a small wooden gate and into a backyard. Another light comes on to reveal old-fashioned metal lawn furniture sitting on a patch of grass and a vegetable garden farther back.

"My landlord grows his own veggies." Colton gestures toward the back of the yard, fenced in with simple chain link.

"Nice."

"The landlord has the bottom two floors and there's another tenant on the top."

I nod.

"I'd like to get out of this basement apartment situation, soon," he says. "I'm saving for a down payment, but the market..."

"Tell me about it." I smile up at him, finding it kind of

adorable that he's obviously embarrassed that he's not a homeowner, even though he's still so young and Toronto is one of the least affordable real estate markets in the world. Very few people his age can afford to buy in this city. Not without a trust fund.

We walk down a few concrete steps, then he unlocks a door and we step inside. He flips a switch and the space fills with warm light, and I pause to take it in as he tosses his keys into a metal bowl near the door. The furnishings are simple and sparse but the apartment is tidy and clean. Near the entrance there's a small kitchen against one wall, a wooden table with two folding chairs, then a sofa against the wall, facing a TV. Past that sits a bed.

"Want the grand tour?" he asks, laughing.

"Sure."

He takes my hand again and gestures with the other. "Kitchen, living room, bedroom. Bathroom is through the door in the back on the right. The other door leads to the furnace room, and there's another set of stairs there that lead up to the landlord's space."

"It's really cozy." I squeeze his hand as we step forward.

"I assume you mean tiny."

"No, I mean, cozy." The wall opposite the bed is lined with trophies and medals. "What are these?" I drag him toward the display.

"I played a lot of sports in high school."

"I can see that." And with his athletic frame it's not hard to imagine. Even the way he carries himself and stands shout athlete.

"What were *you* like in high school?" he asks. "I'll bet you were in the drama club."

"Nope. Not a drama girl."

"Art? Something like that?"

"Art is more like it, but I didn't really go to high school." I pick up a trophy that says Athlete of the Year.

"Home schooled?" he asks.

"More like self-schooled, or library schooled, I guess. Self-taught."

"Oh." His brow furrows, but instead of his expression looking critical or pitying, he seems curious. "Your parents didn't encourage education?"

I look down. "I never met my dad. And my mom… She tried, but when I was six she married this…" My words choke me. I've never told anyone about my stepfather. Not even Lark.

Colton leads me toward the sofa and guides me onto it. "Want something to drink? Beer? Tea? Water? Orange juice?" Staring at his closed refrigerator door, he rubs his head as if that will help him remember its contents.

"Tea sounds nice." I've never actually had tea but it sounds comforting and warm—kind of like Colton.

Leaving me on the sofa, he fills a bright red kettle with tap water and sets it on the two-burner stove. He grabs two huge white mugs and sets them on the counter, then takes two tea bags out of a box and sets one inside each cup.

"How long were you living on the streets?" His voice is calm, even, and completely nonjudgmental.

He doesn't even turn to look at me directly, just goes about making the tea like we're discussing the weather. His question presumed a lot, but his presumption was right, and I'm glad that he's figured out this part of me without having to ask.

"I was on the streets five, maybe six years I guess, on and off. Maybe longer in total. I guess I've never had a truly stable living situation."

"Not even now?" He turns toward me, concern in his eyes.

"I'm good at the moment. Staying with a friend."

"One of those men." Colton leans back against the counter, looking so sexy I almost drool.

"Yes. With Grayson."

"Grayson's the fancy-looking hipster dude?"

"Hipster?" I laugh. "Hipster is the last adjective I'd choose to describe Gray."

"His sideburns." Colton shrugs. "I associate facial hair with hipsters, I guess. At least he doesn't have a beard or handlebar mustache or anything."

"Ah, I guess I get the hipster thing, then." Gray does look out of this time, out of fashion, but at the same time he's by far the most fashionable, put-together man I've ever known.

"How old were you when you ran away from home?" Colton asks softly, presuming correctly again.

"A few weeks after I turned fourteen."

"That must have been rough." He puts cookies on a plate, the kettle starts to squeal and he pours boiling water into each of the mugs. "How did you get by?"

"Washed dishes in small restaurants—ones that would pay me under the table. I cleaned houses, did odd jobs, made enough to buy food and stuff."

"And where did you live?"

"I crashed in a few homeless shelters for a while, but at some point they'd always ask about my parents, and so I'd move on. Lived in a bunch of cheap rooming houses, that kind of thing."

"How do you like your tea?" he asks. "Milk?"

"Sure, if you take it that way." Not a tea drinker, I have no idea how I take it, but milk sounds nice.

After pouring a little milk into each mug, he carries them over to the coffee table, balancing a plate of chocolate chip cookies on top of one. He settles on the sofa a few feet away from me.

One of his arms stretches across the back of the sofa as I reach for my tea. Again, this seems like something out of an old movie—a subtle way to almost put his arm around me.

Steam rises to warm my face and I take a tiny sip. "Oh, that's so good." The warm liquid drifts through me and helps bring me back to the present, away from the cold and dangerous nights of my past.

"I'm so sorry," he says softly.

"Why? The tea is great."

"No, sorry you had to go through so much—and all alone from the sounds of it."

The tea is the most comforting thing I've ever tasted. "I did have one friend…" I stare at the tawny liquid in the mug and the steam rising from it. If I could still cry, I wouldn't be able to contain my tears right now.

"Are you still friends?"

"No." My voice breaks. "She's dead."

"Oh, I'm so sorry." His hand falls to my shoulder and squeezes.

I take another soothing sip of the tea.

"And your mother?"

"I'm not sure." I watch the milky tea swirl. "I used to check on her a few times a year, just to make sure my stepfather hadn't killed her…"

"She never tried to leave him? Or report him to the police?"

I shake my head.

"Sadly, that's pretty typical. Domestic violence is a

complicated thing." He takes a sip of his tea. "Your stepfather. Did he beat you too? Is that why you ran away?" His voice is so kind, his eyes understanding.

"No." I look down. "He didn't beat me."

"Sexual abuse." His tone is gentle, the words coming out on an exhale, and while part of me hates that he figured out my darkest secret, a much bigger part of me is grateful that someone else finally knows, without my having to confess it.

"Yes." The word is a whisper. "Starting when I was eight."

I squeeze my eyes shut as memories flash through my mind like I'm back there—the creak of my bedroom door, the sliver of light from the hall, my stepfather's shuffling steps and the smell of beer on his labored breaths.

"Are you okay?" Colton asks quietly.

I nod, coming back to the present but not sure I can talk. The bad memories are scraping out of me like barbed wire, but as much as it hurts, exposing this painful part of my past, showing Colton a piece of me that's so private and raw, is a release.

Having shared even that small amount, I feel lighter, like the memories were heavy stones in my head and I've finally knocked some free.

"You didn't report him?" he asks softly.

I shake my head. "I didn't want anyone to discover I was on my own and risk getting sent back to that house."

"That does happen," he concedes, and I'm so glad he doesn't argue with me on that. "But you more likely would have landed in foster care. He should have been arrested."

"I didn't trust anyone." I shake my head. "Especially not adults. And I didn't want to ever have to face him again. Even if it was in court."

"That must have been horrible." Colton shifts on the sofa and I feel the cushions move beneath me. "I can't even imagine."

Staring into my tea, I nod.

"You know," Colton says gently. "It's not too late to press charges, even though you're an adult. I can help you with that."

I shake my head.

"What about your mother? Is she still with him?"

My breath catches in my chest in a half sob and he lightly rubs my shoulder. "I haven't seen my mom since my transition. They moved. I searched on the Internet a bit, but I can't find them."

"Do you want me to look? If you give me their last known address, full names, whatever you have."

"Please." Nodding, I turn toward him, and his expression is so full of kindness, understanding and utter compassion. Warmth floods me. It's like Colton sees inside me, like we've known each other for years. I slide over a few inches and rest my head against his outstretched shoulder.

I'm not entirely sure I want to know whatever he finds out, but I'd at least like to know that my mother's still alive. Even if I don't want to see her, I'd love to hear that she's safe.

As I lean against him, Colton's body's heat absorbs into mine and I want to move even closer, to press my leg against his, to slide my hand onto his chest. I want him to wrap his arms around me, to kiss me, but that would increase the chances of him discovering my *real* secret, plus I sense Colton's reluctant to make a move beyond his arm draped lightly around me.

I could make the first move, let him know it's okay to

touch me, kiss me, but I can't forget the main reason I came here.

"Do you really have the serial killer files here?" I ask. "Or was that just a line to lure me into your lair?"

"My lair?" Leaning back from me, he lifts his arm off my shoulder. "Selina. You're safe here. I would never—"

"I'm just joking." I grin, hoping he realizes that I do feel safe—incredibly safe considering I'm with a vampire killer. It was a bad joke to make given our discussion. "But I am serious about the files."

His head tips to the side. "Are you sure? There are photos, descriptions of the wounds. Some are pretty graphic."

"I can handle it."

He gets up, grabs a stack of file folders from a box under the kitchen table and sets them down in front of me.

"You're allowed to take files home from the station?" I ask as he returns to get more.

"Yeah. The rules around vampire case files are different."

I flip open the first file. On top is a photograph of a man in a suit slumped over a sofa, his neck twisted at an unnatural angle. Behind it is another photo, a close-up of fang marks on the man's neck.

Colton drops the second set of files on the table and sits down beside me. "That first pile has the cases without the characteristic wound. Nine cases over twenty years. But keeping files for vamp murders wasn't procedure until recently, so I bet there are tons of bloodsucker killings I don't have files for."

I nod, not wanting to push back at his assumption

that vampire killings are common. "Can I see a file where the victim does have the wound?"

He fishes a file from the other pile. "Here. This one shows it clearly." He shows me a photo of a young woman's leg, carved with the same symbol I have at the back of my neck.

"And all of the victims in that pile have the same mark?" I ask. "Are they all female?"

"Yup. All young women. All carved. This vampire has a sick fetish."

"But none of *these* have the mark?" I tap the first pile.

"That's right. Although for some of the older murders autopsies weren't done and the crime photos weren't thorough enough to be sure."

Nodding, I open another file in the non–serial-killer pile.

The photo on top makes my blood freeze. I can't move, can't breathe.

"What's wrong?" Colton asks.

It's Lark. The murderer in this unsolved case is me.

I can't stop staring. Can't even blink as I'm confronted with a photo of my best friend lying in the alley where she died. Where I killed her.

"You look like you've seen a ghost." Colton touches my shoulder, and I jump.

"Sorry." He lifts his hands up, palms forward.

"No." I touch his leg lightly. "I didn't mean to be jumpy. It's just that…" I consider how much to tell him. "This is my friend. My friend from when I was living on the streets. This is Lark."

His eyes open wide. "Your friend was killed by a vampire?"

I nod.

"I knew it." His eyes fill with tears and he takes my hand.

"Knew what?" My breath stalls in my chest.

"I knew you and I had something important in common. We both had loved ones murdered by vampires. It's so hard, isn't it?"

I look down. My throat is choked closed like I'm about to cry but I know tears will never come. I wish they would.

"I finally get why you're so interested in my work." Colton slowly closes the file and slides it away. "If it's any comfort, your friend wasn't tortured by the serial killer. The timing of her murder falls into the right time period, but she didn't have the mark, and her autopsy was thorough enough to be sure of that."

I want to look through more of these files. I want to ask more questions. I want to see if I recognize any of the serial killer's victims or notice something about the murder locations. Did she drain any others in the same alley where she attacked me?

And even more than that, I want to stay here with Colton. I want to drink tea and eat cookies and get back the warm tingly feelings I felt earlier. But I can't think straight right now and all those great feelings have been contaminated by pain and grief and the guilt I've fought to keep buried.

When I opened Lark's file, everything bad burst out of the cage where I store it and devoured my happy feelings of connection and safety.

But even if I could get back to how I felt before opening that file, it would be a mistake. It's dangerous that I'm so comfortable—verging on confessional—around Colton.

I've told him things no one else knows. A chilling thought races through me. Maybe this is all an interrogation technique to get me to confess what I am.

I set the mug down and bend forward, gripping my head in my hands as sobs build inside me, threatening to erupt. I want to cry, I want to let it all escape, but don't want to let Colton see that I don't shed tears.

I don't need to lay out any clues for this cop. At some point he's going to figure out the truth, and when he does, he'll try to kill me—and my survival instincts won't let him. I'm terrified at the knowledge that I might kill Colton before he can kill me.

I don't want anything bad to happen to Colton, and around me bad things are pretty much guaranteed.

Colton softly rests his hand on my back. "You okay? Can I—"

I leap up from the sofa and stagger toward the door. "What time is it? I've got to go. Thanks for the tea, but I lost track of the time."

He stands and follows, keeping a respectful distance. "I'll walk you home."

I shake my head.

"Then I'll call you a ride."

"It's not necessary." I hold the doorknob to his apartment, trying to keep it together, trying to hide all the things that I'm feeling.

"I'm sorry I upset you." He rakes his hand through his hair. "I knew I shouldn't have shown you those files."

"That's not it. It was seeing my friend..." I shake my head. "Her photo. The memories..."

"I get it." He reaches toward me. "As someone who's lost a loved one to those monsters, I totally understand."

I look down to the ridged black doormat, avoiding his face, certain he'd see the truth in my eyes.

"I'd like to look at the files again," I tell him, "but not tonight. I can't… I've got to go." I open the door.

He steps up behind me. "Selina. It's the middle of the night. I am not letting you go on your own."

"I can take care of myself." Plus, Astrid is nearby. I can almost guarantee it. But I certainly can't tell Colton that.

"Even if you can handle yourself." He pulls out his phone. "I'm calling for a ride. What's your friend's address?"

I take a deep breath. Revealing Gray's address to a cop is something I cannot do. I give him the address of the warehouse where we trained before Pike took me, the only other address I can think of right now.

"Is that place residential?" He frowns as he enters the information in his app.

"It's a loft."

"Okay…" He nods. "The driver's close. Just a block away. He'll be out front in two minutes."

"Great. Thanks." I wrap my arms around Colton and hug him tightly, loving the sound of his heart, the heat of his chest, the promise of power in the muscled strength of him.

I want to hold on to him forever, to live here in his arms and forget all the horrible secrets I can't tell him. But with every ounce of willpower inside me, I let go, open his door and run out into the night.

CHAPTER 21

Gray

The front door opens, and I vault from the foyer up to the second floor landing, hoping to hide the fact that I've been waiting at the door for Selina's arrival. I'm starting to need her like darkness.

But instead of Selina, Rock comes through the door and closes it behind him.

"Where is she?" I ask him.

"Are you telling me she's not home yet?" Looking up toward me, he slams both fists against his thick chest. "Feck!"

I jump back down to the main floor, landing directly in front of him. "Why isn't she with you?"

He shakes his head. "Astrid is with her."

"Where did they go?" I walk into the living room and drop to the overstuffed sofa. I can hear the front door from here, ready for when Selina walks through.

"She wanted to talk to that cop."

"What?" I get right in the giant's face. As close as I

can get to *in his face* with my feet on the floor. I'm six two, but Rock…I'd guess he's got more than a foot on me.

"Why the fuck did you let her go off with a cop?" I want to smash his face, rip out his throat, drain the life from his body.

"She was pretty determined." The giant man paces across my living room, making everything shake. "What would you want me to do? Hold her captive? Make a scene in public?" He stomps forward, then lifts his hands to his head. "I should have stopped her."

I steady a porcelain vase sitting on a pedestal next to the fireplace. "Fuck, Rock. This is a Ming vase."

He sits on the chintz sofa that I hate, and the legs strain from his weight. I hate the Ming vase too, but right now I hate Rock even more.

"Astrid promised she'd keep her safe," he says, his voice strained, "but Astrid's not answering her phone." He puts his head in his hands.

"That's not like Astrid." I'm pissed at Rock, sure, but now I'm genuinely scared. Selina could be in real danger. If the cop figured out what she is, she could already be dead. Maybe Astrid too?

Dread floods my body, starting in my stomach and quickly drowning my wits. My head feels like it's about to explode with fear and dark thoughts. I can barely hear or see anything around me.

I want to smash everything in the room and then impale myself on a stake.

The huge weight of failing in my sacred duty to find her feels minor compared to the thought of never seeing her again, never holding her, never telling her how I feel.

"Shit, Rock," I yell. "Why the hell did you let her go

off on her own like that? With a human? A cop no less? What the fuck were you thinking?"

Rock shakes his head where it's cradled in his hands. He's scared too. Hurting. I don't give a shit.

"I can't *believe* you let her out of your sight, you incompetent fuck! She should never, ever be left alone."

"*Excuse me*?"

I spin toward the entrance. "Selina!"

In a microsecond she's enveloped in my arms, my nose buried in the silky hair next to her throat, but through my intense relief, I realize that she's not hugging me back. Her body is rigid, almost like she finds my embrace repulsive.

Releasing my tight hold, I step back, hands on her shoulders so I can look into her eyes. "I was so scared," I tell her.

"We both were." Rock takes a house-shaking step forward. "I never should have let you go with him."

My anger toward Rock returns, and I point at him. "That is the last time I leave her alone with you."

She backs away from me and my arms fall to my sides.

"I can't believe you two." The anger in her eyes is so clear I feel it. "What I do, and where I go, and who I speak to…" Her voice is shaking. "It's not up to you—either of you."

Fists have formed at her sides and for perhaps the first time I see the powerful vampire she's become and hints of her still-untapped potential.

"I can make my own choices," she says forcefully. "I *need* to make my own choices."

Rock approaches. "Yes, but—"

"But nothing!" She holds up her hands, and he stops.

"We just want to protect you. If anything

happened…" My voice catches, and I look down to the patterned Persian rug at my feet.

"Look." Her voice is gentler now. "I get it. I'd be devastated if anything happened to either of you. But you can't be with me 24/7. If I don't have any freedom…" She takes one of my hands, then takes one of Rock's too.

With the three of us joined like this, Selina the glue between us, I feel happier than I ever thought possible. It's such huge ricochet from my earlier fear that I feel dizzy.

"I get that you want to keep me safe," she says, "but there's a limit. I didn't escape from Xavier and Pike to be prisoner to either of you."

"My prisoner…" I growl in her ear. "That sounds kind of fun. Or maybe you'd like to hold *me* prisoner one night." The thought of that turns me instantly hard. But I could never take Selina into my bedroom, not after what she went through. I don't even want her to *see* it, which is why it remains locked.

"Gray." Fighting a grin, Selina shakes her head. "I'm serious about this."

"I know, princess. I know."

"And I'm tired."

Rock drops her hand and slides his arm over her shoulders. "Let's go to bed."

I put my arm around her waist. "Maybe she wants to come with me." I'll take her to one of the empty guest rooms.

She steps forward, out of both of our holds, then turns to face us. "I meant it when I said I was tired. I'm sleeping on my own tonight."

CHAPTER 22

Selina

I'm in a strange place, confused, as hatred and hunger pulse in my veins. Earthy scents of decaying leaves and flowers meld with the damp night air, and I'm desperate for a landmark, something to give me a clue where I am, but for some reason I can't control where my vision lands. It moves from a paved path, to a stone wall, to grass, to gravestones.

A cemetery. I'm in a cemetery. Why?

My fingers flash before my eyes, as if beckoning for someone to follow, but although the gesture was in my vision, they weren't my fingers. They were someone else's.

A young woman passes under a Victorian-style lamppost, and her blond hair catches the amber-tinted light.

"A cemetery?" she asks. "At night? This seems sketchy,"

"It's a shortcut," I tell her.

I'm sure that I'm speaking, and while the voice is familiar, it's not my normal voice.

"Just through here," I say. "Totally worth it. It's the best underground club in the city. It's where all the movie and TV

stars go when they're in town filming. But if you're too scared…"

"No, I'm good." Putting on a brave face the young woman follows me and I lead her deeper into the cemetery.

We pass a mausoleum. Grabbing her shoulders, I slam her up against the damp granite wall, then sink my fangs into her throat.

She cries out, in pain then in pleasure, as her hot, sweet liquid flows from her body into mine.

I've never felt so powerful, so in control as I drain the life from this woman.

No! *I fight against myself, wanting to stop. I'm determined—desperate—to release my fangs from this woman, but I can't. I don't want to kill. Not ever again.*

I fight against myself, but at the same time I feel like it's not me I'm fighting. Is this some monstrous version of myself? Something I keep deep inside that got released when reminded of Lark?

Feeling more conscious, I suspect that I'm caught in a dream, but it's so much more vivid than a dream.

I'm not asleep, but I can't wake. And I can't stop drinking this girl's blood, even as the flow slows and becomes harder to draw.

Stop! *I tell myself.* Please stop. You'll kill her!

A warm hand lands on my shoulder and shakes me. But it's not the woman's hand; she's dead, and the hand is too big, too heavy.

"Selina. Wake up. Wake up." A familiar male voice slides into my dream.

There's a witness to my crime! Someone will know my deep shame. Who is it? The only person I can see is the limp girl in my arms, dying beneath my fangs.

"Princess," another male voice says, and a hand cups my face. "You're having a nightmare."

My eyes snap open. My own eyes.

My chest heaves as I try to catch my breath and get back to reality. I'm back in my own body. In a bed. In a guest room in Gray's house.

Gray slides into the bed on my left and strokes my face as my body trembles. "You're okay," he says gently. "It's over."

The bed dips on the other side, and Rock's in bed with me too.

"Acushla." He slides his arm under my neck and shoulders, and I turn to snuggle into Rock's chest, resting my fingers on soft hair covering hard muscles.

"You're safe." His deep voice seeps into me. "You're okay."

Gray's body presses against my back, and I'm sandwiched between the two men on the bed, their bodies surrounding mine. I've never felt so safe and it's such a sharp contrast to my nightmare.

Gray's hand rests on my body and gently caresses, stroking up and down over my hip and thigh and up to my ribs, his touch tender and innocent, like he's soothing a child.

My mouth is dry and my heart beats wildly from the nightmare. But I'm safe, and I can't imagine feeling more protected, more nurtured, more loved.

Still, I hate that I had a second nightmare involving a murder. The graphic details in the files at Colton's—Lark's lifeless body as stark photographic evidence of my crime—dredged my guilt up to the surface and conjured the dream.

I hope that's what it was. I shiver.

Rock pulls me closer and Gray's hand strokes down my side, over my back and hip.

"Shhh, princess," Gray says. "You're safe. Just sleep now."

But I'm not sure I can sleep. The dream was so vivid it felt like I was really there. Like I was killing that young woman, a woman just like the ones the serial killer targets.

"Do vampires ever have psychic connections?" I ask Gray. "Let's say, with their Maker?"

"Nah. That's just in books and movies. Most vampires can't affect anyone's mind beyond our venom taking a human's memory of a feeding."

"*Most* vampires."

His fingers caress my arm. "*All* vampires. Okay, almost all. Some of the Ancients possess unique powers, and there are rumors of others, but powers like that are extremely rare and developed over millennia."

"What about a vampire invading someone's dreams?"

"Princess." He pushes up onto one arm and strokes my hair. "You were dreaming. Just dreaming."

"Acushla," Rock adds. "You're safe here with us."

I nod. Seeing Lark's file, discovering a connection between my Maker and the serial killer, all the stress I've been under… All those factors piled on to mess with my mind and give me the vivid nightmares.

Gray is right: the nightmare meant nothing. And Rock is right too: I am safe.

Engulfed in their arms, sandwiched between the two men I care for so deeply, I drift back to sleep.

Selina

I WAKE, WARM AND COMFORTABLE, AND BURIED under what I assume is heavy bedding, but I soon realize it's the heat and weight coming from Rock and Gray's bodies around me.

"You're awake." Rock smiles at me, my cheek resting on his fuzzy warm chest.

From behind, Gray kisses my shoulder.

I stretch, and my ass brushes against an unmistakable pulsing hardness. I shift my ass and his hand slides onto my belly for leverage as he presses his erection against me.

"Oh, princess." He groans. "I could get used to waking up next to you. My cock could, anyway. I don't think I've ever woken up so hard." He growls the words low against my ear, but he must know Rock can hear him.

I look up into Rock's eyes, but he doesn't look jealous, or angry. Instead, he looks at me lovingly, heat filling his eyes too.

Rock's hand slides under the thin T-shirt I wore to bed and cups my breast. His thick calloused thumb brushes over my nipple, and instantly it's hard and so sensitive my sex squeezes as if Rock's hand is there instead of on my chest.

Breaking eye contact with me, Rock nods, clearly looking at Gray who's still grinding his erection against my ass.

"Acushla," Rock murmurs. "If you desire…" His hand drifts from my breast and slides between my legs.

I groan as his thick finger parts my wetness, and I shift one leg over Rock's body to give his hand better access. Gray shifts too, keeping his erection against me.

"If I desire what?" My voice is breathy and catches.

Rock's finger slides over my clit.

All the air pushes from my lungs at once. "Yes, I desire

—yes." Whatever Rock's asking me, I want it. "Oh, yes. Please."

Gray's cock slips between my ass cheeks, and strokes there as the two men work together to slip my T-shirt up and over my head.

Rock takes the back of my thigh and urges my body over until I'm straddling his huge body, my hands on his shoulders.

Is this it? Is Rock finally going to fuck me?

Gray's hands slide over my back, and he straddles Rock too, pressing in close behind me.

Hooking his arm behind my neck, Rock pulls me down for a kiss—a deep and passionate kiss that instantly transforms me to a liquid state—my body molten and flowing, needy and wet.

As he kisses me, Rock's fingers continue to stroke between my folds, teasing my entrance, and then Gray's cock arrives near my entrance, and Rock's finger switches all of its focus to my clit.

Kneeling behind me, Gray shifts up my hips, then moans as he pushes forward. He's not in very deep, but it's glorious and I rock back against his shallow thrusts as Rock's tongue slides against mine and one of his fingers stays on my clit, while his other hand moves to my nipple and gently caresses.

Gray deepens his penetration, and I gasp against Rock's mouth.

Our kiss breaks, and I push up so I can see his face. I need to know he's okay.

And looking into his eyes I see that Rock is more than okay. The desire and love I see in his gaze is powerful and passionate, and it heightens my pleasure, my fiery need.

Pushing back against Gray's deepening thrusts, I take

him in fully. His pace accelerates, and Gray moves his hands to my shoulders, pulling me back against him to better meet each drive.

Something hard pulses against my belly.

"Gray, back up a bit," I say as he thrusts.

Holding himself deep inside me, Gray tugs back on my hips and moves us both back so that I'm lower over Rock's body.

I can no longer kiss Rock from here, but I find his huge cock with my hand and stroke it gently through the fabric of his shorts. I look up into his eyes.

Fear invades Rock's expression, and he shakes his head as I fumble to push aside the fabric.

"Clever idea, princess," Gray growls from behind me. "Very clever."

"No, Acushla," Rock moans. "I can't…"

"Relax," Gray says from behind me. "I'll take care of the fucking, big guy. You just lay back for the ride."

Imbedded deep inside me, Gray pulls up my ass, and realizing what Gray has in mind, I shift Rock's cock under his shorts to better position it under me as I lie between the two men.

Rock closes his eyes, then moans as I move my hands back to his chest and press my lower belly against his erection.

Gray thrusts, and the stroke creates friction not only where he's impaling me, but also between my lower body and Rock's massive cock.

Gray drives again, then again and again, and I'm no longer able to control the movement, no longer want to. It's perfect.

Gray keeps his strokes constant and controlled, the slowest he's taken me since the first time, and I tip my pelvis so that every one of Gray's thrusts slides my clit along Rock's hardness.

This is perfect for me, but Rock's eyes close and I can tell he's fighting his body's reactions, holding himself back.

I kiss his chest, lick his nipples as my body strokes his cock propelled by Gray's long, hard strokes.

Rock's face grows redder and veins rise over his temples, but his jaw remains tight, like he's in a fight with his body. I understand the pain and humiliation of having physical reactions against my will, and I hope more than anything that Rock doesn't feel violated like I did.

"Rock," I say softly. "Look at me. Please."

He opens his eyes and the connection between us deepens until I feel like I'm inside of Rock's eyes and he's inside of mine.

Rock's arousal and our connection seems to melt the restraint from his expression, and Gray continues to drive from behind, sliding me along Rock's huge member. It's not difficult to imagine that Rock is the one inside me, although I'm loving that the three of us are doing this together.

It didn't seem possible, but Rock's erection grows even bigger beneath me and the sensation of sliding along his thick hard ridge, with Gray penetrating me from behind, brings me to heights I'd never imagined.

But I do start to imagine other things, like having both of them inside me at once, and then it grows difficult to think about *anything* but my pleasure as Gray's pace takes off.

He thrusts fast and hard, and Rock moans. It's possible Gray moans too, but it's hard to hear anything above the rumbling sounds of pleasure from my giant's chest.

Gray slows, then shifts, changing his angle until he's

lying on top of me, on top of us both, and I'm pressed flat between my two lovers.

I grip Rock's sides, pressing my cheek against his chest, and I realize that Gray's hands are now braced on Rock's shoulders, and he's using the giant's body as leverage to continue to drive inside mine. We're so tight together the friction between my body and Rock's ignites.

The intensity and speed of Gray's thrusts increases again, and Rock's body vibrates beneath me, his breaths coming quickly, and I have to struggle to hold myself in place as Gray's vigorous thrusts push me along Rock's monstrous hardness.

Rock roars.

I feel it as much as I hear it, and I struggle to catch sight of his face, but Gray's body keeps my head pinned down, my ear against Rock's beating hearts.

Hot liquid shoots between us, coating my belly and chest and increasing the lubrication between our bodies. Rock moans, but it's so tortured I'm not sure if it's in pleasure or pain.

After Rock's climax, Gray pulls up my hips, rises onto one knee and drives so hard and fast I can no longer think, no longer breathe. The side of my head is still against Rock's chest and my only possible focus is on the sensation of Gray's pounding cock, on the heat and pleasure rising almost to the point of glorious pain.

Rock's finger slides between us to find my clit, and I only know it's Rock's finger because of Gray's tight grip on my hips, pulling me back against him with each punishing thrust.

An orgasm slams through me with unimaginable strength and fury.

Gray shouts. His thrusts grow erratic and forceful as he comes too with more vigor and violence than ever before. Then, even after he comes, Gray continues to move inside me as Rock strokes my super-sensitive clit, and I ride the final waves of an orgasm that feels like it might last forever.

As the last of my inner contractions subside, Gray collapses to the bed, his leg draped over my body as I melt onto Rock.

Trying to catch my breath, I stroke Rock's chest as both of them caress my body, and the long, languorous strokes of their fingers and palms trigger aftershocks inside me, reawakening my orgasm with small pulsing contractions deep inside me.

"Holy fuck, princess," Gray says. "That was what I call intense."

I reach up to touch Rock's neck, then his face, and find his cheeks are wet.

"You okay, big guy?" Gray asks, and Rock turns his head to the side, facing away from us both.

I gather enough energy to lift my head and coax Rock's tear-filled eyes toward mine.

"I'm sorry," he says softly.

"Sorry?" I kiss him gently. "Why? That was amazing. Seeing you come, seeing the pleasure in your eyes…" I suck in a sharp breath. "Or… did that feel *bad* for you?"

Closing his eyes, he shakes his head. "It felt so fecking good."

I stroke the side of his face. "If that felt good—for all three of us—then I don't see why anyone should be saying sorry."

Opening his eyes, he nods.

"Thank you," he says, then turns toward Gray. "And

thank you, too. Thank you for letting me be part of what you have with Selina."

"Buddy," Gray says. "I think it's me who should thank you. Our princess came so hard on my dick I almost passed out." His hand slips over my ass.

"You're both wrong." I arch up to kiss Gray, then turn back to kiss Rock's chest. "I'm the one who should be thanking you both."

Rock shifts me farther up his body, then holds my head in his hands and kisses me—tenderly, passionately—while Gray caresses my body, licking along my spine, pressing hot damp kisses over my back and ass and legs, exploring my highly sensitive skin with his fingers and lips and tongue.

What have I done to deserve so much pleasure? So much happiness? I don't deserve this.

The sex between the three of us was the hottest thing ever, but it was so much more than just hotness and pleasure. Enveloped in their protection and love, I can almost believe that I've finally found a place where I belong—and that it could last forever.

CHAPTER 23

Selina

Stiff and bruised from a training session with Gray, I wince as the two of us slide into our usual booth in Rock's bar. I'm beat up, but I know I'll be back to normal soon.

Gray, on the other hand, doesn't seem to be suffering *any* aftereffects from our vigorous fight training.

"Aren't you sore at all?" I ask.

"Sore?" He tips his head to the side as if he doesn't know the meaning of the word. "From the threesome this morning? That was hours ago."

"Ha." At the memory, a blush rises on my chest and heat blooms between my legs. "You really don't feel any pain?" I ask him, shifting the topic back. "I know I'm still the beginner, but I took you down a few times."

"Sex, sex, sex." He winks at me. "Is that all you ever talk about? I'm starting to feel like a sex object."

"Very funny." I kick him lightly under the table. "Seriously. You know I'm talking about the combat training.

You're not bruised at all?" I rub my ribs that are knitting together from the last time Gray got the better of me, slamming me into Rock's basement floor and breaking them.

"The more powerful you get—" Gray signals for Chelle to bring us a round of drinks "—the quicker you'll recover."

"So how do I get more powerful?" There are still so many things about being a vampire I need to learn. While the combat training we've been doing—both here and at Gray's—is excellent and makes me more confident to be out in the city on my own, self-defense isn't the only thing I need to learn about being a vampire, and I feel like Gray's neglected teaching me much beyond the physical stuff.

How he holds back information is kind of like how he is about sex and our relationship—ignoring the meaning behind the actions.

Chelle sets a bottle of wine and a glass on the table for Gray and slides a double whiskey across the table toward me.

"Thanks," I say, smiling up at her.

She nods, but her gesture is stiff and I wish I could melt the tension between us. It's only gotten worse since Chelle saw me talking to Colton. It seems like some kind of cruel joke that not one, but two men Chelle likes are more interested in me than in her. At least she doesn't seem to be after Gray, but I suppose she knows he's a vampire and probably isn't into that.

Gray fills his wine glass then holds it toward me. "Cheers, princess."

"What are we drinking to?"

He leans across the table. "To us, of course. The three

of us." He tips his head toward Rock, who's behind the bar.

Gray's words warm me inside. "I'll drink to that." I take a sip of the whiskey and let its heat flow into my bloodstream. The pain and stiffness from today's training has already vanished. My ribs are completely healed.

I look over to the bar, hoping Rock can join us, but he's busy preparing an order. "At the risk of bringing up sex again, I hope Rock was okay about this morning."

Gray snorts. "I'd say he was more than just *okay,* princess. I've never seen so much come."

"I don't mean *physically.*"

"Yeah, I know." Gray nods as he takes another sip of wine. "Big chap's clearly got some hang-ups."

I look back toward Rock. We need to talk privately. As much as I love the three of us living together—possibly *sleeping* together from now on?—I haven't had a chance to discuss the threesome with Rock.

After we got out of bed, we all showered together, even though Rock refused to take off his shorts. In the shower, we reenacted the bedroom scene and it worked just as well standing up. Maybe better.

Rock leaned against the tiled wall, his legs spread wide, and bent to lower himself as Gray took me from behind, pressing me firmly against the giant's hard rod. Gray's pounding cock lifted my body right off the floor and slid me against Rock's erection, taking him hard and fast to completion.

It was intense, and my only regret was that Rock held my head close to his chest so I couldn't look up and into his eyes when he came. After Rock's ejaculation, he wanted to wash off the come, and Gray pulled me away from Rock's body.

I wanted to join Rock under the stream of water, but Gray bent me over, and I had to brace my arms on the glass wall of the shower while he pumped hard and fast to his climax, bringing me to another.

By the time Gray and I were done, and my ability to focus returned, Rock was toweling off, and then Gray was all about my training schedule, and Rock had some daylight business at the bar to take care of so I didn't see him again until we arrived here.

Since our usual booth was taken when we arrived, Gray suggested we go down to Rock's gym for more training and then…

"Hey!" I tap the table between us. "You never answered my question."

"The answer is yes, princess," Gray says with a grin. "I would *love* to fuck your ass while Rock finger bangs you."

"Gray!" My cheeks heat at his words, burning my ability to form the words to scold him for evading my question. At this rate I'll never learn more about being a vampire—even if my sexual satisfaction will be off the charts.

Gray leans across the table. "Oh, I see. You'd prefer Rock's fingers up your ass, with *me* driving into your pussy." His eyes widen. "Or maybe you want to ride Rock's monster cock?"

My insides pulse and dampen, and I take a sip of whiskey to clear my throat. "Stop it, Gray. You know I was asking about how vampires gain power."

"Okay, okay." He cups the bulb of his wine glass. "I can tell you about the *normal* ways vampires gain power, but princess, *you* are not normal."

"Enough teasing." I frown, even though frowning at Gray takes effort. "Answer my question."

"I'm not teasing." He sits back. "You are highly unusual. Very different."

"Different how?" I can't decide whether to be flattered or insulted, but Gray's clearly uncomfortable with the topic. It's written all over his face.

"Okay." He shifts on the bench. "Let's start with your spontaneous transition, shall we?"

"Does that affect how I gain power?"

"Frankly, my dear, I have no idea." He twirls the stem of his wine glass. "But even setting your unexplained transition aside, you've only fed from me once. And you claim that was your one and only time taking a vampire's vein."

"It *was* the only time."

"Well, that just proves my point." His hands lift off the table. "And it makes your current power all the more remarkable." He holds up his index finger. "First, you transition without feeding… Most baby vampires need *multiple* feedings from their Maker to even have a chance of living through their transition. Multiple feedings over several days, if not weeks. Sometimes weaning takes months."

I chew on the inside of my lip. Is it possible I *forgot* that I fed from my Maker? But everything about that night is so crystal clear I can't imagine forgetting such a supposedly important part of the process.

"Okay, so let's set that mystery aside," I say. "After transitioning, how do vampires normally gain power?"

He shrugs. "With age. Time. Feeding from other vampires."

"I felt that when I fed from you."

He takes my hand and strokes my palm with his thumb. "And that? How you felt that first night?" He whistles softly. "That was *nothing* compared to what you'll feel when you feed while you fuck."

Slickness builds between my legs. "Then..." Instantly highly aroused and hungry, I can barely speak. "Let's go back downstairs so we can feed and...and have sex."

He shakes his head, pulls his hand out from under mine and picks up his wine glass. His lips twitch. "Tempting, princess, but it won't demonstrate what I mean. The power transfer I'm talking about won't be there for us." His gaze is focused on my forehead, not my eyes.

"Why not?'

"Because you're not my mate." His words hit like a slap.

"You have a *mate*?" My voice is thin, almost a squeak.

"No, no, no." His hands rise. "That's not what I meant." Sadness flashes across his face, quickly replaced with his usual expression. "No, I do not have a mate."

"What if..." *What if we were mates?* I think but can't voice. My mouth is dry and refuses to form those words.

It's confusing. I love Rock, I have no doubt of that, but I've fallen for Gray too, and my feelings for both continue to grow.

And the prospect of experiencing the power exchange that Gray describes, the thought of being his mate, feeding while we make love, has woken a need inside me so powerful I can barely breathe. I want Gray so badly. Need him in every sense of the word.

Gaining courage, I take his hand again. "What if you *were* my mate? Maybe we're meant to be together." I swallow to soothe my dry throat.

Gray pulls back from my hand like I burned him. "Alas, princess, that's not in the cards. Never will be."

"Why not?" I croak.

He smirks at me, a cruel smile that stabs into my heart. "Princess, I am not what you'd call the take-a-mate type. You knew that from the start."

My body slams back in the booth. "How can you say it like that, so casually, especially after…after all we…" My hurt turns into anger. "And how do you know that we aren't meant to be mates? It's not like a priest has mingled our blood to test it!"

His eyes widen. "Who told you about the mating ceremony?"

"No one needed to tell me." I shake my head at him in disbelief. "I suffered through *thirteen* failed wedding ceremonies with Xavier, remember? Thirteen!"

"Xavier has a high priest in his court?" His brow furrows. " A legitimate one?"

I slap the table in frustration. "How would I know the difference? You refuse to explain anything! He seemed legit to me. And since the ceremonies kept failing, the priest must have been doing *something* right. If that ceremony's a test for true love, or compatibility, then I'd say the priest was pretty fucking legit! Thirteen times he mixed my blood with Xavier's and nothing happened."

Claiming that nothing happened as a result of those failed wedding ceremonies is far from accurate, though. Each one led to rape and torture that got worse and worse over time.

Rage rises inside me, wiping out my hurt at Gray's rejection. And I'm grateful to the rage for that. Grateful and somewhat surprised that my go-to emotion when I think of Xavier is rage now, not fear.

Xavier no longer scares me, not as much, anyway, and I will not rest until he's punished for what he did to me. I will not rest until Xavier's dead.

"What is it?" Gray tips his head to the side.

"What is what?" I snap.

"Something changed in you just then." He whistles low through his teeth. "I swear I just saw your power grow before my eyes. I can see it in your posture, in your skin, your eyes."

"Really?" But he's right. I do feel more powerful. I close my eyes for a moment, getting used to the feeling. "Can vampires get power from rage?"

"Not *most* vampires." He leans toward me. "Are you that pissed at me, princess?"

"Maybe I am!" Looking down at the table, I shake my head. "No, my rage is all saved for Xavier."

"Well, that's good to hear."

I raise my gaze and find him grinning, his expression back to normal—a lethal combination of teasing and lust.

Gray keeps saying I'm different, and I know he means it in a positive way, but to me my so-called differences are more things that set me apart and make me alone in the world.

My whole life I've either been homeless or living under the constant threat of danger, and as much as I love and appreciate Rock's and Gray's affection and protection, I still don't have a place in the world where I truly belong.

The belonging I felt this morning was a sex-fueled illusion. Not real. I should have known better.

And it goes beyond not having somewhere I belong. No one can even explain why—or how—I even exist!

"Don't be upset," Gray says, clearly sensing my mood. "Some day you'll understand why you're special."

"What aren't you telling me?" I lean forward. "Gray. If you know something more about me, you've got to tell me!"

The entrance door opens, and Colton walks through. Spotting me instantly, he waves and walks straight toward our booth.

Gray lets go of my hand and leans back.

"Hi, Colton." I smile as the human reaches the table.

"Selina, I have news about—" He glances at Gray, then back to me, and the excitement in his green eyes dances between us.

Colton reminds me of an eager puppy, unable, not even wanting to contain his emotions. It's like the idea of containing emotions has never occurred to him.

"Sounds like you two have things to talk about." Gray slides toward the edge of the booth. "Guess that's my exit cue."

"Wait." I reach over the table. "Colton, this is Gray. Gray this is Colton."

As they nod toward each other, both men's expressions change in a flash—not filling with animosity, exactly, but definitely with caution tinged in coldness.

"You don't need to go," I tell Gray, but as I say it, I realize I don't mean it. If Colton has news about the serial killer case, I want to hear it, and he might not tell me in front of Grayson.

Gray unfolds his elegant form from the bench, and Colton steps out of the way as the vampire leans over to plant a soft kiss on my lips.

"If you'll excuse me, princess, I have some business to take care of. Are you comfortable if I leave you alone here with Carlton?"

"Colton," he corrects.

I swallow the laughter bubbling up inside me as I gaze into Gray's mischievous eyes. He knows the right name.

"I'll be fine," I tell him. "Go."

"She's *very* safe with me," Colton interjects. "I'm a police constable."

"Goodness," Gray says with obvious fake respect. "That *is* impressive." He slides his arm across my shoulders and bends toward me again. "Seriously, princess. You okay alone with Coleman?"

I nod, not acknowledging that he got the name wrong again. He's doing it for attention.

Gray kisses me again, this time more deeply than he should with someone else standing by.

"See you at home," he says. Then without even acknowledging Colton, he strides away, out of the bar and into the night.

Colton takes a black backpack off one shoulder, slides into the spot vacated by Gray. "Is he always such an arrogant son-of-a..." He shakes his head. "Sorry...I hate to use foul language, but that man... Is he your boyfriend? Your roommate?" He glances back toward the bar where Rock's serving customers.

"Gray is my housemate and my friend." I'm not sure what Gray is. How can I possibly explain when I don't understand myself? "But enough about him. You said you have news?"

"Yes... Which do you want first? Good news or bad news?"

"Bad news, I guess."

He reaches across the table and takes my hands, his eyes filling with concern.

"What is it?" My insides twist, even though I can't imagine what news Colton might have that could be that bad.

"It's about your mother."

I suck in a sharp breath. "Oh." A rush of joy flashes,

quickly extinguished when I remember the *bad news* lead-in.

"I hate to be the one to tell you this, but she's…dead."

"Did he kill her?" I squeeze Colton's hand so hard he winces, and I let up. "Is he in jail?"

He looks down, then back up. "He took his own life too." His lips twist to the side for a second. "I'm not sure if I should tell you the details."

"Tell me." I swallow hard. "I need to know. Please."

He nods slowly. "I'm so glad you ran away from that man." He shakes his head and his expression grows colder. "He was clearly psychotic. The murder was brutal. I can't…I *won't* tell you the details but suffice to say it was horrific. He got the easy way out—self-inflicted gunshot through the temple. But he didn't use the gun on your mother."

I close my eyes as my mind and body absorb the information.

"Are you okay?" Colton asks. "I shouldn't have told you."

I look into his eyes, and squeeze his hands. "No, I'm glad that you told me." And in some strange way I'm glad my mom isn't suffering the abuse anymore, even if she suffered horribly when she died.

I mourned my mother years ago—mourned a mother and child relationship that barely ever existed in the first place.

I try not to imagine what the stepmonster did to her, or to wonder if I'd have been able to save her, convince her to leave…

I take a long cleansing breath. "You said there was good news too?"

"Yes." He strokes my hands with his thick thumbs.

"But it seems trivial after what I just told you." He shakes his head. "I should have waited until a time when I could spend more time with you… I have to work…"

"That's okay." I smile weakly. "Rock's here if I need to talk."

Colton swallows hard. "I'm glad you've got support."

"Me too. So, what's the other news? I could use the distraction."

Colton glances around to make sure no one is eavesdropping, then leans across the table. "There was another bloodsucker slaying last night."

"Really?" I gulp down the last of the whiskey in my glass.

He nods. "I was at the crime scene all day. Every cop in the city is out staking bloodsuckers tonight, so I can't stay long. "

Discomfort stirs inside me. And fear. Gray just walked out into a city filled with stake-wielding cops.

"How do the police identify someone as a vampire?" I ask, realizing that no one has ever even mentioned this to me. I can tell—vampires' beauty and power waft off their bodies, but humans don't seem to notice.

Colton leans back. "To be honest—and I don't want to scare you—but sometimes it's hard to tell. The bastards are masters of disguise." He gestures around the room. "For all we know, one could be in here right now."

I lift my glass, hoping to hide my reaction in whiskey, but my glass is empty.

"Don't be frightened." Colton takes my hand. "I shouldn't have said that. If one of the monsters was in here, I'd know."

"That's a relief." I do my best to smile. "But how *would* you know?"

"Scientists are working on solutions, but for now our biggest gets are when we find a nest."

"A nest?"

He nods. "A group of the monsters sleeping the day away, out of the sunlight. I tell you, there's nothing like opening a dark curtain or smashing a blacked-out window to guarantee a positive ID. The screams and burning flesh give it away."

I shudder, then my body relaxes as I realize humans have zero idea how to spot vampires, which explains how our kind remained a myth for so long. "What about tonight?" I ask. "How will you know when you find one?"

"We follow suspects for several nights. Watch for a pattern of behavior. Are they extraordinarily strong? Do they avoid the sunlight? Avoid garlic, silver and crosses—known vampire repellants. Do they lurk in alleys waiting for prey?" He shrugs. "To be honest, we often rely on tips. Like the one we got about this bar."

All the things he listed are true about vampires except the garlic and crosses—as far as I know, anyway. I've never had issues with either. And I still have no idea who called in that tip. Was it Chelle? A customer?

"You okay?" Colton asks. "I know you're curious, but maybe I said too much?"

I shake my head. "I'm just thinking it through. Vampires sound really hard to spot. How often do you kill humans by mistake?"

Colton again glances around to see if anyone's listening. "Can I tell you a secret?"

"Of course."

He pats the black backpack beside him. "I told you about scientific advances?"

I nod.

"Well, the VTF just got a prototype for advanced vampire detection."

"What kind of prototype?" My heart beats faster. Has be been playing me all along?

Colton seems like the most transparent person I've ever encountered, fully incapable of subterfuge, but if he's got a vampire-detecting machine sitting right beside him, then either it doesn't work or he already knows the truth.

"Do you want me to show you?" Excitement beams from him. "I can take it out and demonstrate. Prove that there are no vampires in here."

"That's not necessary." I shake my head, then lower my voice. "But how does it work?"

"They're special goggles. They make vampires glow."

"Glow?"

"It's kind of an eerie blue color." He frowns. "Actually, based on the training video I saw, it's kind of beautiful—that is, if you ignore the evil exposed."

My stomach tightens. "Why don't all police have these goggles?" Or every human, for that matter. Not that I mean this as a suggestion.

"This baby here?" Colton pats his backpack. "The prototypes are rare and worth a small fortune. There are only two in the entire country right now. The Vancouver police have one set and we have the other." His chest broadens. "And I get to use them tonight."

"How come I've never heard of this?"

He leans across the table again. "That's why you can't tell anyone. Why I shouldn't even have told you. We don't want the vamps to know."

"Why?"

"The inventor, a scientist in Europe—Switzerland, I think—anyway, she thinks that if vampires ever got their hands on a set of goggles, they could figure out a way to beat them."

"If they figure out what creates the glow."

"Exactly." His grin widens.

His phone chirps and he looks down at his smartwatch. "I've gotta go. Can I see you tomorrow? Maybe lunch?"

"I'm busy during the day."

"Not even time to eat lunch? It'll be breakfast for me. I'm working most of the night."

I shake my head. "But I'll be here tomorrow night."

"With your boyfriends?" His cheeks flush and he looks like he wishes he could kill them both. He actually *does* have a license to kill Gray, and certainly would if he ever pointed those goggles in Gray's direction. Or mine.

"Rock and Gray, they're both..." My mouth is dry again. "Our relationship is complicated, but they're both...they're both very important to me."

"And yet you spend time with me? Hold my hand..." Colton leans over and entwines our fingers together. "They're okay with that?"

"No one gets to dictate who I spend time with," I tell him, "and I like spending time with you." I like it a lot, in fact.

In spite of our scary discussion, I feel comfortable around Colton. It doesn't make sense for me to trust him, but his prejudice is based on misinformation and underneath his bias he's good and kind and warm, and so devastatingly handsome my stomach flutters every time he's near.

"I like spending time with you, too," he says, his voice deep and sincere. "I like you, Selina. I like you a lot." A massive grin spreads across his face. "See you tomorrow night? Maybe we can look at the files again? At my place?" He's back into puppy mode and the expectation in his eyes is adorable.

I nod. "Can we meet here?"

"Sure. I can't wait." His boyish charm is so attractive, bringing out the teenaged girl in me that I never got to be. Every part of me smiles and blushes and tingles and flutters at once.

He stands. "Off to the cemetery."

"What?" My heart starts to thump a little harder. "Why a cemetery?" It's just a strange coincidence. It has to be.

"Don't worry." He grins. "I haven't switched to ghost busting or zombie hunting." He chuckles at his joke. "Last night's bloodsucker victim was attacked in a cemetery. Out in the east end."

He bends and presses a chaste kiss against my cheek. Then he whispers, "I can't wait to see you again."

I try to smile, but I can't breathe.

The latest victim was killed in a cemetery—just like in my dream.

CHAPTER 24

Pike

The one called Grayson leaves the bar, alone, no sign of Selina, and I walk to the edge of the condo-building roof where I've been keeping watch.

Why did he leave her alone in the bar? Frustration and fear rise inside me as I follow the filthy rich vampire's path through the streets, but he tucks into an alley, and I lose my line of vision.

I jump across to another rooftop, then another, but I've lost him. Not that I was trying very hard. My priority is Selina. I return to my normal perch with its great view of the big man's bar.

The night is full of sounds: honking car horns, shouting men, screeching commuter trains, and beneath it the low rumble of the subway beneath the earth. And above all that there are voices. So many voices.

It's been torture since I stopped tuning in to Selina's voice each time I found her at dusk, so I caved and did it tonight. But it's a different kind of torture. Eavesdropping on her every conversation raises such a deep longing inside me I might implode from the pressure.

Fingering the razor in my pocket, I'm tempted to quash the desire rising inside me now.

"Nice view from up here," a male says.

Ready to attack, I spin toward the speaker.

Grayson is leaning against a metal air conditioning unit.

Turning away from him, I cross my arms over my chest, pretending that I couldn't give a shit that he managed not only to find me, but get up onto the roof without my noticing. I am slipping. Losing it.

But my focus must remain on Selina. When she leaves that bar tonight, I will protect her.

Gray steps up beside me. "You're following her."

"I need to be sure that she's safe."

"I keep her safe."

"Safe?" I glare at the vampire in his fancy clothes. "You left her alone in that bar with a cop!"

His eyes narrow. "How do you know she's with a cop?"

"The football player guy she went off with the other night. He's a cop." Gray is an idiot if he doesn't realize this. "He's in the bar. "

I shake my head with disgust. Grayson claims he wants to keep Selina safe, yet he lets her wander around the city alone. He let her go into the home of a cop—a human sworn to kill vampires.

"Tell me I'm wrong." I step toward him. "Tell me that cop didn't approach her the second he went inside."

Gray shrugs. "Bloke's harmless."

"*Harmless*? He carries fucking stakes! A crossbow!"

"Selina can handle herself with a human. She's gotten stronger since you *kidnapped* her. Since you *tortured* her."

It's all I can do to keep my fist out of this asshole's teeth.

"And that cop won't hurt her," the asshole continues. "He's a smitten kitten."

"Smitten what?" How can he be so flip about Selina's safety? I want to throw him off the roof. To make it worse, his expression is a near smirk.

"The cop's in love with her," Gray says. "Head over fucking heels."

My chest tightens. I'd already guessed as much from the human's body language—and hers—but hearing it in words… I dig the razor under my nail to transfer the pain.

"That cop is *infatuated* with Selina—" Gray winks "—just like you are."

"What?" I turn away from him as rage rises inside me. He's right, but I'm not going to admit it. Still, I can't bring myself to deny it, either.

"Can I ask you something?" he asks.

I shake my head, without turning back.

"How did you end up with that asshole Xavier? You don't seem that stupid."

"Fuck you."

"Sorry, mate. But I do want to know. It's important."

"What's it to you?" I drop down to sit on the roof, my legs dangling over the edge.

Gray sits down beside me, making it even easier for me to push him off, and my arms twitch with the desire, but it's not worth the effort.

Unless… If he broke enough bones in the fall, maybe a stake-wielding cop could finish him off before he healed.

"If Xavier's after Selina, we need to know everything

we can," Gray says. "In fact, we're hoping you might help with that."

"Who is *we*?"

"Me, friends of mine. Friends of Selina's. We're looking for Xavier's so-called palace."

I spin toward him. "Do *not* let Selina go anywhere near Xavier." Rage and shame tremble inside me along with memories of that dungeon.

I didn't participate in the horrific things that happened to Selina, but I didn't do nearly enough to stop them, either.

From the first day she arrived at court, my urge to protect her was stronger than it had been for Xavier's previous playthings, but soon my protective urge turned into a driving need.

And then once I had a taste of her blood… I close my eyes as the memory storms through me. Since that small taste, I can't think about anything except making her mine, keeping her safe—and killing Xavier.

"What do you want to know?" I ask. They'd better not do anything to put her at risk.

"How did you end up with Xavier?"

"You were right. I am stupid. Or was back then."

"When was that?" Gray asks.

"Not long after I transitioned. I was a mess." I rub the scar on my cheek. "Mess before I transitioned, too." I shake my head, thinking back to the trash heap of a man I became in Vietnam. And the literal trashcan I landed in once I came back.

"When did you transition?" he asks.

"Early seventies."

"*Nineteen* seventies?"

I nod.

"Hey!" Gray claps me on the back. "We're almost twins! I was late sixties."

I glare at him and he raises his palms toward me.

"How did you get those scars?" he asks.

"Vietnam."

"That must have been tough. Wow. Sorry, man."

Yeah, I bet you're sorry. Rich assholes like him let the rest of us get maimed and killed, then treated us like garbage or worse once we got home.

"How'd you get out of the draft?" I ask him.

"I'm British," Gray replies. "Or at least I was. Don't know what I am now."

Explains his fucking pretentious accent.

"I was in Morocco when I got turned," Gray adds.

"Am I supposed to give a shit about that?"

"Just making conversation." He leans back onto his elbows and looks up into the night sky. "Was Xavier your Maker?" He glances at me sideways, almost like he suspects I'm *still* with Xavier.

"Transitioned in Vietnam."

"You're kidding." He straightens, obvious curiosity in his posture, in his voice. "Our side or theirs?"

"Nothing like that. It was in the hospital. I thought she was a nurse."

"Gives a whole new meaning to donating blood, I guess."

I swallow a laugh, reminding myself that I hate this vampire. "Her name was Binh. She was beautiful. Kind."

"Kind...but she turned recovering patients into vampires? Against their will?"

"It wasn't like that." I draw a long breath at the memory. "She talked to me about it, first. My burns were terrible. Over ninety percent of my body. I was in constant pain." I close my eyes. Some burns had healed, that's why I still have scars, but if she hadn't turned me I wouldn't have survived. Maybe that would have been better.

Binh explained how it would work. How I'd never fully heal from all my burn scars, but how my pain would go away. How I'd live forever—unless I was staked or burned again.

"Where is she now?" he asks. "Binh?"

"I have no idea."

"Sorry, man. How were you separated?"

"I got shipped home."

"How did *that* work, exactly?"

"I was reported dead and shipped home in a box. Binh set it up. She was supposed to come with me, but she got caught trying to break into my coffin." My heart nearly collapses at the loss. I loved Binh. Not like a lover, but like a friend, almost like a mother.

"How did you get them to think you were dead, versus…"

"Versus a vampire?"

He nods.

"Binh gave me herbs that slowed my heart rate, cooled my skin. She organized the whole thing. Made sure I'd never hit sunlight."

"And once you were back in the US? I assume you were buried in a military cemetery?"

I shake my head. "Nope. Got out of the coffin before that. But then I was alone, lost, confused. I'd never even fed without Binh's help. Had no idea how to survive as a vampire."

"That must have been tough." The vampire's eyes show compassion, but not pity, which I appreciate. For an uptight super-rich asshole he's not so bad.

"It would be even worse these days, like it was for Selina." My voice breaks and I cough to cover it up. "Humans didn't know we existed back then."

"Those were the days, my friend."

"Not for me." Every memory of the early days when I arrived back in the US is a nightmare.

"How did you end up here? In Toronto? With Xavier?"

"It was fall, so I headed north. Figured the fewer hours of sunlight the better." I shake my head at my stupidity. "'Course shorter winter days just means more hours of sunlight in the spring and summer."

"The Earth does have that pesky tilted axis thing."

"Whatever. Anyway, one night I got into a brawl. To tell the truth, I got into a brawl *most* nights. I fought humans, other vampires. Anyone who looked at me."

Fake frowning, Gray lifts his fists like an old-fashioned boxer. "Should I raise my dukes?"

"Jury's still out on that."

He laughs.

I don't. "Santos, Xavier's scout, saw me fight one night. He's the same asshole who found Selina."

"And?"

"And nothing. That's pretty much the story. Santos took me to Xavier's court." I draw a long breath. "Xavier was an asshole—that was obvious from day one. But down there I had shelter from the sun and it was easy to feed."

"How *did* you all feed down there?"

"Mostly runaway teens."

"Down there willingly?"

"Are you fucking kidding me?"

"I don't know. You tell me."

"None were there willingly. Not at first. The ones who

did figure out where they were—some of them thought it was a big adventure, goth fantasy fulfillment or something. I dunno. The blood slaves down there are treated okay, I guess." Most of them. "But the prettiest ones…" My throat closes at the memories of things I saw, things I didn't stop. Girls and boys used as sex toys. Bled beyond what they had to give.

"Some don't live long," I tell Gray. "A few get turned. Some die in that process. Most of them are just used for food until they're too pale and anemic to be fun, then they're put out like garbage."

"Released?" he asks, a hopeful look flashing over the horror that landed there during my story.

I shake my head. "Can't take enough of their memories away. Even if we could, there'd be too many questions."

"So…"

"Killed. Fucking murdered."

"By you?" He pulls back a little, just enough so I notice.

"Nah. Garbage man was below my pay grade."

"You got paid?"

I roll my eyes. "Yeah, right."

He half grins. "So, other than Santos, who in the so-called court gets to go above ground and into the city?"

"Officially, only Santos and Philippe. They're the scouts. I followed them, though. Figured out most of the routes."

"Why doesn't everyone do that?"

"Because of me." I shrug. "Because of what Xavier would make me do to them if they got caught."

"But you got out."

"I'm not afraid of me." I cross my arms over my chest.

He nods, clearly putting most of the pieces together and searching for missing ones to fill the holes. "Once you knew how to get out, why did you ever go back, if you hated Xavier so much?"

Isn't that the million dollar question... It's something I've thought about often, but never figured out. "After living on the streets," I tell him. "I guess I liked having someone in charge—like back in the army." It's the first time I've put it together that clearly.

Gray could have a career as a psychologist. For all I know, he does, or did.

Gray turns toward me. "And down there, you didn't need to fight all the time."

I chuckle. "You'd think, right?" I shake my head. "Pretty sure I was addicted to violence. Beating the shit out of other vampires is how I landed a spot in Xavier's Guard. How I rose to the top. Earned the king's trust—"

"He's not a king."

"He was *our* king and I did his bidding." For the most part.

"Like torturing anyone who didn't want to fuck him?" Gray's voice is cold, angry. And I can't blame him.

Looking down to the roof's tar, I dig the razor under my index finger's nail. "I did what I could to protect her—all of them—from the worst."

"Selina says *you* were the worst."

I shake my head slowly. "She assumed that. They all did. Everyone in the fucking court."

"And you let them."

I raise my chin. "I sure as fuck did. When everyone thinks you're a monster—"

"You can get away with not being one." Gray finishes my sentence.

I nod. This prick gets me—at least a little—and I can't remember the last time I felt that. If I ever did it was so long ago I barely recognize the sensation of being seen, understood.

Last time had to have been back in the war, some of the men in my platoon, or maybe Binh? But with her it wasn't the same. The main thing Binh understood was my pain.

"Where are you living now?" Gray asks.

I shrug.

"I've got a big house."

"No fucking kidding."

"Listen, I'll have to talk to the others, but—"

What he's saying sinks in. "You want me to *crash* at your pad? You're kidding, right?" The idea is both horrifying and the best thing I've ever heard. To be that close to Selina. Better able to protect her...

But to live in a fancy house like that, all civilized and shit. I bet Gray serves tea and crumpets twice a day.

"What's so funny?" he asks.

"Nothing."

"Because I'm serious. It's my house, but since Rock and Selina are living there now, I want to clear it with them before I make the offer official."

I nod, the idea starting to surround me, like a heavy coat in winter. "Are you..." My heart rate accelerates. "Which one of you is her mate?"

"Mate?" Gray laughs. "Neither of us." His expression turns serious. "Speaking of mates, Selina said there was a vampire priest in Xavier's court. That true?"

I nod.

"A real one?"

"How the hell would I know?"

"But he performed mating ceremonies, combined blood in a sacred vessel?"

I nod. "It all seemed like fake shit to me. A cheap magic show."

"Probably." Gray's brow furrows.

I lean back. "But the only marriage ceremonies I saw that failed were the ones where Xavier tried to mate with Selina."

"Interesting. Look." Gray leaps to his feet and points ahead. "The cop's leaving O'Malley's. Alone."

CHAPTER 25

Selina

"I doubt she'll go for it, but it's up to Selina," Rock says to Gray as I enter the kitchen. Warm light from the setting sun radiates through the protective-glass window and bathes the men in a delicious glow.

"What's up to me?" I lean onto the center island.

The two men smile as they turn toward my voice, both wearing expressions that tell me I'm the best thing they've seen all day. I don't think I could ever get sick of this—this potent feeling of being wanted, of belonging.

Stronger emotions swirl under that surface, combining to amplify the warmth inside me, but the most powerful, the emotion buoyed to the top is the unmistakable sensation that I belong here, belong to these men and they to me.

And for a girl who's never belonged anywhere or with anyone, not even in her mother's home, the feeling simultaneously anchors and lifts me off the ground.

First I kiss Gray, who's closer, then Rock, who *literally*

lifts me off my feet as we kiss and then sits me down on the island.

"I've got to get to the bar." Hands spanning my waist, Rock presses another kiss against my forehead. "I'm gonna let Gray talk to you about this solo."

"Some backup you are," Gray says with faux anger.

"Hey, it's your idea." Rock chuckles. "And like I said, it's up to her." He kisses my hand, then leaves the room.

My eyes follow Rock until he disappears, and when I turn back, Gray's staring out the window, tension in his back as he grips the edge of the ceramic farmhouse-style kitchen sink. "What's up?"

"Coffee?" he asks as he turns.

"Sure."

He grabs two mugs from an open shelf above the counter and the heady scent of fresh coffee fills the room as he pours the dark liquid from the stainless steel carafe of his fancy coffee maker.

He takes a quick sip. "It's a bit strong. Want cream or sugar today?"

"Stop stalling." I reach out a foot to block his path as he tries to pass me to reach the refrigerator. "You know I take it black."

He sets both mugs down on the island counter beside me and then grabs the leg I extended, running his hand along the outside of my thigh. His hand rests on my hip as he parts my legs and steps between them, bending to kiss me again—a long, slow, coffee-scented kiss that almost succeeds in melting me into the counter and distracting me from whatever it is we need to discuss.

Scooping his hands under my thighs, he tugs me against him.

My sex makes contact with the strong form of his

body, and I almost relent. Reluctantly I push against his shoulders. "What's going on, Gray?"

He steps back to lean against the sink opposite me, and I take a sip of my coffee, loving the immediate hit of caffeine that races through me. Caffeine is different since my transition, its effect faster and stronger but quickly extinguished with no lasting impact. I could drink coffee all day.

He takes a sip of his coffee too. "I had an interesting chat last night."

"With who?"

"Pike."

At his name, my body experiences a rush very different from the caffeine hit—much stronger and incredibly confusing. Fear and lust battle for control inside me.

"And?" I ask, my voice shaky. Whatever I'm feeling, my heart is beating too quickly, and I take another sip of caffeine to give the symptom an excuse—at least for a few seconds.

Gray rakes back his long dark flop of hair and sets his coffee cup down next to the sink. "I might as well cut to the chase."

"That would be good."

"I invited Pike to move in here."

"What?"

Coffee splashes onto my thigh and Gray takes my cup from me and presses his hand over the scalding damp spot on my leg. "You okay?"

"Why?" My voice is smaller than I'd like, almost breathless, so I gather my wits. "What were you thinking, Gray? You know what he did to me."

"That's the thing, princess." He strokes my thighs and steps back between them. "I don't think he did."

"Did what?"

"Any of the things that you think he did."

"You don't believe me?" I lean away, flashing back to the last wedding ceremony, how Pike tugged on that leash, making me so aroused I almost came just from walking, and then how his fingers pressed inside me at Xavier's command, in front of the entire court.

At the memory, I'm wet. My sex throbbing with a need I resent. A need I can't begin to explain or understand.

That moment was humiliating, but it was nothing compared to all the other things Pike did to me while I was captive—horrible, sadistic things. The weeks and months I was left blindfolded in that dungeon, strapped down and fucked roughly.

And the cruel laughter when I cried out at the pain of penetration, how one of them would force a dick into my throat to quiet me as I fought my body's unwanted reactions to the aggressive intrusions.

Pike and his buddies would take breaks to let me recover, just so they could laugh about how painful I found the initial thrusts once they started up again.

It became like a competition—who could drive into me harder and deeper after I healed, and sometimes they'd used a steel dildo instead of, or along with, their own cocks.

I've shared some of these horrors with Gray. He knows what I suffered. "Why would you even suggest this?" I ask through my anger and shock.

Gray cups my face and raises my gaze to meet his. "I believe everything you told me," he says. "Always. But the horrific things that happened to you—are you certain it was Pike?"

Shaking, I pick up my coffee to distract me from the shuddering memories threatening to take hold of my emotions and ruin my evening, my whole night, even before it begins.

I don't *want* to remember the details of the long months of torture I endured.

"Didn't you say you were blindfolded?" Gray asks softly, running his hands gently over my sides. "How can you be sure it was Pike?"

Closing my eyes, I shake my head. I do remember Pike's menacing voice in the mix. But at this moment, the only words I can clearly attribute to him are ones like, "Get the fuck out!" and, "Leave her to me!" and, "My turn. Go!"

And each time those words were followed, not by more torture, but by sips of blood from that tiny cup, by the loosening of my bindings, by being allowed to move, even slightly, to ease the pressure of being forced into one position for so long.

Sighing, I open my eyes to find Gray's expression full of concern.

"I'm not sure anymore." I shake my head. "But even if he wasn't as horrible as the rest of them, why didn't he stop them?"

"I think you should talk to Pike about that," Gray says, but even before he starts to answer I realize that Pike *did* stop them. Many times. And by ultimately freeing me, he was the one to put an end to my torture.

If only he'd done it sooner. For that, I'm not sure I can ever forgive him.

"Selina," Gray says gently. "This won't happen if you're not okay with it. And even if it does, Pike can sleep on a cot down in the basement. Rock and I will make sure that you're never alone with him. We'll make sure he never touches you."

Closing my eyes, I nod. No matter what went before it, Pike saved my life at least twice that I know of. And after the second rescue, he let me come back to Gray and Rock. He initiated that, he found Gray and brought him to me, even though he knew he was risking his own life to do it.

"Princess," Gray says softly. "Pike's all alone. He told me a bit of his story. Like you, he was separated from his Maker right after his transition. He never learned how to survive in his new body and got sucked into Xavier's court before he had a chance to find a way to belong in the vampire world."

At the word *belong*, I suck in a sharp breath.

"I wouldn't suggest this," Gray says softly, "if I believed for one moment that it would put you in danger." He pulls me into a tight embrace and I melt into the comfort of his arms, his chest, his scent. "Your safety is paramount, and if it's too uncomfortable..."

I shake my head against his chest, then lean back to look into his eyes. "It's okay. I'm willing to try it—at least for one night."

CHAPTER 26

Gray

Selina's heart pounds against my chest as I hold her. She's so brave. I trust Pike and trust is something I don't often grant, but I wasn't the one who spent months believing he was the inflictor, or at least the instigator, of my pain.

I hate knowing that he could have saved her sooner, but based on what I've learned about Xavier's court from Pike and from Kwana—the cult-like atmosphere, how Xavier rules with fear, how Pike knew nothing of vampire life beyond isolation and what he'd seen there—I can understand how it was hard for him to act against the vampire he thought was a king.

I can't condone his months of inaction, but I do understand how it could have happened.

Whether Selina ever forgives him, or will ever talk to him, or even look at him, is up to her. This is a big house. She'll never have to see him if she doesn't want to.

As I hold her, Selina's hands travel over my back,

pulling me more tightly against her, stroking my ribs and my shoulders.

Her breathing changes and her heart rate's still high, but now it's driven by a different force. Her hands slide down to my arse, and I'm instantly stiff.

Wiggling on the counter to adjust her position, the intersection of her splayed legs finds the wood rising from between mine, and she pulses her hips, gently stroking against my need while squeezing my arse cheeks with her hands and making my need rise even higher.

She leans back on the counter to rest on one arm, and with the other she holds my hips tight against her. Her desire is obvious in her eyes and takes me over the edge of restraint.

Unwilling to waste time, I grab the waistband of her jeans and tear them open, ripping the button and zipper in one motion. Shifting my hands lower, I rip the center seam of the garment, exposing her warm body to my touch.

Her panties are damp with desire, and so I tear those too and quickly press a finger inside her. Her head drops back and she moans at the initial penetration, and I wait for a moment, every muscle in my body tight with the restraint of holding back until I sense her body yielding, relaxing around the intrusion.

As soon as it does, I add a second finger, slowly pumping inside her and readying her tight pussy for thicker penetration.

"Turn over." I take her waist to help guide her onto her belly so I can fuck her.

Shaking her head, she reaches down and frees my cock from my pants, stroking me and then guiding my rod toward her wetness.

Apprehension courses through me. We've fucked so many times I can't begin to count, but it's almost always from behind, and I'm not sure right now whether I'll be able to bear the intimacy of the act face-to-face.

Looking into my eyes, she places the head of my cock against her opening and pulses her hips, mixing her juices with my pre-ejaculate and inviting me in.

It's been a few moments since my fingers were inside her and I fear that my initial thrust will hurt.

I try to pull back so I can finger her again to be sure, but she tucks her heels behind my arse and forces me forward. My body can't resist complying, and I slide into her, hard. My moan joins her yelp of pain.

I stop. I should withdraw, but her heels and the needy expression on her face urge me forward.

Determined to control my thrusts until she's ready, I make shallow strokes, giving her only the top half of my cock and giving myself the most excruciating pleasure as her tight muscles tug against the sensitive nerves of my head.

One hand on my shoulder, the other bracing herself on the counter, she moves her hips, swiveling and thrusting and increasing the depth of penetration at her own pace.

Her cheeks grow pink, her pupils widen and her pretty pink tongue peeks out between her lips with short gasps as she takes me in deeper. Fucking her like this, slowly, face-to-face, is better—and so much worse—than I could have imagined.

I can't go on like this, looking into her eyes and feeling so connected, so connected I might die if I wasn't inside her.

Forget about *might*. I *will* die. I'll die the second my

cock leaves her body. How will I ever breathe, how will I survive if I'm not inside her?

"What's wrong?" she asks softly. "Are you okay?"

I get a hold on myself. "Princess, I am way more than okay."

I tear the remnants of her jeans from her body, then holding her arse, and my cock still inside her, I lift her and climb onto the counter. I bend her knees up by her ears, then, bracing my hands on the island, I close my eyes tightly and pound.

My hips drive as fast as I can move them, creating friction between us that I hope will wash out every other feeling inside me, that I hope will wipe my emotions away and replace them with lust—pure lust and the pleasure of her wet cunny around my stiff cock.

She moans. I open my eyes and the sight of her nearly slays me.

I rise to my knees and her legs hook around my back as I hold her hips aloft. Her body rests on her shoulders as I pump like a piston, trying to focus on the grain of the marble countertop to avoid the sight of her.

But her hand lands on mine, and I look into her eyes.

"Slow down, Gray." She licks her lips. "Slow down."

I lower her hips to the counter and position myself above, staying still but seated inside her. Missionary position. I don't think I've experienced this sex position since before my transition.

Even as a human, I preferred to fuck from behind—or above—putting the woman in any position that avoided my seeing into her eyes.

Selina smiles softly. Her hands caress my back, my shoulders, my arse, and then her hips start to move, small gentle pulses that contract around me, shifting the depth of penetration a quarter inch at a time, such a subtle stroke that I imagine it would be imperceptible to an observer, but for me it's the opposite. I perceive it all.

With each tiny movement, the place where our skin is joined—where my hardness makes contact with her wet softness—sparks with intense pleasure, and that bond is nothing compared to what is going on between our eyes.

No words are spoken and yet everything is said. I fucking love this woman.

Slowly, deliberately my body joins her motions, keeping the same slow pace, but increasing the depth of each gliding stroke.

Our hips work in tandem to guarantee the inside of her body touches every inch of my rod every time, and our combined motion pulls my cock out to the tip and absorbs it up to the balls with each long, languorous stroke.

With each deep plunge it's like I'm drawn under water, pulled into a luxurious pool of pleasure where I'm more than willing to drown.

Lost in her eyes, in her cunt, my pace accelerates, just perceptibly, and her breathing changes, too, turning more shallow, more erratic. With each stroke, her hips lift up to meet me, harder and harder. She's using so much power now, I have to use all my strength to keep from being thrown off her as she bucks.

She cries out and her climax pulses around me, quite clearly filling her body with intense pleasure. And at the sight of her writhing body, her open mouth, her wide pupils and flushed skin, my heart bursts.

Yes. Fuck. Holy fucking hell. There is no longer any doubt. When Selina is taken from me I am going to die.

CHAPTER 27

Selina

I pace around the foyer in Gray's house, fighting the instinct inside me that's urging me to go outside.

Rock went to the bar hours ago, Gray had to go into FJS for something and I assured him I planned to stay in tonight, at least until he got back.

But my theory that my Maker is involved in the murders has grown stronger, and after Colton told me about the cemetery connection, other locations in the city started flashing through my mind, like dreams coming back.

It's unsettling, and yet my curiosity is driving me to know more. In fact, it's more than just curiosity. I have trouble thinking of a word to describe the compelling drive I have to learn more about my Maker, to find her.

Giving in, I leave the house and head out into the night. I know I'm breaking my word to Gray, going out on my own, but I couldn't stay inside a moment longer.

The night air can barely begin to cool the warmth

that's been burning inside me since Gray and I made love on the kitchen counter. It's the first time I've wanted to use the *make love* verb instead of the "F" one for something that happened between Gray and me. What happened moved the needle on my feelings for Gray by several degrees toward love.

He's still holding back, keeping so much of himself closed off to me. I know very little of his life, before or after he became a vampire, but even without words, his eyes, his actions today told me so much. Even if he can't express his feelings with words, his body and his expressions told me what I wanted to hear.

And all of that joy counterbalances the news that Gray invited Pike to move in. That idea terrifies me, but not for the reasons I told Gray.

Pike is intimidating and exudes danger, but for me he exudes something else entirely—raw masculinity and a sexual energy that generates a matching energy inside me that I'm petrified to explore.

But something completely different tugs at me tonight. Something that drew me out of the house on my own and is leading me through the city with a strong sense of direction toward several unknown destinations.

I head from place to place, drawn around the city by a force I don't understand, and at each stop my nerves are heightened, but so is my drive to continue.

Stopping at the entrance to a residential alley in the Annex, I'm slammed by a strong sense of déjà vu. The reason soon becomes clear. One of the serial killer's victims was found in this back lane, and one was found in Humewood Park, a place I felt drawn to earlier. In fact, my route through the city tonight has been like a connect-the-dots game—visiting all the places where the murders occurred.

Every nerve in my body tingles with fear—or awareness—or both. It's like my prize for connecting the dots is a powerful sense of unease.

I should end this crazy scavenger hunt and head to Rock's bar.

"Why are you stalking me?"

I spin toward an anger-filled female voice.

It's her. The vampire who Made me.

Her jet-black hair and ruby lips, her tanned complexion, her deep brown eyes. Even her clothes are similar to that night, tailored, expressive, expensive. A frisson of fear snakes through me, but it's quickly usurped by a stronger emotion.

I fly at her, taking her by the throat and slamming her body against a nearby garage door. The vibrating bang fills the night air. Down the lane, a dog barks.

"Who are you?" she asks with a strangled voice. "Why do I know you?"

"Who are *you*?" I demand. "And why did you Make me?"

I want to feel revulsion when I look into her eyes. She's a murderer. This vampire stole my human existence, left me for dead, but instead I feel drawn to her, like she's an old friend or a family member I haven't seen in a long time.

"Make you?" she chokes.

I drop her to her feet, but keep hold of her throat, less tightly now so she can talk and breathe.

"You've mistaken me for someone else." She shakes her head. "I have no Progeny."

Something in her eyes tells me she's lying, or not telling the whole truth. "But I have met you," she adds. "I know you."

"My name is Selina. We met in an art gallery two years ago. You lured me into the alley, then fed from me, drained me and left me to die."

Her eyes widen at the memory, but then she shakes her head.

"And you left me with this." I turn my head to the side and lift my hair to reveal my scar.

"It's not possible." Her voice is thready, but her face fills with excitement. "That's why I know you. Feel so much affection toward you." She reaches toward my face. "But you didn't feed from me. I didn't perform the transition ritual. I don't even know how to do it."

"I don't know how it happened," I snap. "I just know that it did. And you're going to tell me how. What is it about you that allowed you to make a vampire spontaneously?" That makes me different, too.

"Selina." She pronounces my name like it's a delicious treat she just discovered. "I'm Zora."

Zora. The name brings back a vague memory, but I can't be sure it's the name she used the night that she killed me—or tried to.

"And since that night? Are you all alone in this world too?" She touches my face.

I flinch away, but seeing the hurt in her eyes, I relent and let her thumb stroke my cheek, my lips, and it's oddly comforting.

I'm about to answer, to tell her all about my life since my transition, like she's an old friend, but then I remember who she is—*what she does*—and it squashes the warmth I inexplicably feel.

"You're a killer," I say coldly.

"I'm a vampire." She half shrugs. "It's what we do."

"No, it's not!" I back a few feet away. "It's *not* what we do."

"Selina, vampires need human blood to survive. You must know this. It's been two years. You must feed."

"Yes, but I don't ever take more than I need. I don't harm humans." *Except one.* I shake my head. "Because of you, the police are hunting and killing every vampire they find. Because of you hundreds, maybe thousands of innocent vampires are dead."

I rediscover my anger, but it's joined by a strong belief that I can change her—convince her that what she's doing is bad, evil. She doesn't understand. She's alone and lost, just like I was. It's not her fault.

"Who was your Maker?" I ask, wondering if the vampire who Made her taught her this despicable behavior. Learned behavior can be unlearned.

She blinks as if remembering what tears felt like. "My Maker's name was Andreas. He was beautiful. And kind. And he was my entire world. We were going to be married, *mated* he called it. That's why he changed me. So we could be together forever."

Sighing, she wraps her arms around herself. "But the first time he took me out to feed from a human, we were attacked."

"Attacked how?"

"Ambushed by one of your *precious humans.*" The hate in her voice is so palpable I can almost feel it spread over my face.

"How many humans attacked you?" I ask. "Two vampires can easily escape a dozen humans. Unless they were armed with a silver mesh net? Or caught you unaware?"

"You are so naive." She shakes her head. "Humans are more dangerous than you believe. More cold-blooded."

I don't want to point out that she's the cold-blooded killer, plus she used to be human. I bite my tongue and let her continue.

"I'd already fed. We were on the way home, but the smells…" She closes her eyes and draws a long breath. "The scents and sounds of blood pumping through every body that passed us, the blood of everyone in the entire city, made me hungry for more. Made me think my thirst could never be satisfied."

"I know that feeling." I know too well how blood sings to me, and how it sang way too loudly at first, how I felt like no matter how much I drank I could never be sated. And I remember too what that unrelenting hunger drove me to do. I swallow my sadness and shame.

"I spotted a young man," she continues. "He was taking a piss in an alley. I meant to approach him slowly, carefully, and just take a short drink, but I underestimated my speed and strength, and my hunger."

A wicked smile washes over her. "Andreas came to help me, to tell me to stop. But before he reached me, he was shot. From behind."

"Shot?" I frown. "Vampires can heal from bullet wounds."

"Shot, spiked, staked, speared. I don't give a shit what verb you use. The little bitch used a spring-loaded wooden spike at point-blank range and it went straight through his heart.

"Bitch shot him in the back. I saw the blood trailing out of his mouth before I even noticed the wood pushing from his chest or the blood blooming on the white fabric of his shirt, like a rose opening in fast motion.

"And when he fell to his knees, I saw her behind him. The vicious little human who shot my love in the heart."

"I'm sorry for your loss," I say softly because it seems appropriate.

"I killed the bitch," she continues. "I tore out her throat while her boyfriend watched. Then I ripped out his throat too."

Nausea rises inside me. I remember Colton telling me about this double murder, one he'd deemed unrelated to the serial killings, because of the gory violence and the absence of the telltale scar.

"That's terrible," I say.

"Thank you," she replies, totally missing my meaning.

A smile washes over her face, and I hate how my emotions react. I pleased her. I feel proud that I pleased her. *What is wrong with me?*

I mentally shake my head, hoping to rid my mind of all warm thoughts toward her. "What's with the scar?" I lift my hair again.

She traces the outline of my scar and it sends a shiver through me. "It's a symbol Andreas wore on a pendant, close to his heart."

"What does it mean?" I ask her stepping out of her reach.

She shakes her head. "I don't know. I just know that the symbol is beautiful, and it was important to him, part of who he was, so I leave a trace of my beloved Andreas on every one of the humans I take in his name."

I should ask her where she lives, so I can tell Astrid. Better yet, I should drive a stake through her heart right now.

"I should go," I say instead. I'm so uncomfortable, so

conflicted and feel like the longer I stay near her, the worse my confusion will grow.

"Please." She reaches toward me. "Don't go. Join me. Together we can avenge Andreas. Avenge all the vampires murdered. Exact revenge." Her expression seems diabolical, and yet I'm still drawn to her.

"Revenge on who?"

"On humans. All humans. Starting with the monster who killed Andreas."

"But you already killed her. You got your revenge, why keep killing?"

"Andreas will *never* be avenged while humans walk the Earth."

I step away from her, disgusted.

"You don't understand, my pet." Her hand lands softly on my shoulder. "But I will teach you. As your Maker it's my responsibility to guide you."

"You murder innocent people."

"Humans murder innocent vampires! All humans deserve death, but—" her eyes narrow "—*especially* ones like her." Her eyes open wider. "That must be why I went after you." She shakes her head. "But you're different. Special. It was clearly destiny that I attacked you. Your transition was a miracle. Clearly we're meant to work together."

I detest what she's saying, and yet something about it tugs at my heart. Gray keeps saying I'm special. What if Zora is the reason why?

And I hate how she makes it sound logical that I belong at her side, or that what she's doing is right. In her mind it's kill or be killed, and by Colton's own admission, humans kill every vampire on sight without fear of consequence, so why shouldn't vampires do the same?

But even if I can talk myself out of that logic, something else about Zora calls to me. Her blood. It's calling to me like a siren, a force that's rendering logic or morals irrelevant.

I lick my teeth, my fangs pulsing to release as my body is pulled toward her, as my thirst continues to grow.

"Come, my pet," she coos. "I know an underground club where we can feed from each other, where vampires gather without fear of humans or the ridiculous syndicate rules. A place we can stay after dawn, without fear of the sun."

"Where is it?" At least if I learn the location I can let Astrid know.

But I'm fooling myself. I want to go with her—feed from her—and the warmth of temptation spreads inside me. I want this. I want her. Zora is my true mother. My real family. Where I belong.

Someone lands at my side, and I gasp with shock. It's Pike.

Zora disappears the second he arrives and my heart sinks. I miss her already.

"Come," he says. "You're not safe here."

"Have you been *following* me?" Anger rises inside me, but my sense of loss at Zora's departure is replaced by a hint of relief.

He looks away. "Just come. The pigs are raiding this area tonight."

"Pigs?"

"Cops. Humans. They've killed dozens of vampires already. And more than a few homeless humans. They're less than a block away." His voice is filled with urgency and fear.

I nod, he takes my hand and we race into the night.

When Pike finally slows, we're back in the Junction neighborhood, not far from Rock's bar, and I'm shocked how much it touches me that Pike took me someplace I feel safe.

Dropping my hand, he steps into a shadow as a group of young women pass, one of them opening her eyes in obvious alarm when she spots Pike's scars, or perhaps just his size.

"Thank you," I say softly, and I wonder if he realizes he saved me from more than just the police.

He nods, but doesn't look up from the sidewalk. He shoves his hands into the pockets of his leather jacket and pain flashes across his face.

Watching him in the alley as he stares at the ground, seemingly in pain, my hand itches to trace over his scars, to compare that part of his face to the smoother skin on the other side. To use my lips to soothe whatever torment he's experiencing now.

"I am grateful for tonight," I say, "but you can't keep following me—"

He looks up, his amber eyes catching the light. "I need to keep you safe."

I chew the inside of my lip, chewing on the conflict inside me too. I hate that he was following me, but I can't deny that it gives me a sense of safety knowing I wasn't as alone out there tonight as I felt until Zora arrived.

"Stay away from her," Pike says, his eyes casting down again.

"Zora?"

He nods. "She's dangerous. Crazy. A killer."

"She's my Maker."

He lifts his gaze to meet mine, then looks down again.

"Resist the pull I know you must feel then. She might not ever hurt *you*, but she will get you killed."

"I feel so connected to her." I close my eyes for a moment, shocked at how easily I'm sharing this information with Pike. "Is that normal?"

His shoulders jerk almost as if he's laughing. "How would I know about normal?"

"Do you feel connected to your Maker?"

He looks away from me, his jaw hardening.

"Do you ever feel…*psychically* connected to your Maker?" I probe again. "Like you can hear his thoughts? See through his eyes?"

"Her." He tips his head to the side. "Sure I felt connected. I loved my Maker. I loved her with all my heart. But a psychic connection?" He glances toward me, then down to the pavement. "You mean, like ESP?"

"I guess so." I take a deep breath, eager to admit this to someone who might understand. "I have dreams. Vivid dreams. Dreams where it's like I'm seeing through my Maker's eyes, feeling what she feels." *And doing what she does.*

He looks straight into my eyes for the first time. "That's trippy."

"No kidding." I can't help but grin at the word *trippy*. It must be from another time, and in spite of my fear, I want to know when the word is from, how long he's lived, where he's been, how he got his scars. I want to know everything about him.

"Do you still see your Maker?" I ask.

He shakes his head, then looks away from me down the street. "I lost her. Forever."

"I'm sorry." I reach forward, my instincts wanting to

take his hand, even just brush the cuff of his leather jacket, but I drop my hand down before I do. "Was she killed?"

"I don't know." He shakes his head. "Last time I saw her was 1974. In Vietnam."

"Oh." That was during the Vietnam War, I think. I know very little about that war, none of it good. "Were you a soldier?"

He nods.

"Is that how you got your scars?"

He nods again.

I sense we've both just shown parts of ourselves we haven't shown others, and the silence feels intimate, wrapping around us like a warm blanket, and somehow, while we've been talking, I've moved closer toward Pike. His blood hums under the surface of his skin, singing to me in the most alluring voice I can imagine.

I shift my gaze to his heavy boots as I lick my lips, knowing I have to resist, that it would be wrong to drink Pike's blood. Very wrong.

Gray is the one and only vampire I've fed from, and for some reason he won't let me do it again. But my urge for vampire blood is building. I don't know how often my body needs it, but it's calling for more right now. In fact the call is so strong, at the next opportunity I may plunge my fangs into Gray without asking permission.

I have yet to understand all the intricacies and implications of feeding from another vampire, but based on the pull I felt toward Zora's blood and feel toward Pike's right now—vampires who scare and repulse me—it's not hard to understand the act's power.

And the even stronger power that must come through feeding from your Maker. If that's what triggers a transition, then it must be the most powerful feeding of all.

What would that feel like? Taking Zora's vein?

I shake my head. I'll never know. Zora's evil and she needs to die.

I raise my gaze, letting it slide up over Pike's powerful, leather-clad legs, his solid torso and up to his face. I catch him looking at me and his eyes send a shiver of fear-tinged desire shooting through me.

He looks down.

"I hear Gray invited you to stay at his house," I say to break the thick silence.

Pike scrapes his boot along the pavement and nods.

"Is that something you want?"

He lifts his head quickly. "More than anything."

"Really?"

"To keep you safe." His voice is deep and low, like a growled whisper, and it rumbles inside me.

That's not necessary, I plan to say, but instead what comes out is, "That's thoughtful."

"Not thoughtful." His voice seems to emerge from deep in his chest, maybe lower. "Selfish. If anyone hurt you I'd die."

"But Pike, you—" How can he say that after he's hurt me so much?

As if knowing what I'm thinking, he hangs his head even lower than before, and his hand tucks back into his pocket. Pain spreads over his face.

"I should have stopped it sooner," he says. "I should have stopped Xavier *years* before you even came to court. You suffered—so much—and others too…" He shakes his head. "I have no excuse."

His jaw hardens and then I see him wince again. It's almost as if his regrets cause him physical pain.

"Let's go to the bar," I say quietly. "You can meet Rock."

He shakes his head.

"You don't want to meet Rock?"

"I don't want to go inside."

"Why not?"

He kicks his heel against the brick wall behind him. "I'd be bad for Rock's business."

"Don't be silly."

His chin lifts. "You think I'm silly?" The corner of his mouth quirks in the slightest hint of a grin, and it's the first hint of lightness I've seen in the man—ever.

It's hard to contain the joy that small morsel of humor makes me feel.

"You *are* silly," I tell him. "Silly if you think your coming into the bar would hurt Rock's business. Do you think the other customers will run screaming? You give yourself too much credit." Although I have to admit, there was a time that the mere sight of Pike did that to me.

"I don't do..." He frowns. "I don't do *people.* Never have. But especially since..."

"Since your transition?" I finish his trailed off sentence.

"Before that. Since the war. I don't know." He winces in pain again.

I nod, then reach out to touch his sleeve above where his hand is tucked into his jacket pocket. "I'll go in on my own then. I'll let Gray know you're out here. Okay?"

He nods.

"See you at Gray's later?" I ask.

His breath hitches, but then he nods, and it flashes so quickly I can't be certain, but I think that he smiles.

CHAPTER 28

Selina

I'm charged with nervous tension as I open the door to the bar. Hearing or merely thinking Pike's name used to generate an intense fear inside me, something worse than fear, but now… Now what I'm feeling is equally strong, but I'm not sure how to name it.

It's like a strange excitement that anything could happen—something dangerous, something sexual—but there's also something tender underlying that energy that's almost like a strong desire to make sure that he's protected.

Pike strikes me as the type of man who's never had anyone looking out for him.

And as much as it scares me, I actually do hope he comes to live with us, if only to know that he won't get caught in one of these police raids or burned to death by the sun. I want to make sure that he's safe.

The second I enter the bar, I spot three handsome and smiling faces, all directing their attention to me. Joy rushes to surround me.

Rock smiles and raises a half-filled wine glass, the relief in his eyes is so obvious I feel it stroke inside me.

Gray's leaning against the far end of the bar and his smile is knowing and lustful, like he knew I'd show up here, and knows what he wants from me right now—wants all the time.

Near the back of the bar, Colton's chair scrapes along the hardwood floor under his table that's close to the booth where I normally sit. His face and his posture exude happiness, like it's all he can do not to bound up to me and lick my face. Lick me everywhere.

That thought heats my blood.

I pause. I want to go to all three of them. But after tonight's events, the two I most need to speak to are Colton and Gray—but for very different reasons.

I'm still doing mental triage on who to go to first, when Colton strides toward me, his puppy-dog grin an injection of joyfulness.

"Hi." He reaches for me, then stops himself, clearly unsure whether or not to hug me.

This time I'm the one to make the decision. I reach out and we embrace, and his strong arms envelop me along with his clean, soapy scent. The hug is so familiar, so comfortable, like we've done it dozens of times before, and his heart is pumping so hard and fast that even his blood sounds happy. The only thing marring the experience is all the wooden stakes I feel in the lining of his jacket.

"I'm so glad you're here," he says. "I've got so much to tell you."

I look up, swept away by his sparkling green eyes and his dimples, so deep from his permagrin.

I fake a pout. "Is a chance to talk about your work the only reason you're glad to see me?"

His eyes open with concern and he raises a hand to his hair. "No, Selina. It's not… I *always* want to see you. For…for lots of reasons."

I tug on the sleeve of his jacket. "I was kidding."

His smile returns. "Thank goodness."

"Listen," I say. "I need to have a quick chat with Gray. Can you wait a bit? Then maybe we can go for a walk or something?"

Disappointment flashes on his face so quickly it's almost imperceptible, then the puppy returns. He nods and smiles. "A walk sounds fantastic. It's such a nice night. And I'm armed, ready to protect you." He pats his jacket, taking a bite out of the joy I feel when I'm around him.

I brush his hand lightly. "See you in a bit, okay?"

He returns to his table, and I join Gray at the bar.

"Everything okay, princess?"

"Yup."

"You said you wouldn't go out on your own."

I smile. "I changed my mind. I needed a walk." Why aren't I telling him the truth? Pike knows…

Rock comes over, pours me a glass of whiskey and tops up Gray's wine. "You were gone for a long time." Rock's eyes broadcast concern.

"I saw Pike."

"What?" Rock leans toward me. "Are you okay? Did he hurt you?"

I shake my head and put my hand over Rock's on the bar. "It was fine. I'm fine. And—" I turn to Gray "—I told him it's okay if he moves in. He's outside right now."

"Are you sure?" Rock asks.

"I think his bark is worse than his bite." I take a sip of the whiskey. "I may have misjudged him." I judged Pike harshly, but based on our brief conversation, no one has judged Pike more harshly than himself.

"As you wish, princess." Gray grins.

"Can we talk for a minute?" I ask Gray, nodding toward the booth.

A customer down the bar signals for Rock.

"You staying until closing?" he asks before leaving.

"Not sure," I answer. "If not, I'll see you at home?"

Rock leans over the bar to kiss me lightly, then I head over to the booth with Gray.

"What's up, princess?" he asks.

Nerves scramble inside me. I do *not* want to tell Gray that I've met Zora. I didn't think I'd want to keep it from Gray or Rock—or even Colton—but now that it's real I can't bring myself to do it.

I need to build up to it. "I'm hoping you can answer some questions about vampires," I tell him.

"I don't like garlic." He winks. "In fact, I detest the stuff, but it's not enough to scare me away."

"Thanks." I kick him lightly under the table. "That's *exactly* what I was going to ask you."

He twists the stem of his wine glass between his thumb and index fingers. "Whatever you want to know, princess, ask away."

I try to decide where to start. Zora's warped sense of ethics got me thinking. "When Xavier's Guard swooped in on us, and some of them were killed…was that murder? I mean, no one got arrested. No one from our side anyway."

"It was self-defense, not murder."

I nod. "What happens if it's *not* self-defense?"

"There is no worse crime than murder." I've never seen Gray look so serious. "The sentence when a vampire kills a human is a minimum forty years in prison—based on the average life expectancy of a human when the law was last changed." He looks like he's thinking. "Guess they should update that."

"And for killing another vampire?"

"Three hundred years. Or death, depending on the circumstances."

I suck in a sharp breath. "What kind of circumstances?"

"Killing another vampire when there are human witnesses, killing your Progeny, killing your Maker…stuff like that."

"Oh." Even if I could bring myself to kill Zora, I would be put to death, and I'm actually relieved to have a strong deterrent, an excuse not to even think about it.

"You thinking of killing Pike?" Gray asks. "Is that why you agreed to let him move in? Plan to stake him in his bed?"

"No!"

He reaches over the table and takes my hand. "Princess. I'm joking. Wow. Are you *actually* thinking of killing Pike? Because that's a really, really bad idea."

I shake my head.

"Then who?"

"No one. I've just been realizing how much I didn't learn from my Maker."

He nods and his expression changes.

"What are you thinking about?" I ask.

"Shagging you senseless."

I kick him under the table again. "No, you're not. You look like you're worried—or hiding something. What aren't you telling me?"

"Can't a man have a little mystery?" He shoots me a mischievous grin. "Or is mystery only for femme fatales?"

He crosses his arms over his chest. "That's gender discrimination."

"Very funny." I stare into the amber liquid in my glass, letting it swirl. "When a vampire is killed, how do the others determine if it's self-defense? What if there are no witnesses?"

"Shit, princess. Seriously. Who are you planning to kill? Should I be worried?" He puts his hands over his heart.

"Very worried." I wink at him. "Just don't cross me."

"I would never." His playful expression turns serious. "I will always protect you. I will always defend you. And I will never do anything to betray you, my princess."

I suck in a sharp breath at the power of his words and their delivery. It was like he was declaring some sacred oath, not just reassuring his girlfriend in a bar. Gray is such an enigma—all joking playboy one minute, then this fierce defender the next.

"Why do you call me princess?" He gave me the nickname almost from the start.

"Because…" He leans across the table, his lips close to my ear. "I live to serve your cunny."

"Gray!" I push on his shoulder to move him away, and shoot him a scolding look, but inside, my body responds in an entirely different way. "Why do you do that?" I ask.

"What?"

"Turn everything dirty. Put up walls."

He glances around, pretending he's confused. "Walls? I see no walls."

"You know what I mean. Every time something gets serious between us, you make a joke, or reduce it to something crude or sexual. You never let me in."

He shoots me a wicked look. "If you want in, we can

talk about that. Are you thinking fingers up my bum or wearing a strap-on?"

I lean back. "You're impossible."

"And that's why you love me." He has a visible reaction the second he says *love*, as if the word escaped by accident. Then he looks away from me. "Your admirer is staring again."

I glance over to Colton and smile. With Colton, I know where I stand. We haven't so much as kissed, but in some ways I feel like I know him better than I do Gray. Or at least I know more about him, his family, his life, his job, how he feels about me—and vampires. I wish I didn't know that.

I know none of those things about the vampire sitting across from me now—my lover. Our bodies have done the most intimate things, and yet there's no true intimacy between us, and I long for that, I crave it. I've been so blessed I feel greedy to want more, but it breaks my heart that Gray may never give me everything that I want.

"Any other questions?" he asks.

"Does this symbol mean anything to you?" I dip my finger into my whiskey and trace onto the table the symbol of my scar, the one found on all of Zora's victims.

Gray goes white. "Where have you seen that?" he asks.

"Well, here for one place." I turn and show him the back of my neck.

"Holy shit." His finger traces my scar.

Even though I'm angry with him right now, the contact rips an excited thrill through my body.

I drop my hair. "What is the symbol?"

"Not sure."

"Bullshit."

He shrugs.

"You've never seen it before?"

He shakes his head, but I can tell that he's lying.

"Then why did you react like that?"

He leans back, like this is the most casual conversation in the world. "I was just surprised I never saw that while I was fucking you." He leans forward. "You know I like you from behind."

I glare at him. He's clearly hiding something. And it's pissing me off.

"Guess I should open my eyes once in a while," he says jokingly. "Pay more attention to parts of you beyond that deliciously tight, wet hole between your legs."

"That's it." I slide out of the booth.

Gray reaches for my hand, but grabs my wrist. "Where are you going?"

"None of your business." I tug at my arm, but he tightens his grip on my wrist.

"Your safety *is* my business." He's all serious now. Like this actually is business for him, not even a bit personal. Like he doesn't even realize how his crudeness just hurt me.

"I'm going for a walk—with Colton."

"Everything okay here?" Colton steps up beside me, glaring at Gray and the way he's holding my wrist.

Gray releases me. "See you later, princess." Turning his gaze toward Colton instead of me, he adds, "We'll finish this discussion at home, after a good hard fuck."

"Excuse me?" Colton's chest widens. "That is no way to speak to a woman."

"He's just joking." I rub Colton's arm, take his hand.

"Yeah, Calvin," Gray says. "I'm a bona fide comedian."

I lean into Colton. "Can we go to your place?"

A blush rises on Colton's cheeks and his neck, contrasting with the blond stubble on his chin.

"Absolutely," he says. "Whatever you like."

"Great." Without even glancing back at Gray, or Rock for that matter, I leave the bar with my handsome puppy-dog cop.

CHAPTER 29

Colton

My body, my heart, my mind have never felt like this. Not in combination that's for sure. Selina's hand in mine, I push open the door of the bar and then follow her out.

Selina chose me tonight. She chose to spend time with me over both of those other men.

My dick twitches, growing stiff in my pants, and I hope I can control it enough that it doesn't show. The last thing I want to do is embarrass or offend her—or worse scare her off.

I cannot believe what that English pervert said to her. But I'm almost glad it happened. Her obvious disgust with his crude behavior and language proves he's not good enough for her and that she knows it.

I don't get why men like that can be so obscene. The things I hear in the locker room at work sometimes make me cringe, and it's hard to imagine that these men I know and work with treat women with so little respect.

When I think of my mother, or my sister…

Okay. That helped. My dick calmed down.

Not that that part of me is ever fully in neutral when I'm around Selina or thinking of Selina.

Damn. It's getting hard again.

"What did you want to tell me?" she asks.

For a moment I'm caught off guard, thinking I might have said something aloud about my stiffening dick, but then I remember what we were talking about.

"We're closing in on the serial bloodsucker," I tell her.

"With your murder sweeps?" Her voice is quiet and tight. "How many vampires did you kill the last few nights?"

"Me, personally?"

She sucks in a sharp breath. "I was asking about the police overall, but now that you mention it."

"None. Didn't have the pleasure."

"Killing gives you pleasure?" Her fingers are tense in my hand.

I stop and look into her eyes. "That's not what I meant." *I am screwing this up.* "Selina, death is what vampires deserve. They're killing machines. But even so, taking a life, even from one who's technically dead. No, it would never give me pleasure."

"I'm glad." Her expression is tense, her shoulders lifted. She's so tenderhearted that she even empathizes with monsters, and it's one of the things I love about her. "So how are you closing in?" she asks.

"We caught her red-handed!"

"Her?" Selina's hand twitches in mine.

"I know. It's very unexpected."

"Interesting." She's so tense I can see her cheeks quiver. Or is it fear? I'm not sure.

"And you caught her? The killer?" She sounds hopeful, I think. I'm not sure, but I'm glad we got this conversation back on track after I put my boot in my mouth.

"Yup." I grin.

"So she's— Is she *dead*?"

I glance down to get a better read on Selina's emotions as she asks me this in a surprisingly neutral tone. I pride myself on being able to read people, but Selina's confusing. At least she is tonight.

"Not dead." I stop and turn to her, taking her other hand too. "But we caught her in the act."

"She killed again?"

"No."

"I don't understand." Selina looks almost ill. "What act?"

"Let's sit down." I gesture toward a nearby parkette, and we walk there in silence.

I brush some leaves off a bench for her, and then take a seat myself.

"I should go back to the beginning." I stretch my arm across the bench behind her. "I was so excited to tell you the news that it came out all jumbled."

She nods, a soft smile on her face, but not one that makes her seem happy. If she were a suspect under interrogation, I'd think she was hiding something—hiding a crime—but in Selina's case I think the smile means she's trying to encourage me, trying to make me feel better after my bad case of foot in mouth disease.

"So…" I consider where best to start. "Last night two constables on foot patrol caught a vampire in the act. A *female* vampire, if you can believe it, feeding on an innocent young woman. Someone not unlike you."

My chest tightens at the idea that Selina might ever be

attacked by one of those vicious monsters. "But the vamp got away."

"So how do you know she was the serial killer?" Selina asks.

"The mark!" My hand tightens on the bench rail behind her. "The villain had already carved her calling card onto the poor woman's…" I look down "…her breast, if you can believe it."

"Wow." Selina slides closer to me, and our thighs touch, and although there are two layers of denim between our legs, the connection's electric. My hard-on problem returns full force.

I want to adjust myself to make sure it doesn't show, but that might break the connection between our thighs and that's not worth the risk.

"So you know now that the killer is female," Selina says calmly. "Did they get a good look at her face?" She's sitting so close now that I can't see her expression. "Do you have a description?"

"Better than that. The killer is getting sloppy. We caught her on camera."

"Really?" Selina's breathing faster now. She must be so frightened.

I take a chance and wrap my arm around her shoulders. She doesn't resist, so I pull her closer, and she rests her head on my chest, sending me straight to heaven. At least I'd be going to heaven if I weren't so certain that what's going on between my legs will send me to hell.

"Yup. It's only a matter of time now." I reassure her.

"What does she look like?" Her voice is breathy.

"I can show you, if you like." Am I being too forward? No. Selina's been to my apartment a couple of times, and asked to go there earlier. "If you still want to come over…"

"To your apartment?"

"Yeah. I have to log in to the department system on a secure line to show you."

"Then let's go." She stands and my arm slides off her shoulders.

She looks agitated, but interested, and any second thoughts about sharing this confidential information disappear under the promise of spending more time with Selina.

We walk the first two blocks in silence, my arm over her shoulders, her arm around my hips, and although she's small, it's like she fits perfectly under my arm. I barely even have to slow my normal pace for her to keep up.

"How many other vampire-related murders have there been in the city that weren't her?" she asks when we're nearing my house. "Ones without the carved symbol."

"None since I joined the VTF…"

"And how many vampires has the task force killed?"

I open the gate, we pass through and then I let her go ahead, keeping close behind her as we walk down the breezeway toward the backyard and the entrance to my basement apartment.

"Not sure of the exact number." The motion detection light turns on over my back door as we near.

"How many last night then. Last week?"

"Dozens. No, probably hundreds." I unlock the door, and step to the side to let her enter first. "The east end team found an nest the day before yesterday."

"They killed the vampires while they were sleeping?" Walking into the apartment, she sounds vaguely horrified.

"No, that would be dangerous. Vampires don't sleep all day like most people think."

"So…" She prods me to continue.

"It was ingenious, really." I take off my jacket and hang it on a hook, only then realizing I should have let her wear it home. It's a chilly night, and without a coat she must have been cold.

"How?" She leans against the side of my cheap IKEA bookcase.

"Are you sure you want to know?" I step toward the kitchen table and turn back, trying to read her.

"You said it was ingenious." She's engrossed, but why…

I love that she's interested in my work, but every time I talk about exterminating vampires her tenderhearted side comes out along with what feels like disapproval. She needs to understand how vicious they are. How devious.

"The bloodsuckers were found in a warehouse in the docklands," I tell her. "The place had windows so high the sun didn't angle down to the floor."

She nods, but looks tense.

"It was sunny yesterday, remember?"

Again she nods, but her gesture's stiff. Still, her eyes tell me she wants me to finish.

"Our team situated themselves on the roof, waited until the sun was directly above, then dropped angled mirrors in front of the windows to flood the floor with light."

"You burned them alive?" She shudders.

"Vampires aren't really alive."

"Yes they… How do you know they aren't alive? From myths? Books? Stories?"

I look at her quizzically. "Everyone knows vampires aren't alive."

"But *do* they know it?" She crosses the room then plops down on my sofa.

I cringe, seeing I left a dirty pair of sweat socks sitting in front of it last night. I toss them in the general direction of my laundry hamper before I sit down beside her.

"Why would you think that they're alive?" I ask. "I mean, now that you've got me thinking about it, it's one of those things that no one ever *can* know, I guess. Not for sure."

She takes a long breath. "But what if you *could* know? That's my point. People used to think that vampires didn't even exist," she says. "That they were a myth. Now we know that they're real. Maybe with a little more understanding, more cooperation between species, instead of all the killing, you could get answers to some of these questions."

I scratch my head.

"Do you guys even consider maybe *talking* to a vampire before you stake them? What if you reversed your policy to stake first and ask questions later?"

I laugh at her joke. "That's *way* too dangerous. Besides, if we don't strike before they see us, they run. They're super fast. They wouldn't stick around to talk."

"Maybe because they know you're about to kill them!"

I shrug.

"What if I told you I've talked to vampires," she says softly, "and they're not what you think."

"Then I'd tell you you're crazy."

"Am I?" She turns toward me, bending one leg up on the sofa. "Am I crazy?"

I tip my head to the side. We're talking in hypotheticals, but she's taking it so seriously. "No, you're not crazy."

She sits quietly for a moment, her eyes facing down so I can't tell what she's thinking. I wish I could figure out her mood, I wish I had more experience with women, like my partner Sanjay does, or some of the other guys at work. But then again, if I were more like them, I'd be bragging in the locker room about the filthy things I'd done to women's bodies.

"You said the police have killed hundreds in just the past few days," she says, breaking the awkward silence.

I nod.

"And was that unusual?"

"Yeah. A real high number for a couple of days, but like I said, I'd guess there've been a thousand, easily, in the past few years."

"And do you think you're making a dent? Do you think you're getting close to killing them all?"

I shake my head. "That's the thing, Selina. I know you're questioning our methods, but the vampire problem is *huge*. These monsters walk the night amongst us. They could number in the *hundreds* of thousands!"

"You call them monsters," she says, "but how many vampire-related killings did you say there have been, ones not involving this one specific serial killer?"

"Very few." I chew my bottom lip, suddenly uncomfortable.

"So, if vampires need blood to survive, and they always kill their victims, why don't the police find bodies scattered all over the city every morning?"

"They dispose of the bodies."

"Where? How? How do they get rid of all of these dead bodies without being noticed? Why is this serial killer the first vampire you guys have ever caught in the act?"

"It's not. I don't think..." My head is starting to hurt. "Want some tea?" I stand. "A glass of water? A beer?"

"Water is fine." She leans forward, hands on her knees as I move to the kitchen area and fill two glasses with tap water.

When I return, she's shifted to sit sideways on the sofa, arm across the back and both legs tucked up underneath her.

"Thanks," she says, taking the glass.

"Do you want me to show you the video?"

She shakes her head. "That's okay. I don't need to see it. I think that might be enough vampire talk for me tonight."

I sit next to her bent knees and her arm extends along the sofa cushion behind my shoulders. There's no contact, but the quarter inch gaps of air—between her arm and my back, between her knee and my thigh—feel on fire.

She may be softhearted when it comes to vampires, but other than that, Selina is perfect. She's everything I've ever wanted, ever needed, without even knowing what it was.

Even her liberal stance toward vampires makes her endearing. She'll make such a great mother—so compassionate, so loving. She's beyond appealing. Even learning more about the negatives, my love for her has only grown.

"What do you want to talk about instead?" I ask, my voice unexpectedly deep.

"Why don't we talk about you?" She smiles.

"Me?"

"Yeah. You told me about your sister. Shelly, right?"

"You remembered."

"Of course I did." Her fingers drop to my back and lightly stroke just below my neck.

In response, my dick pounds, and I shift, hoping she doesn't notice the rising bulge.

"What about your parents? Are they still in Ajax?" she asks.

"You remembered that, too." A grin warms me from inside. "But no. My dad…" I look down and realize my fists are clenched. Unfurling one, I reach for her hand, and move it off her knee and into mine.

"My dad was abusive. Just like your stepdad."

Her eyes open wide. "He touched your sister?"

I shake my head. "No. I don't think so. I hope not." Bile rises in my throat. "But he beat my mom."

"Oh." Her fingers stroke across my shoulders, lighting so many fires. "I'm so sorry."

"The first time he hit me, I was seven. The three of us, Mom, Shelly and I, we moved to a shelter the next day, and I never saw my father again."

"Your mom was brave to get away from him. To protect you."

"She was a saint."

"Was?" Concern fills Selina's eyes.

I blink back tears I haven't allowed myself since my sister's funeral. "Cancer. It'll be ten years on August 18th."

"Oh, I'm so sorry." She rises onto her knees and hugs me.

After the initial moment of joyous amazement, I carefully put my arms around her small body and hold her. I'm overwhelmed by loss, the memories of those two women swirling inside me, along with my excitement over this woman that I've found. I'm overwhelmed by the possibilities, by thoughts of the future…

Her body shifts under my arms and she straddles my lap, one knee on either side of me, pressing into my thighs and hips and…and…

Oh! Her body brushes against my hardness. I can't take it.

I lift her away from me and place her lower on my thighs.

Leaving her hands on my shoulders, she smiles, softly. "You okay?"

"Yes. I'm so sorry."

"Sorry for what?"

I glance down involuntarily, then snap my eyes back up, not sure whether or not I even *want* her to get my meaning. If she didn't already notice, it's better not to draw attention.

"You're so different," she murmurs. "Different from any man I've ever met."

"I am?" I shake my head. "No one's more ordinary than me. I'm the dictionary definition of boring."

"Hardly." She licks her lower lip, and my dick tries to push through my jeans. "You're not boring at all."

My hands at her waist, her hands on my shoulders and her legs over mine, I'm painfully aroused and finding it harder and harder to concentrate, to breathe.

"You're kind, plus you're brave," she says, one of her hands moving up from my shoulder to cup my face. "But under all that kindness, you're willing to kill when you think it's right." Her eyes flutter shut for a moment. "You're masculine and confident, and yet…"

"And yet what?" My back stiffens.

"And yet you haven't made a move on me. Haven't even tried to kiss me."

"Oh." My palms tingle where they rest, my thumbs

rising up over her ribs. One small movement and my thumbs could be stroking her breasts. Is that what she wants? How do I tell?

She leans forward and kisses me right on the lips. Her kiss is soft, and my breath shudders as I exhale into her. Her hand slides around to the back of my head and she kisses me more deeply—as deeply as I've kissed any woman—but it's nothing like any other kiss that's gone before it.

Selina's kiss is sweet and dangerous, scalding and comforting, powerful and soft. Her kiss is her—it's pure Selina—full of contradictions and intoxicatingly irresistible. I never want it to end.

Her tongue slides between my lips and she invites me into her mouth. Our tongues slide and intertwine performing an exotic dance so intricate and perfect that I can't imagine how or when my tongue learned the steps.

Her hand accidentally lands over the bulge in my pants—it must be an accident.

It doesn't feel accidental.

Gasping, I break the kiss. "What are you doing?"

"What do you think I'm doing?" She rubs the length of me through the fabric and a moan rumbles up from deep in my chest.

I move her hand off me so I can breathe. So I won't embarrass us both.

"Selina."

"Colton." She says my name like it's a delicious treat. I want her hand on me again, yet I know that I shouldn't.

"Before anything else happens," I say, trying without success to catch my breath. "You should know something about me."

"What?" Her fingers massage the place where my hair

meets my neck and even that touch threatens to cause an ejaculation. It's like I'm twelve years old again, hiding in a boy's room stall every time Allie or Farzana, or any girl for that matter, looked my way.

I put my hand over her other hand to stop its creeping back toward my hard package. "I don't have much experience—with girls—with women."

"That's okay." Her hand is dangerously close to my bulge again.

"I've never…" I clear my throat. "Selina, I'm a virgin."

Surprise flashes in her eyes, followed by what might be acceptance or understanding, but I no longer trust my ability to read this woman. Even to the extent I *could* read her, at this point all the blood in my body has migrated south, and I'm not capable of higher reasoning anywhere above the belt.

She pulls her hand back from my stiffness, and I relax, trying to breathe more normally, and convince my erection to stand down. Or at least not erupt.

"How come?" She slides off me to the side. "Religious reasons?"

"Not really."

"You know, I was a virgin until recently too."

Relief floods through me. "So your stepfather never—"

"Oh, he did." Hate flashes in her eyes. "But I don't count that." Her eyelids close for a moment, her lashes kissing the tops of her cheeks.

Selina smells so delicious, like vanilla and rainbows, and I want her back on my lap, I want to kiss her again, I want to touch her, everywhere, and I want her to touch me, too.

"I guess everyone has their own definition of virginity," she says softly.

But do they? I nod, like I understand, though.

"I don't count the times men used me without my permission," she says coldly.

My heart cracks. "Men? There were…more than *one*?" How much has she suffered? My arms itch to gather her back into my arms, to never let her go, to make sure no one else ever touches her again. No one but me.

Gaze to the side, she nods, then turns back toward me. "Does it bother you? That several men have—"

I shake my head.

"But as long as we're putting our cards on the table," she says. "You should know a few other things about me."

"Okay." I smile. There's nothing she could say that would change how I feel about her, how badly I want her, now and forever.

"Gray was my first," she says. "My first time having consensual sex."

My chest tightens, but I nod. "So it's Gray that you love, not Rock."

She bites her lower lip. "That part is complicated." Her fingers trace the sides of my face, as if she's memorizing the angles and textures, then one of her hands slides into my hair, stroking my scalp, playing with the curls that sprouted since my last haircut.

"My life is complicated," she says. "I care for Rock and Gray. Both of them. A lot."

"I've noticed."

"Is that okay with you?"

"Yes," I say without thinking. I need to explain my answer to her—and to myself. "I mean, it's not *ideal.*

Would I prefer it your life was—less complicated? If I didn't have any competition? Yes…yes I would."

"Don't think of them as competition." She slides back onto my lap. "It isn't like that. It's just that—"

"You're not ready to commit." I finish her thought. "That's okay. I can wait." I can wait as long as it takes for Selina to be mine—only mine. If I try to rush her, or force her to leave the others, I'll push her away.

"That's not it." Her hand slides down my neck and onto my chest and my erection pounds like a prisoner on meth trying to break his handcuffs. "I *am* ready to commit."

I play with her hair, so soft and shiny. "But you haven't found the right man." Not until now, I hope.

She closes her eyes for a moment, as if considering her answer. Then her eyes open slowly, but she keeps her gaze pointed down. "That's the thing, Colton. I think that I have."

A ferocious joy rushes through me, and I take her hand off my chest and kiss each finger in turn, then I move my lips to her wrist, pressing a wet kiss against her pounding pulse.

She sighs. "Colton."

I look up into her eyes.

"I think I should go. I told Rock I'd help close up the bar."

"Are you sure? I mean. If you like…" I close my eyes. "If you want to go further… I mean, I won't stop things again." My throat is tight.

She rises up to her knees and kisses me softly, and I slide my hands onto her waist, hoping to coax her against me again.

"I think we should wait," she says softly. "Your first

time should be special. When there are no obstacles between us."

"Obstacles?" I nod. "Yes. I get it." She wants to break up with Rock and Gray first. She wants us to take our time and do this right.

And that's what I want too. I'll do whatever it takes to win Selina's heart.

CHAPTER 30

Selina

Colton and I walk back toward the bar in silence. My mouth is dry and I don't know what I'd say even if I thought my throat or tongue or lips were capable of forming those pesky word things at the moment.

I can't believe I just did that, that I kissed Colton—kissed a human. If he hadn't stopped me, I would have had *sex* with a human. Not only a human, a cop.

I wanted him—still want him so badly. But taking that step with Colton would be wrong—wrong for so many reasons. And the one I used as an excuse—his virginity—isn't the main one.

As much as my body was urging me to go forward, it wouldn't be right to have sex with him before he knows the truth, but there's the rub—if he figures out the truth he'll try to kill me.

And what scares me the most, is that if he tried to

stake me, my instincts might take over, and with my superior speed and power I might accidentally kill him instead.

We pass by a man leaning against a wall and smoking a joint. Colton's hand lands protectively on my lower back, then he drops it off me once we're past the man.

The power of my desire tonight took me by surprise. There's always been a spark between me and Colton. I find him enormously attractive and liked him from the start, but I'm shocked at how quickly my feelings grew into something more, especially given his intense bigotry against vampires.

Colton's bigotry isn't his fault, and it doesn't define his character. Given all the misinformation he's been fed about vampires, combined with what happened to his sister, I get why it's there, but once he learns the truth, I feel sure his hatred will vanish.

His phone beeps. He pulls it out, then stops dead in his tracks to read a message.

"What's going on?"

"I'm so sorry. I've got to go. Work." In spite of his apology, obvious excitement invades his body. He can't stand still. His hand moves to my back again and urges me forward. "I've got to get you back to the bar quickly. She's been spotted again."

"Who? Z—" I stop myself. "The killer?"

He nods. "Yes. We've been running face recognition software on feeds from surveillance cams all over town."

"Is that legal?"

"It is when we've got a positive ID on a bloodsucker."

My heart pounds like it wants to escape my chest. "Where is she?"

I don't know why I'm asking. Do I want to warn her?

Save her? Do I want to call Astrid so she can get there first and arrest her?

If I believe that Colton could change his mind about vampires, isn't it possible that Zora could change her mind about killing humans? Does she need to die?

"Downtown," he says. "Entertainment District."

I stop and touch his hand. "That's the other direction. You should go. I'm fine from here. The bar is just around the corner." In fact, I'm standing at the end of the alley where I first met Rock.

"You sure?" Colton rubs his hair, a sure tell that he's conflicted.

"I'm positive." I smile up at him. "Go. I'll be fine."

He bends, kisses me softly, and I clasp my hands behind my back to keep myself from turning the kiss into something more. Not only do I want Colton, sexually, I'm hungry for his blood, and as we kiss a thirst builds inside me that's hard to contain.

He backs away from me for several steps, and then turns and heads off at a run.

"Hello, my pet." A voice comes from behind me.

I spin around.

Zora is standing in the shadow of a tree across the street. In an instant she's beside me.

"Why are you here?" I ask her. If the police are all headed to the Entertainment District, they're too late. I hope no innocents die because of it.

"I am here for you, my pet," she responds. "I followed you here the other night when that vampire interrupted us. I took the chance I'd find you here again."

My heart races as I fight the urge to dive into her arms, to dig my fangs into her vein.

"Why didn't you kill that human?" she asks. "He's a cop, the worst kind."

"Because I'm not a murderer," I tell her.

"Well, you should have at least taken his blood. I can tell that you're hungry." She cups my cheek tenderly and looks into my eyes. Her fingers stroke over my throat, massaging my vein.

"I'm fine," I tell her.

But I'm not fine. She's right. I wanted Colton's blood while we were kissing, and after, but didn't realize the ferocity of my hunger until Zora mentioned it. And now I want *her* vein, although it would be an even bigger mistake than feeding from Colton. At least I could make Colton forget, and I certainly don't need to increase the connection I feel to my Maker.

Using every ounce of willpower inside me, I pull myself away from Zora and head into the alley. Ravenous and turned on after my time with Colton, her caress ignited so many confusing sensations inside me.

"Humans hunt us like prey," she calls after me as she follows. "They kill us without reason or mercy. It's not murder when we kill them—it's self-defense. Evolution. Survival of the fittest."

I turn back when I'm nearing the door. "You're wrong." Her reasoning is the mirror image of Colton's, though.

"Humans aren't as evolved as we are, my pet." She puts one hand on her hip. "Their ignorance is rooted in evil and causes nothing but pain."

"That's not true. Not all humans are evil." But I think back to my abusive stepfather, my mother who did nothing to stop him, the many predators I encountered while living on the streets...

Excluding my time in Xavier's court, my experiences with vampires have been a million times better than those with humans.

"Name one human who's been good to you," she taunts as if reading my mind.

I frown. "Humans and vampires lived together in harmony for millennia," I respond. "And we can again." I need both Colton and Zora to see that.

He can help the police and then other humans to understand. Together we can stop all the killing. I reach for the back door to O'Malley's.

Zora leaps in front of me, blocking my path. "You have so much to learn, my pet."

"I'm not your pet."

"You're my Progeny, my daughter." She pulls me into a tight embrace, then whispers in my ear, "And now that I've found you, I will never leave you." Her tongue laps over the vein in my neck. "I have so much to teach you."

I want to pull back, but find myself holding her as tightly as she's holding me. Her blood smells and sounds so comforting, so delicious, and I realize that she's right. It's been too long since I've fed.

She pulls back her hair to expose her throat. "Take what you need, my pet. What I have is yours." She licks my neck. "We will feed from each other and grow stronger."

I lick my fangs, fighting the impulse to dig them into her vein. I've never wanted anything so badly and yet I know it would be a mistake. I remember what happened when I fed from Gray, how passionate and carried away I became although I'd just met him. And Zora's my Maker. Surely drinking her blood will be even more intoxicating. And powerful. I think back to the things Gray told me.

Someone whistles at us. I spot a few laughing young men at the end of the alley, and realize I was rubbing against Zora's body. We must look like a couple badly in need of a room.

"Take my vein," she purrs. "Do it."

A growl interrupts us, and she's torn away from my hold.

I want to attack whoever or whatever took her from me, but I'm breathless, weak from hunger and lust, and high on the promise of her vein.

And then I see that her attacker was Pike.

He holds Zora by her throat, her back against the brick wall. The fierceness in his eyes is something I've witnessed before, many times. But this time, as much as it scares me, it excites me too. He's so powerful, so determined, so sexy.

I shake my head at that final thought.

Zora looks terrified. And she can't breathe.

"You're going to kill her," I tell Pike.

He turns toward me. "Is that good or bad?"

Looking into his amber eyes, fierce with power, I don't know how to answer. *Both* is the answer in my mind. She needs to die so the killings will stop, but I don't want her dead.

"Let her go," I tell him.

Pike drops Zora, and she vanishes into the night.

I slump against the wall, panting, weaker than I've felt since I was human.

CHAPTER 31

Selina

"Why did you let her live?" Pike asks me.

He's standing against the dumpster where Rock and I left my meal container the night we met. The night Pike let me—helped me—escape. Reflected light from the street bounces off his leather-clad body, highlighting the intense masculine beauty of his shape. His thick thighs and biceps, his broad chest and tapered torso—and the obvious bulge between his legs.

"She's my Maker," I whisper. "And killing another vampire is murder."

He nods as if that's enough explanation, at least for him, and I'm glad that there's at least one person in my life who's not arguing with me tonight, who's agreeable and supports my decisions.

Who would ever have believed that person would be Pike?

I take a step toward him, but my legs give out.

In a flash, his arms are around me, the only thing keeping me from hitting the pavement. "You need to feed."

I nod.

He leads me to the far side of the dumpster, away from sight of anyone passing by the end of the alley. "I'll find someone."

I shake my head. "I don't want some random human. I want you."

His eyes open wider as he shakes his head. So much for him agreeing with me.

"Please," I reach out and grab hold of the front of his open jacket. "I need vampire blood. I need you." I can't believe I'm saying this, but I clearly let my thirst for vampire blood build too long, and the unsatisfied sexual tension between me and Colton tonight, and then nearly taking Zora's vein, have left me drained, desperate.

His heart rate triples, and my senses are overtaken by the force generated by his heart muscles. Each thundering beat of his powerful pumping organ pushes what sounds like gallons of thick, hot liquid coursing through his equally powerful body, and its scent and sound is so enticing I can already taste it. I want it. I want it more than I can bear.

An equally strong need is also building between my legs, and my hips pulse slowly, my inner muscles contracting in time with his heartbeat as if that part of me is reaching toward him, begging him too.

One arm around my back to hold me on my feet, Pike's other hand rests on the front of my shoulder to keep me at bay. If not for that, I'd be pressed up against him already. Holding him. Taking from him what I need.

"I'll get Gray," he says roughly.

I shake my head. "Gray won't let me feed." My hips continue to pulse and I lick my lips, my teeth. I feel crazed, my mind, my body out of my control.

"Why?" He tips his head to the side and frowns.

"Gray's refused to feed me. Multiple times. And I need this. Now."

Pike props me up against the dumpster and then removes his leather jacket. Under it, his simple black shirt is well worn and looks soft, and I'm jealous of the cotton fabric because it's already touching Pike's chest, his abs, his back, his arms.

Panting, unable to move, I wait for him.

He approaches me slowly, tentatively, like a mountain lion might. I'm so weak with need that I'm not sure what to do, but he seems willing to take the lead. He lifts one of my arms and slides it into the sleeve of his jacket, and the heat transferred from his body to mine through the leather, combined with the smell of Pike, overtakes my senses. I close my eyes, barely aware that I'm moaning.

He sheathes my other arm in the jacket, and then I realize he's put it onto me backwards, the back of his jacket covering my chest, the collar over my throat.

Pulling me forward from the dumpster, he turns me, gently, then tugs back my arms.

"What are you doing?"

My arms move farther behind my back. I try to pull them forward, but can't. He's tied the jacket sleeves behind my back, putting me in a quasi straightjacket.

Taking my shoulders, he turns me back toward him, and the lust in his amber eyes heightens the dampness and need between my legs, as the pulsing down there continues. I'm drooling with ferocious wetness between both sets of lips. Both sets of lips want him, *need* him. Now.

"You can feed," he says in a near growl. "But no fucking."

A disappointed cry erupts from my chest, taking us both by surprise. I'm so turned on, but the idea of actually fucking Pike hadn't really crossed my mind until he forbade it. I remember how I felt when I fed from Gray. I should have realized sex would be an issue.

"What makes you think I'd let you fuck me?" I ask, breathless, trying to sound convincing.

He grunts, then lifts me and presses me back against the brick wall at just the right height. Tipping his head to the side, he exposes his throat to me.

My entire body reacts, undulating against him, wanting this so badly that all other thoughts, all awareness of my surroundings, the alley, the whole world—all of it vanishes. All of it's gone except Pike.

I pierce his skin. Immediately his hot, meaty liquid enters my mouth, coming in hard pulses that I need to gulp or I'd choke. I'm unable to keep up, yet unable to get enough. His thigh presses against my belly to prop me up, and I part my legs, sliding down slightly until my hot, wet sex finds his thick, hard thigh.

I thrust my hips as I feed, the seam of my jeans grinding against the leather covering his muscles, but instead of relieving my intense pressure, it magnifies it. The pace of my pumping accelerates and my hips shift to maximize the pleasure on my clit. But it's not enough. It's not nearly enough.

Sensing what I crave, Pike slips his hand, hot and calloused, down the front of my jeans, and I release his vein as he strokes my clit, then slips his fingers through my folds and pushes one finger inside.

Crying out, I come, tightening around his digit, and

his thumb presses into my clit as he pumps his finger inside me, gravity increasing the force as my feet dangle over the pavement and my arms remain bound behind my back.

My orgasm seems to go on forever—each time it subsides, it begins anew. And through it all Pike keeps supporting me, his head resting against the metal beside me, his finger plunging, his thumb strumming and his blood coursing through my body, igniting every cell inside me with its powerful, nourishing fire.

His finger slows, then withdraws, sliding up over my belly and rubbing there a few times before I hear the sound of my fly coming up and I realize I never even noticed it going down.

He slowly lowers me to the ground, but won't make eye contact as he unties the jacket, and I pull it off me.

"Pike."

He turns from me, eyes pointed down.

I reach around toward his massive bulge, but my fingertips barely graze the leather before he grabs my wrist.

"No."

"Why?"

He shakes his head.

"Fuck me. Please, fuck me." I can't believe my own words, but I've never felt so powerful, so energized—or so in need of a hard cock inside me. Not just any hard cock—Pike's. "I need you," I tell him. "Now."

"Go." He backs away from me. "Go find Gray." He races away into the night, gone before I can take another breath.

Disappointment stabs inside me, then passes, replaced by the need to do just as he suggested. I need to find Gray. I need to find Gray this second.

CHAPTER 32

Gray

Selina looks wild when she comes through the back door and into the bar.

I leap out of the booth. "What's going on?"

She grabs me by the neck and kisses me, hard, pushing her tongue into my mouth, and I taste the lingering scent of blood. Not human blood. What the fuck has she done?

"Home. Now." Her eyes are wide, her pupils huge, and her small body rubs against mine as if she thinks friction can dissolve the fabric between us.

I take her head in my hands. "What did you do?"

She shakes her head. "No time. I need to fuck. If you won't, I'll find someone else." Her hand lands over my package and strokes the length of me through my trousers. I almost come.

"We're heading out," I tell Chelle who's staring at us, wide-eyed. As is, I imagine, every other patron in Rock's bar. "Tell Rock we'll see him at home."

The moment I get Selina out the door, we run. Run

faster than I've run in years, almost flying, and it's even more clear to me now that Selina fed from a vampire. She's faster, and newfound power pulses off her in rays, and I've never seen anything so sexy.

"Your room," she says once we're in the foyer.

We both leap up to the second floor, vaulting over the railing there. She heads for my room and I remember I left it unlocked.

"No." I say. "Don't go in there!" I call after her, but it's too late, she's already opening the door.

After what she went through with Xavier, she'll leave me once she sees what's inside.

I chase after her, but she's already torn off her jeans and I forget why I wanted to stop her.

She starts removing my clothes, her hands shaking, so I take over and let her deal with her panties, but the moment my fly's open her hand is around my cock, stroking so hard that it hurts.

Maybe if I fuck her up against the wall she won't notice everything in the room and I can coax her into going somewhere else.

"Who was it, Selina?" I ask her between kisses. "Who fed you?" It must have been a woman or Selina would have already been fucked.

No male vampire I know could have ever resisted her. Or has she already been fucked by whoever fed her? Am I round two?

Jealousy and betrayal flash through me. But I don't own her. In fact, I know she will never be mine, but the idea of her feeding from—not to mention fucking—another vampire raises emotions inside me I didn't think I'd ever feel.

She heads for my bed, then turns back to me, questions and lust swirling in her eyes. There's a reason I haven't let Selina in my room. It's full of my playthings.

Toys I loved using with other women, and based on what she's told me about her time in Xavier's dungeon, some of my playthings might seem familiar—and repulsive.

"Are you okay?" I study her face, but she looks more turned on than traumatized. "These things—"

She steps toward my bed and grabs one of the rubber restraints attached to the post.

"Selina. I'm so sorry." I step up slowly behind her. "After hearing what you've been through, I should have gotten rid of all this."

I haven't felt the desire for kink since I met her, but seeing her in my room, my desire for it returns with a vengeance. And if she's not traumatized by this, maybe it will be a way to turn off my emotions, to make this all about sex.

"Don't be sorry." She looks around the room, taking everything in, and relief floods through me when she doesn't bolt. "I trust you, Gray. You won't hurt me."

I smile as my lust shoots through the roof, then I realize she still hasn't told me who fed her. I tell myself it doesn't matter. Not right now.

Clearly she needed vampire blood, and if she fed from me tonight, I would have fed from her too—I'd never be able to resist it again—and our bond would have deepened, and then my pain, and hers, would be that much worse when I lose her.

She rips off her shirt, literally tears it, and throws the scraps of fabric to the side, then unclasps her bra. My shirt gets a similarly rough treatment from me as she grabs hold of the rubber straps attached to the foot posts of my four-poster bed and bends forward, leaning way back, presenting her ass and her sex to me.

Her pussy is bright red and so wet I can't even imagine the power of her need right now, but if it's as half as strong as mine…

Not even preparing her tight pussy with a finger or a slow shallow start, I grab her hips, bend my legs and force myself balls deep inside her, using one long, hard, punishing thrust.

She cries out, but I don't stop. I grip her hips and drive, using every muscle in my body to impale her with my cock as she holds the straps and lets her weight fall back, gravity pulling her down harder to meet each of my drives.

Selina comes quickly, her insides pulsing around me so hard it's difficult to keep moving against the tightening muscles inside her, but I keep moving anyway, and her climax goes on and on, the longest, strongest orgasm I've ever felt around my dick.

I want to come too, but I hold back, wanting to eke out every last contraction from her body.

Her orgasm slows, and I hold her around the waist, supporting her, expecting her to collapse from all that expended energy, but she straightens and my cock slips out from inside her.

"What's that?" She sees the St. Andrew's cross for flogging, then my fucking bench and she turns toward me wide-eyed. "I know what *that* is."

I want to kiss her, but when I try to pull her into an embrace she crosses the room to the bench and discovers the glass-covered cabinet of sex toys beside it.

She bends forward over the bench, ass in the air.

"You act like you've done this before." I chuckle.

She looks over her shoulder. "Who says I haven't?"

An icy shock enters my veins. "The dungeon."

She nods.

"Selina. We can't. How…" I rub her back as she lies draped forward over the bench, her ass at its apex.

"I want this, Gray. Please. I need to be fucked tonight. Hard. And I know this will help. Please. This is what I need. I'm about to explode."

"You just came."

"Not enough. Not nearly enough. And this… If you take me here. It might erase my bad memories, neuter the power that Xavier once held over me."

Her hips squirm. Her sex glistens.

"Are you sure?"

"Yes," she says forcefully. "Fuck me. Fuck me now. Fuck me as hard as you know how."

I can't imagine whose blood she has coursing through her right now, but it's given her not only more power, but a sexual energy I can barely fathom and can only hope to match.

"Strap me in," she says, while grinding her hips against the bench.

"Are you sure?"

"Do it." The strength in her voice takes me by surprise and I quickly fasten the constraints at her wrists, ankles and waist. She won't be able to move. She'll be completely vulnerable to me. Unable to adjust to or lessen the force of my thrusts.

My cock pounds at the idea, so hard I feel like the skin might burst.

I stroke her back. "You sure you're okay?"

"Fuck me, Gray."

Not needing another invitation, I push inside her again.

Her pussy recovered during the time we talked, and my first thrust is like entering a virgin. She cries out and bucks under me as much as the bench's constraints allow.

After several long, hard drives, I grab the straps at the front of the bench to give me more leverage.

Using every one of my arm and leg and back muscles for power, I pound myself into her, using even more force and speed this time, unable to hear or see or sense anything but the pure pleasure concentrated in my balls and cock.

Then she comes around me, even harder than the last time, crying out, convulsing, shouting my name.

This time I can't hold back. I explode with the hardest orgasm of my life, my seed shooting inside her with the force of a fire hose.

Collapsing over her draped body, I love the feel of her hot damp skin against mine, of her heavy breaths matching mine.

"More, Gray. Please. I need more."

"Princess, I'm going to need a minute."

"Then use one of those." She nods toward the case of goodies.

My imagination soars. She thinks that fucking is the only thing that will satiate her need, but I've got other ideas.

I take a small butt plug out of the case, then push it inside her pussy.

"Oooo." She wiggles her hips. "Too small."

"I'm just getting the plug ready."

"For what?"

I slide it between her ass cheeks.

"Oh!"

Her asshole tightens when I circle it there, but I press the plug's tip, lubed with her juices, against her entrance. "Relax."

Her tight pucker loosens, just slightly, and I ease the butt plug inside.

She moans, and I pump it a few times, loving how her ass cheeks pink, how juices continue to flow from her pussy.

"Shall I try something bigger?" I ask.

She nods, so I grab a much bigger plug, one both longer and thicker, and once again I plunge it inside her pussy for lubrication.

She cries out as soon as it goes inside her, and I once again remember how tight she becomes after recovery time. No wonder Rock refuses to fuck her. It's impossible to imagine his huge rod inside her, now that I've seen a glimpse of him.

I pump the butt plug inside her pussy for a while, then move it to her back entrance. This time she's more relaxed, and it's easier to enter, but the plug is long and widens toward its base and it takes a while before I can get it fully lodged, the base against her pink ass cheeks.

"How's that?" I ask huskily.

"Good," she says. "Different."

I lift a flogger, one like a heavily leaved tree branch, but made of leather, and I stroke it over her ass and back a few times.

"How does that feel?" I ask her.

"Nice."

I bring it down hard against her ass. "And that?"

"Oh!"

I do it again, and relish how her body reacts, how her

skin glows, how her breaths break, how her hips swivel in pleasure as I come down on one cheek, then the other, back and forth, watching her writhe against her tight constraints.

Releasing them, I guide her to her feet.

"Oh, that feels strange." I watch as she adjusts to a standing position with the butt plug inside her. "Do we leave it there?"

I nod, then lead her across the room to a corner I don't think she noticed when we entered.

"What's this?"

I turn her and sit her down on the custom raised chair that positions her sex at just the right height for me, then I fasten a padded belt around her waist to hold her securely at the edge of the seat before bending to fasten cuffs around her wrists, pinning her arms up and to the sides. Finished with that, I kiss her breasts, then put soft cuffs on her thighs and ankles keeping them wide.

"What are you doing?" she asks as I attach clips to the cuffs.

"You'll see." I use pulleys to spread her legs open and up, testing her flexibility until she's completely exposed, her knees back near her chest, and her rosy, wet pussy ripe and ready above the disked end of the butt plug still deep inside her.

Her nipples are hard, and I can't resist taking one into my mouth. She moans as I lightly flick its tip, then suck hard, drawing the bud between my lips with as much force as I long to use to draw blood from her vein.

My cock's throbbing and hard again, but I want more time to recover, so I take a dildo from the case and slowly work it inside her. Once it's fully lodged I pump it a few times and her hips struggle to move against the motion, or with it. It's hard to tell which, but her skin is pink, her eyes glassy, her breaths coming hard and thready so I know without words that she's still enjoying this.

I eye one of the larger dildos, one that's a vibrator, and mentally compare its size to Rock's member. It's not nearly as thick, but maybe this is a safe way to test Selina's limits, see how much she can take once she's stretched out.

I hold it up to show her.

Her eyes open wide, but she nods, so I lube it. I slip out the first dildo and quickly replace it with the head of the thick one. She cries out as it pushes past the tight muscle of her opening, but one quick look into her eyes tells me to keep going, so I press it forward, trying to be gentle, trying to ease it forward slowly. But it's too big. Fuck. And I don't think it's as thick as Rock.

"Force it," she says. "Push it as hard as you can."

"I might hurt you."

"I'll heal."

"I don't want to tear you."

"Do it." The force in her voice takes me by surprise. She's different tonight and it's terrifying, exciting.

I can't look into her eyes as I do as she wants, and slowly, I push it forward an inch, back a half inch, then forward another inch, progressing deeper into her tight space until it can go no further.

"Fuck me with it, Gray. I want to feel that huge thing moving inside me."

I lean over her and take her lips, plunging my tongue inside her mouth relentlessly, as I take the dildo's handle and slam it in and out, her increasing slickness helping my progress now, helping it slide.

She moans against my mouth, her tongue just as active as mine and I sense she may be coming again.

I break the kiss to look into her eyes, but they're closed, her mouth open and panting, her stomach muscles contracting and pulsing as I work the huge dildo. Then her body starts to relax and I take the end of the dildo and start to pull it out.

"No," she says. "Leave it inside."

I push it back where it was, then move my attention to her nipples. Licking and biting and sucking as she moans, and I've never heard such a beautiful sound, never tasted such sweet skin.

I accidentally bump against the dildo, and she gasps.

Reaching down to make sure it's still lodged inside her, I remember the switch to turn it on. Pinching one nipple hard, I kiss her equally hard as I press the on button for the vibrator.

She screams into my mouth, but her kiss intensifies, like she wants to devour my tongue, devour me, and she climaxes again.

I squeeze both of her nipples tight, then tease the tight buds as she writhes within her constraints and rides out her powerful orgasm.

Sliding one of my hands between us, I find her clit, unbelievably swollen and hot, and as I graze it, she bites down on my tongue.

She sucks, swallowing my blood.

I pull back, nursing my bit tongue as it heals. The kiss turned into a mini feeding and her body is wild, absorbing the vibrations of the huge dildo.

Her every muscle taut, her legs strain, testing the limits of the pulley system so hard the entire chair creaks, like the wood might break as she tugs against the cuffs around her wrists.

My cock is solid, raging. Harder than ever.

Jealous of an inanimate object, I wrench out the vibrator, tossing it to the floor, and then thrust myself inside her.

It feels so good to be inside her again, but I can tell that she can barely feel me. After that huge vibrating dildo, my thicker than average knob is no competition.

While kissing her and fucking her slowly, I release her wrists, and her hands fall onto my back, and then she reaches down to my butt. Driven by her squeezing there, I increase my pace. But then I have a better idea.

I pull out.

"Stay inside me, Gray. Please, I need more. I need *you*."

Her words make my heart sing and my cock throb. "Soon, princess, soon."

While I let her pussy recover, tightening far faster than a human woman's ever could, I find some nipple clamps and place them carefully.

"That okay?" I ask.

She nods, so I tighten them a few twists. When she moans, I add one more twist but the tips turn white, so I ease off a bit, then grab the flogger again.

Instead of spanking her, I drag the leather strands over her torso, gently stroking her and watching her body react each time the flogger's branches brush over the nipple clips.

Dragging the flogger lower, I brush it gently back and forth over her pussy and the backs of her exposed thighs.

"Oh, Gray." She sighs and I can see her insides pulse. "I knew you were hiding a part of yourself from me, but I never imagined it was this."

Her grin is delicious, and I avoid looking into her eyes

so she won't see that this bedroom isn't the half of what I've been hiding.

"You like my toys?" I ask, licking my lips.

"Very much."

"Want to join me in here again sometime?" I softly stroke her pussy lips with the flogger while we talk.

"Yes," she says on a sigh. "But next time, I'm in charge."

My cock jumps at that thought, turned on and more than a little nervous about reversing roles. I've never done that before.

"Oh, Gray," she sighs. "I never thought I could feel like this."

"How do you feel, princess?"

"Pleasure. I feel pleasure all over. Everywhere. Inside and out. Pleasure in places I never knew existed. And I feel powerful but boneless at the same time. Hot and cold. Soothed and in pain. I feel in love."

At that, I look up into her eyes.

My chest constricts. I can't take it anymore. Forget about pleasing her, my cock is making demands.

Grabbing the back of the chair for leverage I thrust, driving into her—over and over and over—until I collapse from exhaustion.

CHAPTER 33

Pike

"Holy shit!" my new host says when he sees me in his kitchen. "It's you!"

I brace for a fight, every instinct built up over the past forty years screaming for me to rip out Gray's throat.

I take a deep breath, then shake my head. If Gray didn't want me here, why the fuck give me the code to the front door?

"Fine. I'll go."

"Go? Why?" He takes a couple of crystal goblet type things and a bottle of booze out of a cupboard. "Cognac?"

I shrug, and he puts a few inches in each glass then hands one to me.

He cups the base of his glass, just above the stem and swirls the liquid around, then raises his glass toward me. "Cheers, chap. Welcome to my humble abode."

I take a gulp of the drink. It's smooth and warms all

the way down, leaving a taste in my mouth that's sweet, then smoky, and keeps changing even after I've swallowed.

Gray sets his glass down, and cups it in both palms as he leans against the counter in the middle of his kitchen. "Sorry, about the outburst, mate." He grins at me. "I just realized something when I saw you."

I narrow my eyes. "What?" I take another sip of the drink. It's a tiny bit like bourbon, but not.

He rotates the glass between his palms. "You're the one who fed her."

My body tenses. If he'd fed *my* mate I'd want him dead.

If my mate was Selina, I'd more than *want* him dead—he'd already have a stake through his heart. But he doesn't even seem angry.

He is the one who got to fuck her, after all. She must be upstairs, resting.

"You pissed?" I ask.

"Nah." He straightens to his full height and I realize he might actually be as tall as me. His wiry build and fancy clothes make him seem smaller. To me, anyway. Not a threat. Someone I could easily take down.

Looking at his relaxed posture and friendly expression, I shake my head. When was the last time I looked at a man without sizing up whether or not, or how, I would kill him? Have I ever?

Drafted into that infernal war when I was still a kid, it's hard to remember a time when my reactions to people were in the same ballpark as normal.

I don't belong here.

I set down the glass and the base clatters against the stone counter. "Shit." I steady it to make sure it doesn't break.

But I'm the thing that's broken. Smashed into so many spiked shards that I don't belong anywhere near polite company. And this dude and his fancy pad are the dictionary definition of polite company—whatever comes six levels above polite company.

I head for the exit. I've still got a half hour to find a safe place to crash before dawn.

Gray's hand lands on my shoulder, and I freeze, fighting the instinct to turn and fight.

"Don't go." He squeezes my shoulder then claps me on the back. "Come on. Let's take our brandy into the sitting room.

"Sitting room?" I say with disdain.

He grins. "Yeah. Whatever the fuck you want to call it. This house…" He shakes his head. "Is so not me."

"Bullshit."

"No, seriously." He hands me my drink, then walks through the grand entranceway to the house, and I follow.

"My parents *did* have money," he says, "or more accurately, they came from money, I suppose. Enough so I didn't ever really think about how much they had, or where it came from, but you could say I rebelled against all that."

"Rebelled?" I glance up at the two-story-high entrance with all its wood paneling and marble floors and fancy paintings. Sure as shit doesn't look like rebellion to me.

"Yeah." Gray goes into one of the rooms off the entrance. "I did the whole hippie thing. Ran off to Morocco. You know the drill."

"And yet, here you are." I take in the room, full of expensive furniture and other shit that's so fancy even the legs of the chairs are carved like statues.

He drops into the corner of a couch, crosses one leg

over the other and rests one elbow on the arm. Lifting his glass toward me, he nods. "And yet here I am. Please—" he gestures with the glass "—sit. Make yourself at home."

I grunt. No chance I could ever feel at home here.

"I am grateful," he says, "that it was you who fed Selina—not some stranger."

I take another gulp of the drink and it tastes even better than I remembered. If booze like this is what comes with money, I'm all in. "Why won't you give her your vein?"

"It's complicated." He swirls the booze in his glass.

"Something wrong with your blood?" I ask, because I can't imagine a reason not to feed Selina. I'd give her everything and anything she wanted. I'd rip my heart from my chest if I thought that was what she needed.

"Nothing like that."

"Then what the fuck?"

"I fed her once." He looks down. "I can't. Not again. Trust me, it's a really bad idea. But I'm glad that you did. She needed it."

"No fucking kidding."

Gray chuckles and then takes a sip of his drink. I take a seat on the leather-covered chair that looks least likely to break and take a swig of the booze.

"Have you fed from *her*?" Gray's voice is deeper now, almost menacing, and he stares at me intently as I decide how best to answer.

"No."

"But you have had a taste."

I look down, shame crushing me so hard I'm not sure I can ever move again.

"When?" Gray's voice is hoarse, like he's remembering how she tastes too.

I keep my eyes focused on the pattern of the rug between us, its reds and blues and blacks in repeating swirls. "I didn't feed from her vein. Someone else made her bleed. I took a taste. I couldn't help myself." The memory of her blood, so sweet but filled with power and an exotic flavor I've never before sampled—likely never will again.

"How was it?" Gray asks.

"As if you don't know."

"I don't, mate. I really don't."

Shock lifts my gaze. "Bullshit."

His expression convinces me he's not lying. "Really? How the hell is that possible?" He's fucking her—I've heard them in the act—and I can't imagine the self-control it would take to keep my fangs out of her vein while doing that.

"Why not?" I ask. I don't get this man—*either* of these men she's with. One refuses to give her his cock, even though she's practically begged for it, and the other won't feed from her vein or give her his. It doesn't make any sense.

Gray pushes back the dark hair that flops over his forehead and looks up to the ceiling for a moment. "It just doesn't seem right."

"What doesn't seem right?" Selina asks from behind me.

I leap out of the chair and turn. She's leaning against the oak-trimmed entrance to the room, wearing a dark red silk robe that's way too long for her and I realize it must belong to Gray.

Jealousy rises inside me. But it's not like she's mine, and even if she were, Selina is a woman worth sharing. I'd share her with three-hundred-and-sixty-four other men if it meant I got her one night a year.

Her skin is flushed and glowing, and I can still sense my blood inside her, part of me mingling with her as it pumps through her body. My cock goes hard, thinking back to the feeding, thinking of how our blood has been joined, even if our bodies have not.

"Pike." My name on her lips is like opera. "I'm glad that you came."

I nod, unable to take my tongue off the desert-dry roof of my mouth.

"How are you feeling, princess?" Gray asks her. "Not too *constrained*, I hope?"

She looks down for a second as if embarrassed. "I feel great. Thank you for tonight. Both of you." She floats into the room. At least, it seems like she's floating to me.

Selina moves quietly and smoothly, and the red silk flows around her, brushing the floor and carpet, and hiding her legs and feet.

She stops and looks from one of us to the other as if trying to decide where to go. I drop back into the leather chair opposite Gray.

She crosses the rug and chooses a velvet chair at the end of the seating area between us. Sinking into the soft cushions, she pulls her legs up to sit cross-legged under the robe.

Selina's sexy as fuck. I can't quite put my finger on why I'm so drawn to her, but the way her lavender hair falls over that red silk makes it look like one is caressing the other and my palms itch, wanting to get in on the action.

"What are you guys talking about?" she asks.

"Your beauty," Gray answers without missing a beat. "And how we both live to fulfill your every need."

"Well, you get full marks for that tonight. Both of you." Blushing, she looks from me to Gray, and he looks like he might pounce on top of her for another round of fucking. The look between them is so intense I feel like a Peeping Tom. I start to stand but then she turns in my direction again.

Her soft smile makes my heart leap and my dick pound. I don't deserve attention from this tiny, perfect creature. Shit. I don't deserve any of this.

"I feel so grateful right now," she says. "I don't know what I've done to deserve this."

I gasp.

"What's wrong?" she asks.

"Nothing." I shake my head. "Just had the same thought."

But *she* said it symbolically, to show her gratitude. When *I* think it it's literal and true. I do not deserve to be here. Not one bit.

After all I've done, the only thing I deserve is hell, and instead I'm sitting in this posh house, not eight feet from the woman I most desire and across from a generous vampire I've genuinely started to like.

"Thank you," I say to Gray.

He raises his glass toward me. Then turns toward Selina. "Princess, fancy a glass of cognac?"

"Sure."

They both rise, but she holds up a hand. "I'll get it." She goes through some secret back way I hadn't noticed, and we both watch until she rounds a corner out of our eyesight.

"I mean it, man," I say to Gray, then take another sip of the cognac. "I owe you—big-time."

"It's just a cot in the basement."

"Not just that." I look back down to the rug. "You trusted me when I had Selina. You didn't try to kill me after I let her go. You invited me to stay here. And you didn't kill me when you found out I'd fed your mate."

"I'm not his mate," Selina says as she steps back into the room carrying a glass of cognac and the bottle. "Gray keeps reminding me of that." She holds her glass of cognac toward him before returning to her chair, this time folding her legs underneath her.

"What is...the situation, then?" I look at her as I ask this. Her answer is the only one that matters.

And she seems to be looking for it inside the cognac. She takes a sip then rests the base of the glass on her knee.

"I feel like Rock should be here for this conversation," she says.

"He's sleeping," Gray says. "Humans need way too much of that shit."

"Rock is human?" I ask.

"He's not sure," Selina answers. "He thinks he's part giant and part human, but he never knew his people."

I nod. Part giant makes some sense, even though I never knew such creatures existed.

A soft smile graces Selina's lips as she draws a long breath. "I love Rock," she says. "And he loves me. I don't think he'd mind me telling you that." Her expression is soft and contented.

She takes another sip of the cognac and her cheeks bloom with a fresh flush. "But he doesn't feel the need for us to be exclusive."

She turns toward Gray. "As for *this* one..." She turns back to me. "Gray and I are still figuring out where we stand. But there's something between us. At least, from my side." She looks down to her glass.

"For me too, princess," Gray says. "There's something there for me too."

"And the cop?" I ask.

Selina sighs as she shrugs. "I enjoy being around Colton. He makes me feel special. He reminds me of what it felt like to be human." She shakes her head. "But it will never work."

"And what about our latest houseguest?" Gray leans forward and winks at me.

"Don't answer," I say quickly. "Please."

Tonight has been near perfect, the best five or six hours I've had since the 1960s, maybe ever, and I can't face hearing her rejection.

Her desire for me earlier in the night was a side effect of the feeding and meant nothing. Even if she's hiding her hatred and fear right now—her utter revulsion for me—I know they're there.

"Pike." Uncurling her legs from beneath her, she stands and crosses the few feet that separate us, then sits on the thick arm of my leather chair, her legs dangling over one of mine. I nearly come from the contact of her calf against mine.

"Look at me," she says.

My vertebrae are rusted gears as I force my head to turn her way. Then I look up into her eyes and nearly melt from the compassion and affection I imagine seeing there.

"I realize the truth now," she says softly. "I know that you freed me from Xavier. I know you did what you could to protect me while I was down there." She reaches out and puts her soft palm against my scarred cheek. "Stop shaking your head."

I didn't realize that I was. "You're wrong. I didn't do enough. I let things happen to you. Bad things. So many, and I'm sorry. So sorry." My voice sounds like I'm choking. Thank God I'm not human, or tears would be pouring down my face.

"It's okay, Pike." She caresses my cheek. "I forgive you."

I look down, unable to bear the tenderness in her eyes. I can't quite believe that she could ever forgive me. I don't deserve it. And it's not enough. It will never be enough because, even in a million years, I could never begin to forgive myself.

CHAPTER 34

Selina

Lying on my back on the floor of Gray's basement gym, I fight to recover. The three men I live with might care about me, they might want to keep me safe, but they sure don't hold back when it comes to my combat training.

Tonight it was three against one, with me being the one. The fact that I survived makes me feel like I could take on Xavier and his remaining Guard if he ever dares take me again.

"Holy shit, princess." Gray rolls over on the mat and strokes my leg. "You really gave us a run for our money tonight."

I put my hand over his. "I was just thinking the same thing."

"At least you guys have healing powers." Rock steps into my view, stretching his neck toward his shoulder and wincing.

"You okay?" I reach up toward him.

He grabs my hand and pulls me to my feet, and I lean into his hard, sweat-soaked body. "Better now." Rock's arms encircle me, and his hearts pound their rhythmic music through my body.

I lift my head off his chest to see Pike sitting against the wall, elbows on his spread knees and head in his hands. I let go of Rock.

"You okay?" I step toward Pike. He doesn't answer and I lay my hand on his shoulder.

He jumps, startled, but then seeing me he smiles. "Me? Sure."

"Good." I sit down beside him and lean against the wall. "I've gotten so much stronger since I had your blood."

I can't believe he's been living here for a week. Already it seems to me like Pike belongs with us, but he's quiet, still sleeps in the basement and keeps his distance from Rock and Gray. Keeps his distance from me too.

Sitting next to him now, taking in the scent of him after our work out, I want his blood again. And I want so much more than his blood.

His heart is pumping quickly and it can't still be from the workout, and where they used to repulse me, now his scars urge me to soothe them, to stroke their intricate patterns and salve the pain they symbolize. The pain of his past. The pain he still seems to feel now.

I want to reach out to touch Pike, but fear that if I do he'll bolt like a skittish animal.

Pike's clearly attracted to me, and even more clearly he wants to protect me, but something strong is holding him back. It could be my other two—possibly three—boyfriends, but I sense it's something bigger, something much more important that's weighing on Pike's heart.

"You're getting very strong," he says, and the words sound like they hurt coming out.

"And that's at least partially thanks to you." I smile, hoping he'll see how much I appreciate him.

He looks away. "I should have fed you when you were a prisoner."

"You tried, remember?"

He draws a sharp breath through his nostrils. "Not hard enough. Should have tried sooner. More often." He shakes his head and puts it back in his hands.

I lay my hand on his thigh, but he stands and walks toward the others in the middle of the room.

Moving to join them, I'm surprised that all my aches and pains from the fighting have subsided. Just a week ago, it took nearly a half hour to recover from a rigorous training session. Now it takes less than five minutes.

Gray is still massaging his side like he's not quite there yet, and I marvel that I could be getting as strong as Grayson. My men have made me stronger. Rock's love, Gray's and Pike's blood. I want to return the favor, but Gray holds me away anytime his fangs get near my throat.

"Astrid still wants to talk to you," Rock says to Pike.

"Nothing to tell her," Pike says gruffly.

"So you say." Rock shakes his head.

Pike squares his stance in front of Rock. "You think I don't want him dead?"

I slide between the two males. "We all want Xavier to pay for what he's done. We all want to free the vampires and blood slaves still trapped in his court. We're all doing everything we can."

"Again," Gray says. "Not a court. Stop calling it that. Stop acting like he's royalty. He is not."

"We know," I say. "We know." I smile at him and the frustrated expression on his face turns to a smile.

He knows he can get obsessive about this subject, but if I have trouble not using the terms of royalty when referring to Xavier, it must be impossible not to for Pike. He was with Xavier for decades, not months.

"I for one," Rock says, "won't be able to sleep until I know that threat to you is gone."

"Seems to me you sleep well enough," Gray says to Rock.

The three of us have shared a bed most nights this week, and nothing makes me happier than waking up sandwiched between them.

"You know what I mean," Rock says gruffly. "I want Selina to feel safe."

Gray claps the giant's arm. "We all do."

But even after Xavier's dead, there's another threat I face. I'm reluctant to bring up Zora though. It's not like they don't know she exists but I've only discussed the connection I feel to her with Pike, and even then, I didn't tell him everything.

No one knows how I've dreamed about some of her murders. How so many of the crime scenes were familiar to me, and how much I want to be with her whenever she's near. Even when she's not.

I haven't seen Zora in over a week. Colton says the police can't find her, and there's a deep longing inside me that I fear only she can fill.

I don't want to talk about it. I don't want them to worry and definitely don't want them to curtail my independence. But even with those excuses, deep down I fear my reluctance to discuss my Maker is really out of some misguided loyalty to Zora.

But if I expect Gray to open up to me, or Pike and Rock to share their pain, then it's time I set an example. Maybe they can help me better understand my feelings towards Zora.

"Listen, guys. I've got something I want to talk about."

They all draw in close.

"Is it Rock's snoring?" Gray asks. "Because that's been bothering me too."

I give him a gentle hip check.

"I don't snore," Rock says.

"If you say so, big man." Gray rolls his eyes.

"If you have a complaint," Rock says, "sleep in your own fucking room."

"I'm serious," I interject. "This is important."

"We're all ears, princess," Gray says. "Shall we retire to the sitting room?"

"No, this is fine." I drop down to sit cross-legged on the floor and the three men follow suit, although of the three, only Gray has the flexibility to fully mimic my position. Pike and Rock get comfortable as we sit in a quasi circle on the floor.

"What's up, buttercup?" Gray asks.

"Finally," Rock says. "A nickname besides, princess."

"You're one to talk, *Acushla*."

I shake my head. As much as I'm worried about Pike's long silences, at the moment that's suiting me better than Gray and Rock's banter.

"It's about Zora," I say.

"Your Maker?" Pike blurts.

"What?" Gray shouts. "You know who your Maker is? What the hell, princess? Why didn't you tell me?"

I look into his eyes and see the subtext under his question: *Why did you tell Pike?*

"I'm sorry." I turn to Rock and repeat the apology with my eyes. "I don't know why I haven't told you all more. My Maker's name is Zora and she's the killer."

"What killer?" Rock asks.

"*The* killer. The vampire who's been leaving bodies all over the city. The vampire who left me for dead, who gave me this scar." I lift my hair and turn to make sure they've all seen it.

"That scar's from your Maker?" Rock says. "I just assumed it was another gift from your stepfather." He reaches over, takes my hand and brings it up to his lips. "Oh, Acushla."

"How did you find out?" Gray asks. "And why does she use that symbol?" He's grown paler than normal and his eyes show a hint of panic I don't quite understand.

"She found me, or I found her, I'm not sure." I look down at a seam between the rows of rubber mat flooring in Gray's basement gym. "Remember when I asked you about psychic connections between vampires? Vivid dreams?"

Gray nods.

"Well, I've got some kind of strange connection to Zora. I've dreamed some of her murders. Maybe all of them since I escaped from Xavier and met all of you."

"Since you drank my blood," Gray adds, his voice full of awe.

"Maybe that *is* what triggered it." I think back.

Did I have any dreams about Zora before? Maybe vague ones. Dreams I assumed were just flashbacks to the night I killed Lark. Guilt dreams. But maybe they *were* about Zora. Maybe if I'd realized sooner I could have stopped several murders.

Great. More reasons for guilt.

I draw a deep breath. "I'm not sure when my dreams started, but I didn't begin to understand what was going on until Colton told me that the latest murder happened in a cemetery."

"Colton knows about this?" Gray leans back.

"No. Well, yes. But no. Not really." I swallow hard. Clearly Gray's hurt that I haven't discussed this with him sooner. I certainly don't want to add that I've discussed some of it with Astrid.

But seriously, Gray's one to talk. Every day it's clearer to me that he's hiding something, so to accuse *me* of that... I shake my head. I don't want to get off track.

"That last bad dream I had, it was about the murder in the cemetery. It was so real. Like I was there. Like it was me, not Zora, killing that woman." I close my eyes for a moment as the memory snakes through me. "And then the next day Colton told me that they'd found a body in a cemetery. All the details matched my dreams."

"When did you tell *this* guy?" Rock asks, pointing to Pike.

"I didn't. Well, not directly."

"I saw her with Zora," Pike says. "Selina was about to feed from Zora's vein. I overheard enough to know that was a bad idea."

"You were still stalking Selina?" Gray asks, his eyes narrowing.

"Fucking lucky I was there," Pike growls.

"Let's stay on topic," Rock adds. "Selina, tell us everything you know."

"There's not much more to tell. Zora's Maker was killed by a young woman, and she's hated humans ever since. She chooses female victims because they remind her of the one who killed her Maker. And she carves the symbol into her victims." I turn toward Gray. "Do you know what it means?"

He nods.

"What?" I lean toward him. "You lied before. You said you didn't know what it was."

He shakes his head. "It's the symbol of an ancient order of vampires. Do you know what it means to Zora?" I've never seen Gray so concerned.

"She said it was on a pendant her Maker wore."

Gray can't hide his reaction.

"What does it mean?" I ask him.

"It means I know who her Maker was," he says. "He was a friend of mine."

"Andreas," I say.

"She told you his name?" Gray looks nauseated. As far as I know, vampires never actually throw up, but he looks like he might.

"Gray—what aren't you telling me?"

He shakes his head. "I'm just thinking about Andreas. We wondered what happened to him."

"We?"

"Mutual friends." He straightens his long legs, then bends one back. "Have you told Astrid about this? That you know who the murderer is?"

I shake my head. "I told her some of it. She knows about the symbol… I should have told her more about Zora, but I know she saw the surveillance video the police have." I look down, ashamed that I'm making excuses. "When I'm around Zora, I feel like I'm part of her and…" I squeeze my eyes shut. "If she's a murderer, and I'm part of her—"

"No, princess." In an instant, Gray's at my side his arm

around me and the other two come closer as well. "It doesn't work like that."

"Then how *does* it work?"

"The pull you feel toward her is normal, but her personality traits, her beliefs, her character…none of that will have passed to you through her blood."

"I never drank her blood, remember?"

"Right." Gray takes a long breath. "That's even better, then. All you were exposed to was her venom when she fed from you."

"So why do I feel so attached?"

"This is uncharted territory." He sits, pulling me down, his arm around me. "You're the only vampire I've heard of who didn't feed to transition."

I look down at my clasped hands. Is it possible I forgot? I've gone over that night so many times that forgetting doesn't seem possible, but at this point nothing should seem impossible.

"Zora needs to die," I say.

"You mean, Astrid needs to arrest her." Gray squeezes my shoulders. "Can you track her? Do you know where she is right now?"

I shake my head. "I only get flashes, usually in dreams. She found me when I was visiting her crime scenes. Astrid knows those locations."

"I'll tell her to keep them under surveillance," Gray says. "If she hasn't already. Sounds like Zora returns to the same areas."

"Good," I say. Although I'm shocked at how the idea of Astrid and her team finding Zora makes me feel. I do want the killings to stop, but at the same time I don't want anything bad to happen to Zora.

"Next time I see her," Pike says, "she's dead."

I reach toward him, but he shifts out of my reach. "Pike, if you me or Gray kills her, it's murder, vampircide."

"I could kill her," Rock says. "It's legal for me."

"No." I squeeze his hand. "I couldn't ask you to do that. Our best hope is for Astrid to find her. Or Colton…"

"The cop?" Gray frowns.

"The police have her description. They're using surveillance cameras. Closing in on her." I shiver.

"You talked to Colton again?" Rock's eyebrows rise. "You have to be careful. You can't trust him."

"I am being careful." I smile at each of the men in turn. "You need to trust me." I stand and head for the stairs, and everyone else follows, except Pike who stays behind.

I asked them to trust me, but when it comes to either Zora or Colton I'm not sure I fully trust myself.

Every time I see Colton I like him more, want more from him, and I've come so close to telling him the truth, even though his hearing it would mean my immediate death.

And Zora… I've never felt such conflict inside myself. As badly as I want her dead, or at least locked up, I still want to please her, to be with her, to love her and have her love me.

CHAPTER 35

Selina

My eyes snap open. I'm out of breath and lying in a pool of sweat.

Where am I?

Rock's bedroom. But my disorientation continues.

I sense sheets beneath me, walls around me. I feel the places where Rock and Gray normally sleep, both spaces empty beside me, but overlaying all that I see trees and the sky filtered through leaves. And ahead of me a young woman is jogging, the florescent strips on the backs of her sneakers bouncing along at an even rhythm.

Zora. She's about to kill again.

My perception is so strange, like a movie is playing on top of my surroundings. I'm able to see my reality beneath the scene playing in my mind, and I feel sure the jogging scene is what Zora's seeing right now, what she's doing.

I've never connected to her like this before outside of my dreams.

Am I conscious? Yes. I think so. And deep inside me I feel Zora's drive to kill. Can I get there in time to stop her?

I dress as I race down the stairs to the foyer.

Gray calls out from the kitchen, "That you, princess?"

"Yes!" I yell back, but don't stop.

Where is she?

Zora follows the woman toward a set of wooden stairs and glances to the side. I catch a glimpse of a sign. Glen Stewart Ravine. East end. Beaches. I'll never get there in time.

I slam the door behind me and run, taking leaping strides that get longer and longer until it feels like I'm flying, taking entire city blocks at a time. I'm moving so quickly no pedestrians spot me, no drivers notice when I step off their cars' roofs.

Zora is still stalking her prey, taking her time with it and I can see it in my mind's eye. I've got to get there before she strikes.

I cross the Don Valley in one leap, cross Riverdale Park in two more strides, and bounce over the warehouse lofts north of Leslieville until I'm close. I cross over the houses to the west of the ravine, and then branches scrape my skin as I descend through the trees and land on a bridge above a creek.

I'm between Zora and the woman.

I crossed the entire city in less than a minute. My powers have grown exponentially since I fed from Pike, but all I care about is that I got here in time.

The woman turns toward me, her eyes wide with terror. "Where did you come from?"

"Run!" I tell the young woman. "Run as fast as you can. Call the police. Constable Colton Young. Now!"

She does as I say.

"As if she can outrun me." Zora laughs. "Not even worth the chase. Plenty more where she came from."

I kick a rung on the bridge railing. It splinters and I tear off a piece. It's not exactly a wooden stake, but it will have to do.

Zora laughs again, the tone light and musical, so incongruous with her evil intent. "What do you plan to do with that? Kill me?" She steps closer. "Selina. You won't kill me. You can't. I'm your Maker. You love me."

"I *hate* you."

"I am your only family. Your true family. The only one who has, or will ever love you."

Shaking, I raise my stake. I hate Zora. And I know that she's evil, psychotic. Maybe she was even before she transitioned. I was a fool to think I could stop her from killing. She'll never learn.

And yet I can't bring myself to drive this stake through her heart. Has Zora filled the space that learning of my mother's death left in my soul?

If I stall long enough, Colton and his team will arrive, and do the job for me. But even if that jogger has her phone with her, it could take ten minutes, maybe more, before the police arrive.

"Tell me more about *your* Maker." I lower my makeshift stake, but keep a tight grip on it. "What was he like?"

Zora smiles smugly, clearly thinking she's won. "He was the most handsome man on the planet."

"Tell me more." I need to keep her talking, give Colton time to arrive. "Was he local?"

"He had dark brown hair and skin, so beautiful." Her voice turns wistful and her shoulders relax. "When human, he lived in Cameroon and he had the most beautiful accent and speaking voice, deep and rich, a French accent tinged with something softer."

I glance past her, hoping to see signs of the police. It won't be easy for them to approach unnoticed on this ravine trail, probably one reason Zora chose it for her attack.

If she tries to run, I *will* stake her, I'll have to, but I hope the police will take care of that for me. "How long was he a vampire?" I ask.

"For centuries." She lifts her chin like she's proud. Either proud of him or proud of herself for attracting the attention of such an old vampire. "He was Made by one of the Ancients."

I gasp.

"That means something to you?" She steps toward me.

I shake my head. "Just sounds mysterious."

"It made him very powerful. And that's why he was chosen to help guard the king."

My stomach turns. "Xavier?"

"Who?" She tips her head to the side.

"What king?" I ask. The trees rustle above us and for a moment I'm hopeful that someone is coming, but it's only the wind.

"*The* king. The Vampire King." Shaking her head, she looks down.

"The king who disappeared?" I ask.

She looks up, and her face twists in anger. "Our King went for peace talks with the humans." Her eyes narrow. "Our Sovereign Leader and four of his Guard went to the talks, but were never seen again. Humans are evil!"

"That is a terrible story." I shake my head and make a mental note to ask Gray more about this Vampire King. Or maybe Astrid. Gray is clearly keeping things from me.

Both of them have mentioned the King's disappearance, but I know so little. "Why was your maker, Andreas, in Canada if he's from Cameroon?"

"That's confidential." She looks down. "He couldn't even tell *me*, his true love."

"I'm sorry you lost him," I say with sincerity. "And how he was murdered is terrible, but why do *you* need to keep killing? You can drink blood without taking a life."

"Why would I do that?" She steps toward me. "Why just drink, when I can drain life? Join me. Together we can wipe humans from the face of the Earth. No longer the hunted, we'd be the hunters and embrace our true predator nature."

My grip tightens on the stake. I'm not sure I can wait. She needs to be stopped. I need to do this. As hard as it feels, I must kill her, no matter the consequences.

I raise my weapon.

Pike lands on the path behind Zora.

She turns toward him.

"Duck, princess," Gray shouts from somewhere above me.

I flatten myself on the ground as Gray leaps down from the trees and drives a stake through Zora's back, directly, I hope, into her heart.

Lights brighten the path a few hundred feet behind Pike.

He leaps into the air and disappears.

Zora lies unmoving on the path, the stake through her heart, her head turned to the side and her eyes lifeless.

Gray wraps his arms around me as the police swarm in.

CHAPTER 36

Selina

I can't hide my trembling as I watch the police dump Zora into a canvas bag—treating her like garbage—then they close the bag with a rope.

Colton puts his arm around me. "You don't need to watch this."

"I want to." And I do. I'm glad that Zora's dead, but a huge part of me is grieving. Grieving for what I barely ever had and never will again. Family ties. A familial link to someone who loves me.

I step forward, and Colton's arm drops off my shoulders as I watch two of the cops drag the sack holding Zora. It bounces over a rock in the trail, and the thump and crunch turn my stomach. I doubt they'd treat a dead raccoon this badly.

"Ready?" A tall South Asian cop claps Colton on the back, then he looks down at the goggles hanging around Colton's neck. "Want me to take those in?"

"Nah, I've got the case in my pack."

"Okay," the other cop says. "Let's go."

"I'm going to see her home," Colton tells him. "I'm off duty."

The other cop raises his eyebrows a few times and smiles.

"Selina," Colton says. "This is my partner, Sanjay. Sanjay, Selina."

"Nice to meet you." Sanjay shakes my hand, then shoots an obvious wink at Colton as he walks away.

"I can see that you're shaken." Colton takes my hands. "I was so scared when I heard that the witness mentioned my name, and a woman with purple hair…"

"I'm fine. Gray was with me." Gray's leaning against a huge oak tree at the edge of the dirt path, about fifty feet ahead of us.

I'm glad Gray stuck around. I need to talk to him. To thank him and Pike for following me, for doing what I never could have done. For killing Zora.

"Are the police *done* questioning me and Gray?" I watch as all the cops except Colton climb the stairs out of the east end of the ravine, the bag with Zora's body smashing into each wooden step.

"Yup." Colton squeezes my hands.

"I just thought…I just thought there'd be more." They'd barely asked Gray or me a thing. "Don't we have to make official statements?"

"Your friend Gray did a public service," Colton says. "Exterminated a bloodsucker. But…" Colton nods down the trail toward Gray. "Do you think he expects a medal or something?"

"No, I just… Someone was *killed*."

Clearly Gray isn't going to face any consequences for killing Zora, not even questions, and dread flashes through me wondering whether he'll get off so easily in the vampire world. Killing Zora wasn't exactly in self-defense.

I'll certainly stand up for Gray and tell Astrid, or whoever asks, that Gray's life was in danger, but the stake entered her body from the back so it might be hard to make that claim…

I'll say that Zora was about to kill me. Leave Pike out of it. Gray and I need to get our stories straight before seeing Astrid or her team.

"What were you and Gray doing in the ravine?" Colton asks.

"Just out for a walk."

"On this side of the city? There are ravines all over Toronto, you know." He grins.

"We took a stroll on the Boardwalk, then headed up here."

He nods. "Pretty spot, isn't it? Almost like you're in cottage country. Hard to even know there are all those big fancy houses up there and the city all around us."

"Yeah."

"It's dark, though. We should get out of here. Hey!" he calls toward Gray. "My car's up on Balsam. I'll give you two a ride home."

Colton heads toward Gray, but trips over a rock. "Crap. It really is getting dark. I'll lead you guys out so no one gets hurt. These will help." He puts on his goggles.

The world starts to move in slow motion as I realize the implications of what Colton's just done.

Those goggles. They aren't simple night vision goggles that anyone can get, they're specialized devices for spotting vampires.

He glances down the trail toward where Gray is standing.

Gray pushes off the tree.

Colton stops dead in his tracks and his arm reaches back for a stake-shooting crossbow that's strapped to his back.

"No!" I yell.

But it's no use. Colton has already readied his weapon to shoot, and his body blocks my vision of Gray.

Gray can move quickly, but without knowing Colton's goal, will he move quickly enough?

I take a running leap and vault over Colton.

Twisting in the air, I see the hate in Colton's eyes, and his hate turns to shock as the stake leaves his bow and flies toward me.

I'm midair when the sharp point pierces my chest.

The pain is intense.

Did his stake pierce my heart?

I'm not certain, but as I hit the dirt, I don't think about dying, the only thing I can think is: *Colton knows. Colton knows what I am.*

Continue reading Selina's story in BOUND BY HER DESTINY, coming February 2020. Order now.

Join Mara's Reader Group on Facebook.

Follow on Amazon to make sure you don't miss a release.

And/or sign up for Mara's Newsletter

ALSO BY MARA LEIGH

Follow Mara on Amazon: Click here

PARANORMAL, WHY CHOOSE ROMANCE

Bound by her Blood Series

Bound by her Blood

Bound by her Passion

Bound by her Destiny

Bound by her Love

CONTEMPORARY ROMANCE

Bad Stepbrother

Downey Brothers Series

Bad Boy Next Door

Bad Habit

Bad Princess (coming soon)

Best Kind of Bad (coming soon)

SHORT EROTIC READS

Fantasies Unleashed Series

Dirty Business

Surrender

Bedded by Strangers

Humbling the Boss

A NOTE TO READERS

Did you enjoy this book?
If so, you can make a huge difference.

Not only do reader reviews make my day, they help bring books to the attention of other readers. In fact, no marketing tool is more powerful or effective than honest reader reviews.

That said, I'd be very grateful if you could spend a one or two minutes leaving a review on this book's Amazon page. (The review can be as short as you like.)

Believe me—your review matters.

And thank you so much for reading!
xo, Mara

ABOUT THE AUTHOR

Mara Leigh escaped from the corporate world and now hangs out in coffee shops, letting her imagination run wild. After living in various cities including Edinburgh, San Francisco and Philadelphia, Mara and her exorbitant shoe collection have settled in Toronto where she writes sexy, smart and satisfying contemporary and paranormal romance.

Follow her on Amazon:
https://smarturl.it/MLAmznProfile
Sign up for her Release Newsletter:
https://smarturl.it/MaraLeighVIPs
Join her Facebook Group:
https://smarturl.it/MarasReaderRoom

Or find her on social media

AFTERWORD

Don't miss out!
Be the first to hear about sales and new releases:
Sign up here
http://smarturl.it/MaraLeighVIPs

Or follow Mara Leigh on Amazon:
https://smarturl.it/MLAmznProfile

Made in United States
North Haven, CT
07 January 2025

64083661R00183